GOOD HEARTS

Marilyn Dysart

1

COPYRIGHT

Endless hate abounds

As white supremacy reigns

Racial justice now

- Marilyn Dysart

It is for the living to dedicate ourselves

That these shall not have died in vain.

- Abraham Lincoln

Matthew Ajibade, Tanisha Anderson, Ahmaud Arbay, Anthony Ashford, Aaron Bailey, Sean Bell, Lavante Biggs, Sandra Bland, Rekia Boyd, Rumaim Brisbon, Rayshard Brooks, Paterson Brown Jr., Marcella Byrd, Emantic Fitzgerald Bradford Jr., Michael Brown, James Byrd Jr., Miriam Carey, Philando Castile, Wendell Celestine Jr. Kenneth Chamberlain Sr., Andrew Chaney, William Chapan II, Keith Childress Jr., John Crawford III, Tree Crawford, Alexia Christian, Jamar Clark, Stephon Clark, Dominique Clayton, Terence Crutcher, Michelle Cusseaux, Albert Joseph Davis, Christopher Davis, Shantel Davis, Amadou Diallo, Michael Lorenzo Dean, Samuel Dubose, Jordan Edwards, Salvado Ellswood, Miguel Espinal, George Floyd, Ezell Ford, Ronell Foster, Terrance Franklin, Shelly M. Frey, Korryn Gaines, Peter Matthew

Gaines, Eric Garner, Andrew Goodman, Brendon Glenn, Oscar Grant, Freddy Gray, Akal Gurley, Miles Hall, Megan Hockaday, Darnisha Harris, Eric Harris, Kevin Hicks, Anthony Hill, Dominic Hutchinson, Kendra James, Botham Jean, Atatiana Jefferson, David Joseph, Bettie Jones, Lamontez Jones, India Kager, Rodney King, Felix Kumi, Aiyana Stanley-Jones, Ralkina Jones, Michael Lee, Quintonio Legnier, Charleena Lyle, Asshams Pharoah Manley, George Mann, Joseph Mann, Trayvon Martin, Kevin Mathews, Christopher McCorvey, Elijah McClain, Jeremy McDole, Kendrec McDade, Tony McDade, Laquan McDonald, Shawn McDonald, Willie McCoy, Ariane Mccree, Natasha McKenna, Keith Harrison Mcleod, Kayla Moore, Randy Nelson, Michael Noel, Paul O'Neal, Dante Parker, Dyzhawn Perkins, Richard Perkins Jr., Nathaniel Harris Pickett Jr., Junior Prosper, Daniel Prude, Eric Reason, Dreasjon "Sean" Reed, Jerame Reid, Tamir Rice,Darius Robinson, Tony Lamar Robinson, Tony Robinson Jr., Troy Robinson, Calin Devonte Roquemore, Antwon Rose II, Aura Rosser, Timothy Russell, Jonathan Sanders, Michael Sarbie, Ernest Satterwhite, Michael Schwerner, Antronie Scott, Walter Scott, Demarcus Semer, Frank Smart, Alonzo Smith, Sylville Smith, Yvette Smith, Alton Sterling, Darrius Steward, Breonna Taylor, Christian

Taylor, Terrill Thomas, Bernie Lee Tignor, Emmit Till,
Willie Sherman Tillman, Adam Toledo, Marty Truxillo,
Pamela Turner, Raynette Turner, Walter Wallace Jr.,Phillip
White, Christopher Whitfield, Melissa Williams, Janet
Wilson, Tarika Wilson, Alteria Woods, Dante Wright, and
THOUSANDS OF OTHERS. We carry them in our hearts.

Chapter 1

Mississippi hot. Samantha gazed at the motionless checkered blue curtains framing the tiny open window. She'd hand-stitched the curtains from a dress she'd brought along—a dress she decided she wouldn't need when she got there. *Nope. No wind today.* A few large ants edged their way up the worn barnboard wall. They were pushing a large crumb of bread. Samantha wondered who had dropped that crumb. *Maybe it fell off one of the volunteer's sandwiches.* Then she remembered; she was in Linnville, Mississippi and folks didn't eat sandwiches here like she was used to eating in Chicago. Maybe it was a broken-off piece of biscuit. Her host mother Loretta had served her several biscuits this last week since she'd arrived. *That could be it; one of our group of five could have brought a before-school biscuit snack and dropped some crumbs while eating.* The ants seemed to be working together to push the large biscuit crumb over the windowsill and out into the fresh air. Freedom. *Those ants are us—the*

Freedom Teachers. Here we are in Linnville, and about to teach kids just a few years younger than us. We've read the training manual, but how are we going to reach a group of high school kids? Oh, well, it's up to us to move forward for six weeks to guide the kids toward finding more freedom. We'll achieve our goals if we work together.

Samantha glanced down at her day one lesson plans. What would her education professor at Northwestern University say about such scanty plans? She grabbed a piece of chalk and started to write the agenda on the board—*well, it's the best we could do for a blackboard.* She was glad Everett had found the old bed headboard up in the attic. When he suggested painting it green so they'd have a blackboard, she told him he was crazy; they wouldn't be able to read chalk words on it. *But I was dead wrong. The dark green paint he'd found was a perfect contrast for the yellow chalk.* Samantha was glad the COFO organization had assigned Everett to their group. Not only did he have some decent carpentry skills, but he grew up in Mississippi before leaving for Harvard. *I know he'll help us understand where the kids are coming from.*

Hey, Samantha, a blond, curly-haired young woman, said walking into her small classroom.

Samantha smiled. *Hi, Marla. I'm sort of nervous. How about you?* Samantha put the short piece of chalk down in the make-shift chalk tray and turned to face her colleague.

I'll be honest, Sam. I felt pretty confident on the bus ride down here, but now that we're actually starting our teaching today, I'm a bit nervous myself. And can you believe that I will be teaching a class on African American history? You would be much better suited to teach that subject.

You mean because I'm black?
No, I mean because you are a history egghead. Nobody knows more historic details than you. I should know; I sat by you on the bus and heard millions of them. I know quite a few African-American heroes, but since you brought it up, how are the students going to accept a white person teaching them this subject? She nervously twirled a curl of hair around her finger.

Relax, Marla. You'll do a great job. You read Dubois' book, didn't you?

Of course. My brain is full of theories and knowledge about Mississippi and the people who live here. I just don't want students to think I'm some uppity Northerner who's come here to preach to them. She started

8

to doubt whether the one week of training was adequate for whatever she might face: sporadic student attendance, lack of interest in learning. . . and then there was all the white violence that might erupt across the state just because the status quo was being challenged.

Nonsense. Last evening when Miss Loretta was telling us how she taught in her day, I noticed you kept up with her ideas of best teaching practices. She has some years on us, that's for sure, but just remember that you and I and the other three on our team are trying out a great American experiment. According to Bob Moses, the kids we are about to teach have been neglected educationally and deserve to have a dose of confidence and curriculum. Besides, it's lots better for a white person to teach them African-American history because it will be a totally new experience on many levels. The whites here have stifled the accomplishments of blacks; they've kept the locals in boxes, not even letting them have some of the basic freedoms. They haven't acknowledged the accomplishments of anyone who's black. And they've focused on oppressing the blacks—you've noticed how poor they are. The kids will be impressed that you are recognizing black heroes and teaching about their challenges and victories. The fact that

*a white teacher is gutsy enough to teach black history will
impress them.*

Marla's lips stretched into a smile. *You know, you
are right, Sam. I will put my confident-teacher face on
right now. By hook or by crook, I'm going to do my best to
teach these kids. They deserve it.*

The door to the Vicksburg Freedom School
squeaked open. Three tall teens burst into the narthex
where Gina, a volunteer teacher from New York greeted
them. She perused a list of names—names of kids the five
had combed the black neighborhoods for. COFO had been
a help getting some publicity out earlier about the schools
coming. Two small groups—Samantha and Thomas II, and
the other team of Everett, Marla, and Gina had walked
door-to-door through the black section of Linnville
introducing themselves as Freedom School teachers and
recruiting older students. It had been a challenge; many
were already busy working in the fields. *Well, goo-ood
morning, guys! I think I remember your names—Josephia,
Daniel, and Hector. Right?*

*The jean-clad girl squinted. Hey, are you calling me
a guy?*

Gina realized her faux pas. *Oh, I'm so sorry,
Josephia. I'm from New York where we refer to a group of*

teens as 'guys' whether they are male or female. I stand corrected. Gina put a check mark in the July attendance boxes for the three before engaging the three collected pairs of eyes. *Not only are you here today, but you are early! Oh, Josephia, if you aren't too mad at me for calling you a 'guy,' would you be willing to read a Langston Hughes poem to our group before we break into our classes?*

Gina looked down at her fingernails to give Josephia some time to ponder her request.

Can I choose the poem I want to read, or did you already choose one?

Gina liked the ping pong questions Josephia was asking. It was a definite goal for Freedom teachers to encourage individuality and critical thinking. It seemed that Josephia was well on her way to analyzing and responding to questions.

So, if I said YOU could do the choosing which of his poems would you pick.

Easy, Ma'am. I'd recite 'Down and Out.' 'Cause it reflects on my culture; we are always keeping our eye on the money jar because it never seems to be full enough. Gina wondered why a young woman like Josephia should have to carry the burden of financial solvency on her shoulders. *At her age, she should be thinking of wearing pretty clothes and going to parties with friends.* Gina had been shocked to see the lack of materialism in Linnville. Her host family lived in a three-room house with no running water or indoor plumbing. Her first shower was a surprise. Her host mother, Miss Leila, told her to keep her clothes on and go to the pump behind their house. Miss Leila demonstrated how to prime the pump with several up and down arm jerks, then to be sure and have a bucket under the spicket when the water came out. Pouring it over herself was a new experience. She rubbed a handful of shampoo she'd brought over her hair, arms, and legs and rinsed off with a second bucket.

Her bedroom, if you could call it that, was half of their small back porch. The family had removed some shelves and a table to make room for a narrow cot. *I know the four dollars I pay them weekly for food and board will really help out. I don't mind, though. With so little, it's amazing they want to welcome me in.*

I accept your fine offer, Josephia. 'Down and Out' it will be. I'll cue you in when to share. And did I hear you right that you have it memorized?

Yes, you did, Ma'am.

Please call me Gina. Here at Freedom School, we are not overly formal.

12

Yes, Miss Gina.

Okay, you guys and Josephia, go on into the auditorium over there. We'll all meet together for some songs, and your poem will be after that.

So, what can I do for the program? The shorter boy wearing a t-shirt with some torn armpits interrupted. Gina wasn't sure if he was serious or just joking around. *Just what would you like to do?*

Daniel flashed a grin. *Oh, don't pay any attention to Hector.* He can't really do much of anything.

I'll have you all know that I, Hector Ulysses Jackson, am the best harmonica player in all of Mississippi.

Marla had eavesdropped on the lively conversation and decided to engage with the first students. She walked over to them and grinned. *Did I just hear that the best harmonica player in the entire state of Mississippi is right here in our midst? I sure could use a top-notch harmonica player to accompany me during the freedom songs we'll be singing in just a few minutes.*

Count me in, Hector said. *Daniel, you can function as the audience.*

Hey, someone needs to be the audience; it might as well be a fine brother like me.

*Oh, I almost forgot to tell you, after the sing-along
in the aud, you'll go to Marla's class. Just remember the
letter 'M'.*

Got it. M for Marla.

Marla enjoyed the friendly teen banter. If the other
students were as easy-going as these, then teaching at
Freedom School would be a piece of cake.

Gina gestured toward the area designated as the
school auditorium as Marla walked into the area the
volunteers called 'the auditorium.' Three sets of five
wooden benches filled the horizontal room. Fred Dodger—
the property owner-- had met Samantha, Everett and
Thomas II at the fallen-down shed northwest of town one
week ago. The shed, once a sharecropper's cabin had
collapsed and Everett's host family said they could have the
wood for use in the Freedom School. The community
center, a 2000 square-foot one-story building by also long-
neglected, needed several wooden joists replaced, and some
rooms partitioned off for classrooms. Everett oversaw the
volunteers in tearing nails out of the worn cabin wood.
Miss Loretta had volunteered her wooden cart so the group
of novice carpenters could haul it to the school site.
Originally, the community center was comprised of three
rooms. Everett suggested that the larger room adjacent to

14

the entrance be the 'auditorium,' and he spent two evenings building the benches, simple double-planks over supports. With his volunteer work crew, he constructed a hallway behind the entrance and auditorium off of which he partitioned off five small classrooms, one for each volunteer. An anonymous donor had left four gallons of paint off at the school early one morning and the fresh coat of paint inside and out had spruced up the walls. The volunteers enjoyed their painting party, some getting paint on their arms, legs and hair. Gina's calligraphy skills helped her pen an artistic sign: *Welcome to the Linnville Freedom School.*

Three turned into thirty, thirty to seventy. Gina was overwhelmed. *I'm not sure where we are going to put seventy students.* The benches in the auditorium were filled and students stood side-to-side along the back and sides of the room. *COFO told us to expect about fifty. Yikes!* She had to turn the attendance log onto the back side to add the extra names. She kept sending them into the auditorium. *I have no idea how they'll all fit in that room.*

Hi, and welcome to Freedom School, shouted Everett to the group of attentive teens. *Voices. Voices, please.* It was a crowd quieting technique he'd learned in training. Even though they were only talking softly with

each other, his directive brought them to complete silence.
You are a fine-looking group of high schoolers. Thank you for coming today. We hope you fill your brains with knowledge and your hearts with love.

And how about filling our lives with freedom? Josephia blurted out.

Amen, they murmured.

And definitely freedom!

I'd like to introduce our fine staff here at Freedom School. On my left is Thomas Jenner II—you can call him Tom. He's come here all the way from San Jose, California. Let's welcome Tom. Everett led the students in polite applause.

And let's meet the rest of our staff here at Freedom School. All the way from Madison and the University of Wisconsin is Marla Johnson. More applause.

Next up is Samantha Bryant, a junior from Northwestern University in Chicago, Illinois.

Do you have a lot of snow up there? asked a kid sitting on the front bench. Samantha nodded and smiled. The applause filled the room.

And last but not least, I introduce the fifth member of our staff: Gina Lovick. She came here to Linnville from New York City.

Clap the loudest for me, she teased.

You didn't tell us where you were from, Mr. Everett, Daniel said.

Right now I'm a freshman at Harvard Law School. But my hometown is Jackson, Mississippi.

Everett had to wait a full minute before the applause died out. *As you can see, we come from all over the states. But we have some things in common. All of us like to learn and we hope to share the joy of learning with you. Also, we all are college students who believe in the value of humanity. We believe each of you is important and deserves to have a good life. That good life depends on having basic rights, one of the most important rights is freedom. Under the current government, you are being denied freedom to vote, freedom for a good education, freedom to travel freely, and then, of course, there's justice—the list goes on and on. During our six weeks here at Freedom School, we want you to learn about how to achieve more freedom. Let's get our day started by singing a couple freedom songs.*

It was Marla's cue to lift her guitar and strum the C chord. *Will our harmonica player Hector come up here in front?* Everybody, *join with me in singing some familiar* songs. *Let's start with 'Going to Shout All Over God's Heaven.' Join in when you recognize the tune.*

Is that the song about wanting to have a beautiful robe and finding out that you get one after you've gone to heaven? asked Josephia.

Marla nodded. Soon the room was rocking with song: *I've got a robe, You've got a robe. All of god's children got a robe. When I get to heaven, gonna put on my robe, gonna shout all over God's heaven. . .*

The voices of the teens harmonized as they told the story of hope for a beautiful robe to wear in heaven despite only having shabby clothes on Earth. *And just what will your heavenly robe look like? Marla asked.*

Mine will be white silk with gold trim, a teen in the middle of the room said.

And mine will be made of the finest linen. It will have large embroidered red flowers all around it, said a girl sitting right in front of her.

Daniel stood up. *Mine will be the finest of leather.*

Marla nodded in affirmation. *Now, let's sing another song of freedom. This next song has its roots in a hymn 'If My Jesus Wills,' a beautiful hymn written by Louise Shropshire, the granddaughter of slaves,* she explained. *Shropshire was known for her singing, piano playing and her good cooking. She gave Martin Luther King Jr. permission to revise the words to her song and use it in our civil rights movement. Here we go. The staff will sing through the verse first, then join in with us.* She strummed a few D chords.

We shall overcome,

We shall overcome,

The harmonic voices of seventy students joined in after only two lines of the song. *How do they know this song?* Marla wondered. *Of course, music travels by warp speed. This song has spread across the country.*

We shall overcome, some day,

Oh, deep in my heart

I do believe,

We shall overcome, some day.

Marla had first heard the song in training. Singing it every morning and every evening had cemented the hopes—hers and those of the other volunteers—for the whole freedom project. *The chords are simple and the melody gripping. The message, timely.*

As she belted out the song in second-soprano, and strummed along, her eyes moved slowly from side to side among the vocalists.

We'll walk hand in hand
We'll walk hand in hand
We'll walk hand in hand, some day
Oh, deep in my heart
I do believe
We shall overcome, some day

Gently swaying, the students locked arms as they belted out several more verses.

Suddenly a sweet voice filtered through the room. A teen in the front row blurted out a new tune in perfect pitch. *This little light of mine, I'm gonna let it shine; This little light of mine, I'm gonna let it shine; This little light of mine, I'm gonna let it shine, shine, shine.*

Hector took the harmonica out of his mouth and called out the words: *Here in Freedom School.*

Everyone blended their voices together to sing the next verse: *Shine right here in Freedom School, I'm gonna let it shine; Shine right here in Freedom School, I'm gonna let it shine; Shine right here in Freedom School, I'm gonna let it shine; Let it shine, shine, shine.*

Shine all through the U.S.A! called out Daniel.

Shine all through the U.S.A., I'm gonna let it shine; shine all through the U.S.A., I'm gonna let it shine; Shine all through the U.S.A., I'm gonna let it shine; Let it shine, shine, shine.

Marla strummed a final chord on her guitar to signal the vocal sharing was over. She looked over at Gina to signal her.

Gina stood up. Nice. Very nice. You young people are the epitome of singing with feeling. *Poetry is rich in feeling, too,* Gina said. *It tells a story—not always a pretty story, but always a real story. Today, let's listen to a poem by the legendary black American poet—one of my favorites—Langston Hughes. Josephia is going to recite one of her favorite Langston Hughes poems titled "Down and Out."*

Josephia stood proudly. She paused before speaking. With a confident voice, she recited the powerful words describing a poor woman and her struggle with poverty.

No one needed to tell the students to applaud. Gina wasn't sure who started it, but everyone jumped to their feet and not only applauded but shouted joyfully.

Huzza, huzza! Shouted volunteer Thomas Jenner II. The room quieted and all eyes stared at him.

What? You haven't heard people shout 'huzza, huzza?' His face reddened. *Back in San Jose, whenever my family or friends in a group liked something, that was a typical shout of tribute. Sometimes my old man says it with a glass of California wine as a toast. I guess it's just a California thing we say. I guess you all will be learning some ways of the world in addition to freedom.*

Thomas was glad to be part of the Freedom Project. His mother had squawked about him coming, threatening to prohibit it. *Thank goodness, Dad interceded. He explained to Mother that it would be a good character-building activity that would mold me into a decent human being. She must have thought I needed molding and she gave in. I think she must have put the extra twenty-dollar bill in my suitcase. As far as parents go, they are pretty good eggs.*

Everett spoke. *Now that you all know Tom likes to say, 'Huzza, Huzza,' it's time for us to get going to our Freedom School classes. We'll be rotating through classes, so you'll have each one of us teachers throughout the day. When you checked in with Gina this morning, she told you a letter. That letter represents the classroom you'll go to first. The letters are the first letter in your teacher's first name, so let's see how smart we are. . . If Gina told you the letter 'M', whose classroom are you going to?*

Miss Marla's.

Good. How about 'T'?

Tom's.

Huzza, huzza, shouted a tall boy in the back.

Yes, and S?

Samantha.

Ooh—you guys are good!

Two left—G is ?

Gina's.

And E?

You!

Of course. Okay, head to your first class and show your Freedom Teachers your best conduct.

Everett raised his hands as a gesture for the students to move to their classrooms. *The classrooms will be crowded, but we'll have to make do.*

Marla slipped past Everett and the others and walked quickly to her classroom. She leaned her guitar in the corner and walked over in front of the blackboard. *Welcome, and sit wherever you can find a spot. There are some extra stools along the back wall.*

Thank goodness, we made a contingency plan just in case enrollment was over expectations. The teachers had met early several mornings to build some simple stools from the scrap barnboard.

What are we learning here, Teacher? Asked a girl at the front table. *Are you a good teacher?*

We are learning about some great people. And what is your name?

I'm Shirley. My friends call me Shirl.

Nice to meet you.

Once the fifteen students were seated, Marla pointed to the agenda on the board. *Welcome, all of you. Here's our agenda for this class. First, we'll introduce ourselves. Even though most of you know each other, I want to learn your names and learn more about you. After that, we'll talk about what makes a person a hero. Then there are two heroes I would like us to talk about.*

So, would you, one-at-a-time, stand up and say your first name and tell us something you like to do for fun. I'll start. My name is Marla and for fun, I like to draw pictures. She held up a drawing of a mother bear and her cub. *This is a drawing of black bears I did one summer when my family and I took a trip North and we saw this mother bear and her cub along the roadside. My dad stopped the car so I could sketch it.*

You are lucky they didn't eat you!

Marla noticed that Josephia, Daniel, and Hector were sitting together at a back table. *Let's continue with*

Josephia, then snake our way from the back tables to the front. Incidentally, Josephia, you did a masterful job sharing that poem in the aud. Not only did you recite it flawlessly, but you recited it with a lot of emotion.

Thank you, Miss Marla. As most of you know, my name is Josephia. For fun, I like to memorize poetry. Usually, I just go into the woods and recite it, but I did enjoy sharing the poem today with all of you.

My name is Hector. You all know me and you know I'm the best harmonica player in the area.

My friend Hector is certainly not shy, that's for sure. Hi, I'm Daniel. When I want to do something fun, I break a dry branch off the old oak tree west of my front porch. Then I use the pocket knife my grandpa gave me to whittle small animals. So far, I've made examples of every wild animal you'd see in the state.

At the next table, the introductions continued. *Hi, everybody. My name is Ed. I don't have much time to mess around because I'm always working. In fact, in order to come to this school, I have to work in my uncle's fields during the night. But as I'm working, I like to daydream about floating on a cloud.*

As the snake of students introducing themselves wound to the front of the room, Marla couldn't help focusing on Ed's comments about having to work throughout the night in order to come to Freedom School. She mechanically jotted down names on a seating chart as the rest finished talking.

Marla walked over to the blackboard and wrote the word *hero* on it. She continued to write some definitions. *There are many definitions about what a hero is. One definition is a mythological figure like Zeus, the head god of the Greek gods and goddesses. Another definition is the main character in a story. And a third definition is a person admired for achievements and noble qualities who shows great courage.* She drew a circle around the third definition. *For today's lesson, I'd like us to consider this third definition.*

I want to tell you about two people who I consider to be great heroes—one a woman, and one a man. The woman, lived a long time ago. She's a hero in this country. Born in 1820 in Maryland as a slave. Does anyone want to guess who I'm talking about?

Carolina nodded. *It's got to be Harriet Tubman you're talking about. But I have to say, I don't think she's a hero to everyone in this country—respectfully, Miss Marla, the whites here in Linnville do not like any of us, not to mention an agitator like Harriet Tubman. And I suspect she's not respected in most of the other places.*

You're right, Carolina. It's Harriet Tubman we are celebrating today in class. Harriet had dreams that she would one day be free, and not only did that come true, but she helped free 300 others from slavery. And Carolina, you are also right that some white folks here in Linnville and other southern cities do not respect her. But in many places, she is respected because she faced huge challenges in going back into slave states to free others. I like how she used spiritual songs to hide code words, and guided the groups of people by using stars. She is highly respected in northern states—in fact my high school history book had a whole chapter about her that my class studied

Wha—at? She was in a history book you studied? I simply can't imagine that!

So, students, what else do you know about Harriet Tubman?

She didn't take no guff from the folks she helped, said Hector.

Can you elaborate on that, Hector?

If you explain what 'elaborate' means.

Marla smiled. *"Elaborate" means tell us more information about that topic.*

27

Oh, for sure. Well, what my grandma told me was that Harriet explained the traveling rules to the people before she took them North. The babies couldn't be crying; she'd give them a little medication to keep them quiet. Mostly, the groups would travel at night and if someone started to chicken out about traveling, she'd show them her shotgun and encourage them to keep moving, if you know what I mean.

My auntie Mary told me about Harriet, said Roberta. *Harriett joined up with the Underground Railroad and was the most famous conductor on it. She'd travel at night, just like Hector said. She'd take the people escaping to safe houses where they could hide during the daytime. My auntie's great grandma Mary was one of the travelers with Harriet. Mary was related to Harriet. According to her, Harriett sometimes had spells where she couldn't move. Once Mary helped Harriet while she was recuperating.*

I'm proud to meet you, Roberta—someone who is related to Harriet Tubman. You should keep her memory in your heart. She was truly great. In fact, another reason she's considered a hero is because she just didn't stop working for racial justice when the Emancipation Proclamation was issued. She helped wounded soldiers in

28

the Civil War, served as a spy, and helped newly freed
people adjust to their new citizenship. She even founded
the Harriet Tubman Home for the Aged and the Anti-
Slavery Society.

Teacher, why are we studying about Harriet
Tubman. She's dead and gone, said Gwendolyn. *I mean,*
shouldn't we be dealing with the here and now, not the long
ago past?
How does it help us get freedom today when we aren't even
slaves?

Some mumbling started. Marla's thoughts became
assurances. *I'm glad this is a spirited discussion. Bob*
Moses told us to really encourage critical thinking skills.
I'm off to a good start.

You know, if you look around our side of town, you
see really beat-up houses compared to what the whites
have. In some ways, we're still slaves. We don't have
much to speak of. Daniel squinted and continued. *I have a*
lot of anger in me because of this. Why should we have
smaller schools and worse jobs compared to whites? And
then what about the good-olds who drive around shooting
our people to keep them in place? Respectfully, Miss
Marla, it's still pretty bad here in Linnville.

Thanks, Daniel, for sharing. Thank all of you. You are 100% right. Whites throughout the South are oppressive. They have misused power in so many ways. They want you to clean their houses and work in their fields, but that's about all. In so many ways, they don't see you as equals, with dreams and wishes. And they certainly don't want you to have opportunities. That's exactly why we have Freedom Schools. You need to feel supported in your quest to get more opportunities. Now, I'd like to go back to what Carolina said about why study about Harriet Tubman—why not study about more current figures? The answer to her question is, we should study about both the past and the present. From those that are deceased, we can learn about their strong desires for freedom and how they went about securing it. Similarly, today we can learn from leaders about new challenges we face and how to address them. So, let's move on to a current black hero: Thurgood Marshall. Right now, as we're sitting here in Freedom School, he's in Washington, D.C., making decisions as a Supreme Court Justice. Marla held up a picture of Thurgood Marshall she'd torn from a history book she brought from home. She held it with both hands, moving it corner-to-corner across the room.

I honestly didn't know that a black guy was in the Supreme Court, said Adam.

Yes, he has the distinct honor of being the first African-American member of the US Supreme Court. He started as a lawyer for the NAACP, and although he was educated in a segregated school like many of you, he went on to graduate from college and got a law degree from Howard University Law School. Thurgood Marshall has worked to chip away at segregationist policies. And he is probably best known for convincing the courts to overthrow a case culled Plessy v. Fergusson, a case challenging segregation.

Like Harriet, Thurgood is a hero for more than just being a Supreme Court Justice. In 1961, John F. Kennedy appointed him to the US Court of Appeals, and President Lyndon B. Johnson holds him in high regards, too.

So, we can all be proud of the good work that Thurgood Marshall is doing on behalf of blacks and whites. Now, what I would like you to do is work in small groups and discuss two questions—with each of your sharing your answers in your group.

You mean you want us all talking at the same time? Ed asked.

Not everyone, but in each group, there will be one person talking out loud to the group. It may seem a little noisy at first, but soon you'll get used to this—we expect each of you will participate. Also, in your group, I want you to choose someone who will report a summary of your group's discussion to the whole class in about fifteen minutes. So, the two questions I want you to discuss are 1. What qualities make a person a hero? And 2. What limitations do you face in becoming a hero? She chalked them on the board.

As she continued talking, Marla used her arm to divide the class into four groups. *Now, go ahead and begin your small group discussions.*

Marla stood beside each group to see they were speaking to the topic. She lingered behind Carolina's group which included Josephia, Daniel, and Adam.

I think what Miss Marla wants us to talk about is what made Harriet and Thurgood such great people. I'll start and I'll volunteer to write down each of our ideas for whoever gives the report to the class.

All in favor of having Caroline be our group's reporter, say aye, said Adam.

Marla heard a chorus of ayes.

*Okay, I get it. None of you wants to speak in front
of the class. Well, that's okay; I'll do it. I came here to
learn and seems like speaking out is one good way to
accomplish that goal. Now, since I have the floor, I'll start
be saying that one quality of a hero is bravery. Harriet
was brave because she led groups North when she knew
there were lots of slave catchers looking for her to arrest
her.* She wrote the word *bravery* down on a worn piece of
paper. *Who's next?*

*Since we all have to share a quality, I might as well
go next,* said **Adam**. *I'm going to say a hero shows
foresight.*

What do you mean by foresight, Adam? asked
Daniel.

*Well, my grandpa always told me that if I was going
to amount to something, I should have foresight—be able to
think before something happens. For example, I'm thinking
right now that the freedom teachers better put some boards
over the windows here in school when we're done learning
today. I have foresight that the good-olds will be driving
around tonight and want to throw a little surprise through
one of these windows. And in consideration of the two
heroes Miss Marla is talking about, probably Thurgood
Marshall had the foresight to know that if he studied law,*

he could make a big difference for others and Harriet had the foresight to know that once some got free, others would want the same experience.

I hear you, said Daniel. *Mine is guts. When you try to be a hero, others will try to push you down so they don't look bad in comparison. Heroes have to have guts to stand up to others who make fun of them or challenge them. Sometimes the challengers are their own people. I think they need a LOT of guts.*

I guess I'm last, Josephia said. *While you all have been talking, I was thinking about one quality that a hero would have and I'm going to say leadership. Take Harriet, for example, she had to make plans for the groups she guided and think of ways to get the people to follow her. She was a really good leader.*

Caroline read back the list: *Okay, we came up with bravery, foresight, guts, and leadership.*

I think our list will be the best, said Daniel.

Caroline continued. *So now, we're supposed to talk about why it might be difficult for us to be heroes. Who wants to start. . .*

Marla smiled and nodded at the group. She silently walked across the classroom to listen to another group process the questions. She heard Daniel's voice fade as she

34

distanced herself, knowing that he was contributing a basic challenge.

I think not just for me, but for all of us, a barrier to being a hero is the color of our skin. . .

Marla was moved. Each group was on track, processing the two questions. *They really bought into this small group discussion. Five more minutes and they will share their group summaries with the class. . . A few more hours and day one at Freedom School will be over. . .*

Chapter 2

Mississippi night. A crescent moon hung halfway in the dark black sky, creating shadows of things that may or may not have been real. Pond frogs croaked noisily like angry bulls as they lurked in the small pond behind Loretta E. Mays' modest house. Nothing good ever happened after dark.

In the evening, Loretta always sat in the red upholstered chair in front of the small living room window. It was a perfect lookout; she could see down the gravel driveway from that overstuffed chair. She was extra wary tonight because she knew. She and her black friends were hosting Freedom Teachers. The good-olds had a way of reacting to her people under normal conditions. Now that things were moving beyond normal, there could be trouble. She hoped not. The two nice girls staying with her were trying to make a difference. They'd come down all the way from Wisconsin and Illinois to be teachers. She'd been a teacher, too. She reached her left hand behind the worn velveteen drapes. Her fingers wrapped around it. Yes. The shotgun was there.

Loretta was glad that the organization had insisted in driving the girls back and forth to school in cars with special drivers, drivers trained to spot trouble and try to avoid it however possible. Today had gone well, according to her girls. Marla had had a good experience teaching some history, and Samantha enjoyed her classes, too. She had been hungry for the details. Both girls had eaten a goodly portion of her home-cooked supper: creamed asparagus on biscuits. Loretta had insisted they move into the living room for her signature dessert, honey peach cobbler.

Now the three of them were in the living room, Loretta in her window chair and the girls, feet tucked under, on the worn cloth couch.

In the distance, she heard the faint sound of tires moving over gravel. The road past her house was a gravel one and not only could you hear the sound of tires spitting gravel through the air, but you could see the clouds of gravel dust billowing behind the car. Even in the dark, the gravel dust kicked up fog clouds you could see. She knew she could reach the loaded gun if the driver of the car was one of the good-olds.

Loretta could identify the car drivers just by their engine sounds. She relaxed her shoulders. *Well, I'll be. It's my friend, Mr. Green. He is out awful late. He and his bride must be on their way back from tending to his father. I'm so glad it's not the good-olds out looking for trouble.*

Is Mr. Green's father sick? Samantha asked.

Well, not exactly. You could say he's more disabled than sick. It's a long story that I may tell you another time.

What do you mean when you say 'good-olds,' Miss Loretta? One of my students said that today and I wasn't exactly who he was referring to, Marla said.

I hope they told you about the good-olds—some folks call them 'good-old boys'. Around here, we like to call them the 'good-olds' because more often than not, they aren't boys, but rather grown men.

COFO told us that the Freedom Schools would be considered radical by some and that we should be cautious.

Say, girls, I've been wondering about something. I hear you talk a lot about COFO. What exactly do those letters stand for? I'm a card-carrying member of NAACP, and I know about the Southern Christian Leadership Conference—SCLC—and the Student Nonviolent Coordinating Committee—SNCC, but I hear you young folks referring to COFO all the time.

38

Marla answered. *That's a good question, Miss Loretta, about COFO. As you well know, NAACP, SCLC, and the Student Nonviolent Coordinating Committee— SNCC—have been active here in the state for quite some time. Leaders in the organizations felt that it would be more effective if the organizations would reorganize into one giant organization to really step up voter registration. So, the umbrella organization they formed is the Council of Federated Organizations: COFO.*

Thank you, Dear, for that nice explanation.

Are you afraid of the good-olds coming here? Samantha asked.

Some Latin words I read once, 'In Omnia Paratus,' mean to always be prepared for anything and so I keep my shotgun loaded and ready.

Marla put her fork down on her plate. *You have a shotgun, Miss Loretta?*

Loretta pulled back the drapes, unveiling the gun. *We may never need to use this. But just in case, it's loaded and ready. I don't want you girls to worry, but if any of us gets threatened, we can use Old Betsy here to scare an enemy away. It's best to fast talk someone out of bullying, but sometimes nothing works and we have to do what we have to do. Come over here for a minute, girls, I want to show you how to fire it.*

Loretta gently lifted the shotgun into her lap and pointed the barrel away from the girls. *Look at the carving on the barrel, here. My papa did all of this. Now, look here. To fire Old Betsy, you put the stock against your shoulder, point the gun, and just pull back here on the trigger. There's nothing to it. But as I said, fast talking sometimes works. Other times, it might be better to go hide in the pond. Duck way down in the water with your face covered with some brush. There're other things to do to be safe, too. We can talk about that another day. Now that we know the car going by was our folk, we can relax. I'd sure be grateful if you girls would tell me your stories. How did you get involved in the Freedom Teachers? Hearing your stories would fill my heart.*

Marla's story is intertwined with mine, Samantha said. *Marla, you start.*

Well, Miss Loretta, when I was in high school, a friend of mine, Tyra, invited me to go with her to hear Martin Luther King Jr. speak in Milwaukee. She knew I was writing my research paper on racial justice, so she thought it would be a good experience for me. Later, she told me the reason she invited me was because I was welcoming to a new black girl in our high school. Now that I look back, I think she had an inkling that I might one day help the movement.

Well, when we got to Milwaukee, the bus driver reminded us to show off our good "Madison manners." I'll have to admit, I was surprised to see such a large group of black people gathered outside the auditorium. Someone started singing, "We Shall Overcome," and a man led a chant that everyone seemed to know the responses to— something about wanting freedom now. I saw a white minister singing loudly and gesturing with his hands during the chant. I felt good that white ministers were standing up for equality for blacks. And then I saw the white-hooded protestors— the KKK. Immediately, I looked away from them; they weren't worthy of my attention.

Miss Loretta nodded in agreement.

We worked our way into the entrance of the auditorium and I stuck close to Tyra because it was so crowded. She led us to some seats near the front and it didn't take long before that auditorium was packed.

I bet Mr. King's speech was a mighty one, Miss Loretta interjected.

Oh, yes, he gave a powerful speech about civil rights and about the need to use nonviolence to bring about change. When he finished, everyone stood up and cheered and cheered.

Thank you for sharing your experience with me, Marla. Oh, how I wish I could have been there to hear Dr. King myself. Is this trip to Milwaukee what influenced you to join in Freedom Teacher's program?

Partly. The other big event that influenced me was when I was working on my English research paper about justice in today's world, I got invited to participate in an exchange program. I'd written a letter to Beatrice Donner, the head of the Southern Organization for Racial Understanding, asking for information about racial justice. She mailed me information about their organization, and invited me to participate in an exchange with a student of a different race/culture. . .

***

"Marla, a letter came for you today."

Marla smoothed her polyester mini-skirt as she got up from the kitchen table. She was almost done typing her senior English research paper: "Social Justice in Today's World."

How is your homework coming along, dear?

Quite goovily, Mom.

Is 'groovily' even a real word?

Gee, Mom, anything you want to be a word can be one. That's what Mr. Jones says.

And just how old is your English teacher?

He graduated from college last year, so he's probably about twenty-two or so.

She walked over to the living room divider where the incoming family mail was stacked each day. There on top, was a letter addressed to her. She studied the return address.

Who do you know in Virginia?

No one, really. It's just some information for my research paper. I've written a bunch of places and people to get some primary sources for my paper.

Your experience attending King's speech should be one good source.

Um-hum.

Impossible. The letter was hand addressed to her and the return address read *Beatrice Donner*. Marla got a table knife out of the silverware drawer and sliced open the envelope.

Tell me, dear. Who sent you the letter?

Mom. You won't believe this. I read about the Southern Organization for Racial Understanding and how they worked to end segregation and discrimination. I addressed the letter to the current president of the organization, Beatrice Donner, thinking that maybe her secretary might send me a brochure about the organization's activities. But guess what—this is a personal letter from Beatrice Donner herself!

Very good, Marla! I'm proud of all the work you've put into your paper. I'm sure your English teacher will be impressed with it.

Marla looked up from the letter. *Sorry, Mom, I didn't catch what you just said; I guess I was engrossed with this letter.*

Tell me, dear, what does it say?

Well, the first part is a summary of the organization's accomplishment. It will be a good source for my paper. . .

Wow! Listen to this Mom! ' The future of civil rights in our country rests on the shoulders of young people like you, Marla. You are searching for explanations about the human story and in that search, you are likely to find out about human injustices. Because you are asking questions about the injustices, you will likely be in a position to find out answers and truths and in turn, teach the truths to others. Our society is fluid and people do change their minds and hearts about justice. I challenge you to do your best to change the world by teaching people about having good hearts, not just having a black heart or a white heart.

I sense you want to dig deeper into African-American history and culture, so I invite you to be one of our youth ambassadors. This is an opportunity to host a teen from Chicago in your home. The teen I'm thinking about, Samantha Bryant, is a talented African American young woman, and like you, she is in her senior year of high school. Even though your senior year is over half-way completed, it would be an opportunity for both of you to share your diversity and cultures. Please share this letter with your parents, and ask one of them to contact me. As you are not quite eighteen, we need to seek their permission—and we need to get them onboard as hosting a nonfamily member in your home for several weeks can be time consuming. It is my belief, that this is the way racial justice will proceed: individuals learning about diversity in a very personal way.

If you decide to host Samantha, there will be some requirements that I will share with you at a later time. Rest

assured, that this will be a life-changing experience for you
and your family.
Sincerely, Beatrice Donner'

Can I, Mom? I mean may I host Samantha?

I'd like to say, 'yes,' dear, but I need to talk to your
father and get his blessing.

He'll say it's okay, I'm just sure about it.

He will be home for dinner in a few minutes. You
can bring up the subject then. I'm hoping he will agree.
You know, your project is really mushrooming in size.
First it was a simple research paper, and now it is an inter-
cultural experience.

Life is great like that, isn't it, Mom? One
experience sometimes just propels you into another one.

Yes, dear, it certainly does.

Mom, while we're waiting for Dad to get home, take
a look at these comments Mr. Jones wrote on my research
paper. I guess he really liked the introduction.

She handed her mother the piece of lined notebook
paper.

Marla Johnson
Senior English
Mr. Jones

March 12, 1963

Social Justice in Today's World: an Introduction

Throughout history, groups of people have searched for ways to ensure they and others have a good life. Often a "good life" is interpreted as one in which societal justice prevails. Others define "social justice" as the distribution of wealth, opportunities, and privileges within a society. Early civilizations like the Greeks and Romans had elaborate systems of justice that provided guidelines for living and criteria for punishment for those people who strayed from fairness in society. Early civilizations recognized the human urges for power and possessiveness which counter social justice. The quest for social justice continues in today's world and its parameters vary depending on who has the power to ensure social justice. Sociologists and historians continue to wrestle with the concept of "social justice" in today's world. What are essential requirements for social justice to exist in societies? Can social justice be insured to those who do not have power? How can different cultures unite their views and practices of social justice? These and other questions offer us a basis for investigating social justice in today's world.

Marla, this is a well-written first draft of your research paper's introduction. Your grammar and mechanics are A-okay as usual. Now, as to the theme of your research paper: good topic—social justice—as it is always one with a lot of surrounding questions. I suggest you proceed in your paper by writing more about the tenets of social justice. Is your paper going to include the aspect of racial justice, a component of the broader topic of social justice? I think you would find it interesting to focus on racial justice in light of all that is going on in our world today. You might wish to select two cultures—one that exemplifies social/racial justice and one that does not—and contrast the two in regards to principles of justice. Next time you see me in class, let me know your thoughts on this direction for your paper. Any ideas for two cultures you could contrast???

Overall, great job on your paper so far!

Mr. Jones

Why dear, I'm so proud of your work, too!

Marla heard the familiar sound of her father's Buick station wagon pull into the gravel driveway. She briskly walked to the back door and peered out the tiny door window. She saw her father gaze at something in the back yard; maybe he was thinking about tilling up the soil back there so Mom could plant her treasured vegetable garden. His wide grin and enthusiastic swinging of his briefcase told her he'd had a good day at the office and might be in a good mood—just what she hoped.

Marla cradled the brass doorknob in her hand. With a swift pull, she opened the oak door and pushed against the glass storm door to welcome in her father.

And to what do I owe this special welcome? Marla.

Hi, Dad. Did you have a good day at work?

Leonard set his briefcase down inside the door and extended both hands to give her a quick hug. He stepped back and looked her in the eye. *Thanks for asking—I did have a splendid day. Not only was my heating and cooling design selected for the new city hall, but the general manager asked if I would oversee its construction.*

That's great, Dad! I hope the guys that do the labor will follow your orders.

Don't worry. A paycheck is a great incentive to do a good job at work. The guys are all union, so they know the ropes. They really won't need orders, per se.

Ethel joined the group hug. *Hi, Len. I fixed your favorite for dinner.*

Oh, are we having pheasant under glass?

I guess I fixed your second favorite—lasagna.

49

You do make a mean dish of lasagna, Ethel. He squeezed her before kissing her on the lips.

And what do me two favorite women have planned for me tonight?

Marla has something she wants to talk to you about, and after your tummy is nice and full, I wondered if you'd help me do some yard work.

Hmmm. I fully expected to help till up your signature garden. What's this mystery you want to talk to me about, Marla?

I think I better wait until you've eaten to bring it up.

Oh, is it something about getting a car?

Not exactly. But that would be a good topic of discussion sometime soon.

Ethel took the 13 x 9- inch pan of lasagna out of the oven and set it on a hot pad in the center of the table. A leafy green salad was centered in a glass bowl on the corner of the table. *Marla, will you pour the water for us?*

Len seated himself at his usual spot in front of the bulletin board. He glanced up at two pictures someone had pinned to the board. He hadn't noticed them there yesterday. Underneath the three pictures, was the cutline: *Social Justice Should be for All*

Looks like Martin Luther King Junior in this one, but I'm at a loss who this other figure is.

You guessed number one correctly. These other two aren't quite as famous.

Am I supposed to know these women? He took a bite of lasagna. *Gee, Ethel, this lasagna is over the top. You never cease to amaze me with your culinary skills.*

Dad, you know I'm doing a research paper about social justice for Mr. Jones' class.

Yes. He took another bite of lasagna before continuing. *How is that coming along?*

Great. Mr. Jones likes my introduction to the paper.

Are you going to include something about your trip to hear King's speech? Seems like that should get some brownie points.

Dad. I'm not doing this just to get a good grade; I sincerely want to learn something as I work on it.

Sounds just like my Marla.

To answer your question, this picture is Beatrice Donner, founder of SORU.

Fill me in— SORU stands for. . .

Southern Organization for racial Understanding. This organization wants to equalize rights between African Americans and whites.

Well, they certainly have a big job on their hands. About half the states in this country are unbalanced in justice.

That's just what I'm writing about in my research paper, Dad. Mr. Jones wants me to contrast two groups— one that has social justice and one that doesn't. Don't you agree that African Americans, especially in the South, are way behind whites in equality?

You don't have to twist my finger. I agree with you completely. And it's not just in the South—they face discrimination here, too.

Marla got an important letter today, Len.

Dad, I wrote a letter to Beatrice Donner asking for some information about how her organization was helping, and she sent me a personal message back. Can I read this part to you?

Forward ho.

Marla skimmed the letter and found the section inviting her to participate in the student exchange. She read it with expression, pausing to look up at her father's eyes as she read.

Her father set his fork down on the table cloth and listened attentively.

Hmm. . . a student exchange. Sounds interesting. Are we having dessert tonight, Ethel?

Dad, I have to let Mrs. Donner know if Samantha can come live with us the rest of the school year. I really want to do this. Do you support it?

Having a person of any race live with us is fine with me. I just want you to think seriously about how this might affect your life. After all, you would be responsible for insuring she had a good experience here.

I know my friends would be nice to her. And I have really great teachers that would be understanding, too.

Atwood High School isn't exactly a diverse school, Marla. Don't you think she would have an identity challenge—what are there, two African Americans in the high school?

We have three now, two girls and one boy.

What do you think, Ethel?

I know it would mean extra work for all of us, but it may be a good experience for us to step out and embrace the civil rights movement more.

Let me say this, if I get served a really big piece of chocolate cake right now, then I'm all for you hosting Samantha.

Marla rushed over to the Formica counter and grabbed the metal cake pan. She cut a double portion and placed it on a small dessert plate. *Here, Dad, is a double-piece of cake.* You two are the greatest parents ever!

***

Loretta stood up slowly and carried her empty cobbler plate to the kitchen. She returned to collect Samantha's and Marla's. *What a lovely story, Marla. So that's how the two of you met—in high school—your senior year. It was very brave of you to host someone you had never met. And very brave of you too, Samantha, to move in with a family you had never met. How did you fare in Madison?*

Samantha rearranged her legs, extending and crossing them. *Well, in many ways, my move to Marla's family was not too difficult. Madison and Chicago have about the same climate, so it was bitterly cold when I left Chicago and bitterly cold when I arrived three hours later in Madison. Of course, Marla and I hit it off right away.*

54

She was glad to have a temporary "sister" and was genuinely interested in getting to know me. I appreciated the warm welcome her mom and dad gave me. These were definitely highlights for me.

Loretta rubbed her chin with her forefinger. *But what about your adjustment to your new school? What was that like?*

Overall, it was nice. Marla introduced me to all of her friends. Of course, being in the minority, I got lots of stares. Lots of girls asked to feel my hair. And Marla knows this, a few racist kids put notes on my locker a couple of times.

Did you report them to the principal?

Oh, Miss Loretta, as you told us earlier there are different ways to handle things. I decided just to ignore the notes. And pretty soon they stopped.

Now, just how did the two of you get involved in this Freedom Teacher project?

After we graduated, we went our separate ways to college. Then our sophomore year, we heard about the Freedom Project and both of our sets of parents agreed to let us participate. The orientation week in Oxford, Ohio was the most exciting thing I've ever experienced—Marla, I know you'd agree, too. There was singing, lectures, training sessions. More singing. I can't say they taught us everything we'd need to be super teachers, but we sure came down here inspired to teach.

Loretta leaned forward and placed her ear against the window screen. She snapped off the living room light switch. *I'm sorry to interrupt your fine story, but you girls need to run out the back door, latch it back up, and head directly down to the pond. Let yourself off the dock slowly and then hand over hand, work your way along the underside of the dock as far back to the front as you can go. Don't say anything. I'll come get you when this is over.*

What's going on? Samantha asked.

It's a car load of good-olds heading our way. Hurry now. Remember to latch the door. Go now. Hurry!

Samantha sensed Miss Loretta's anxiety and grabbed Marla by her hand. *Come on girl. Let's get moving.*

The girls half-ran through the kitchen. Marla pressed the screen open and Samantha let it close behind her. She turned the wooden latch to secure it.

Tires crunched gravel as a truck pulled into the driveway. Loretta stuffed the shotgun in a laundry basket and quickly readjusted several folded towels and sheets to hide the gun. She carried the basket out the front door and set it down on the porch. She picked up her heavy-duty flashlight. *I recognize the truck; it belongs to Miles Grimes.* She focused the flashlight beam onto the windshield. She needed to know how many men were riding with him. Good. His thirty-something son Homer was the only other passenger. Miles slowed the truck when he got close to her porch and steered it in a semi-circle so his window was facing the porch.

Well, good evening, Mr. Grimes and Homer. You are out late tonight.

Yes indeed. We've become aware that you might be hosting some Yankees here.

Well, Mr. Grimes, that may or may not be true. But what certainly is true, is your wife gave me a large order of washing to do today. I've got about half of it done and folded in this basket. You know I sure appreciate your family hiring me to do the washing. Since I retired, I don't have much money coming in and your family sure has helped me to afford to buy a few necessities. Say, Mr. Grimes. Would you like to take this basket of already-done laundry home now, or would you like me to deliver it tomorrow with the rest, once I've finished.

Personalize. That sometimes works. Make a connection to the person's family that would make them feel too guilty to try any violence. It had worked before.

Naw. You can bring it tomorrow when it's all done. And Miss Mays, you watch your involvement with the outsiders. We've had a good life here in Linnville. We don't need no agitators disturbing the peace—I'm sure you'll agree with me.

Loretta stifled her impulse to correct his double negatives. *I'm for peace, too, Mr. Grimes. Now when you get home, you give your bride a big smile from me and tell her again how I so appreciate my business partnership with your family.*

He revved the engine and turned the wheel to exit her driveway. *Whew. Good thing it was who it was. Homer could have taken us all out singlehandedly. His mother must have told him she paid me to edit his high school papers. Never could get his grammar straight.*

Loretta sat down in the porch rocking chair. *No need to believe they were really gone.* Sometimes the good-olds got a second bout of racism and returned to a black home to really do some damage. She'd wait a bit 'till the coast was clear.

***

Marla squeezed Samantha's hand tightly. Down three rickety wooden back porch steps and all the way across the scrabbled lawn to the pond. In the dim moonlight the dock could barely be seen. Marla spotted it first. *There's the dock, Samantha,* she whispered. She gave Samantha's shoulder a little nudge in the direction.

Samantha wasn't sure why, but she felt more comfortable crawling along the dock. She lifted her knees high, careful to avoid getting any splinters. She could feel Marla's breath on the back of her neck Both girls slid off the dock into the cool water. Loretta was right; the dock was about a foot and a half above the pond surface—just high enough to keep their heads above the water and their bodies under. Samantha and Marla edged backward by holding onto the underside edges of dock boards with both hands. *This reminds me of doing the rings in gymnastics class,* thought Marla—*only backwards.*

This is as far back as we can go, don't you think? Samantha whispered.

They froze as they heard the sound of a vehicle coming into Miss Loretta's driveway. The conversation Miss Loretta had with the driver seemed to last for hours.

As the time slowly ticked away, their arms ached from hanging onto the boards, their feet suspended in layers of mud. Dozens of slimy leeches found new homes on the girls' arms and legs.

***

The vehicle left. They stayed in place.

Girls, you come on out now, Miss Loretta said in a sweet voice. *Come sit here in the grass and I'll pull those nasty leeches off you.* After they sat down cross-legged beside her, she reached into a little dish of salt and rubbed it along each leech clinging to Samantha. They fell off one by one onto the dirt.

Ooh, these leeches are creepy! Marla started tugging at one that was stuck to her arm.

I'm so sorry, girls, that you had to go through this scare so early in your stay here. It was a good-old and his son passing by to criticize me for hosting. Fortunately, I do the family's washing, so it all worked out. I'm glad I had you hide, though. You never know when a simple encounter with the good-olds can escalate. As my mother used to say, "Better safe than sorry."

Loretta finished picking off the last leech on Marla's leg. She stood up. *Now, don't you think we all deserve another piece of honey peach cobbler?* Loretta E. Mays put her arms around the girls' shoulders and walked them back in silence to the house.

Chapter 3

What would you like to do here in Linnville that you can't do? What would you like to do in America that you can't do?

Samantha decided to start her day two class at Freedom School with a large group discussion.

Fiona raised her hand. *What do you mean, Miss Samantha? When I was a young kid, I couldn't do much because my parents had a lot of rules for me. Now, I can do about anything I want to. They don't impose many rules any more.*

Can you check out books from the white Linnville Public Library? Can you eat at the Linnville Downtown Diner? Can you watch a movie on the main floor at Hunford's Cinema? Can your family who are twenty-one, vote? Can you attend any public school or university in Mississippi? Samantha wanted to direct her students' thoughts.

Joshua Freeman liked speaking out in class. His high school teachers in the black school didn't seem to solicit the same high level of class discussion. It was easy for him to speak up in church; he gave a personal testimony just about every Sunday. This Freedom School was about the same. Stand up and think clearly and logically; then, deliver an opinion or two based on reason. Make it powerful by adding in a few personal examples.

Miss Samantha. I see what you are getting at. Are we as Linnville blacks, as Mississippi blacks, free to do all the things our white brothers and sisters are? The answer to this is definitely no. Because the folks here in the South built their plantation economy on the backs of our slave ancestors, they have been slow to accept us as equals. They do allow us to work for them; but the compensation is low—whether it be for field work or for house work because it's hard for them to get out of the owner-slave model. The examples you mentioned are places that have traditionally been segregated in Mississippi. No whites here want to see us at their restaurants, movie theaters, libraries, or schools. While a few blacks have tried integrating some of the southern institutions, there is a lot of racial anger at those who integrate and at those who support integration in their writings and speeches.

Thank you, Joshua, for sharing these fine thoughts. And what are your thoughts about ways you and we can gain more rights like those enjoyed by whites in the state and country?

*That's the big question, Miss Samantha. I've
thought a lot about this. It's an uphill challenge, that's for
sure. When one of us or a few of us tries to integrate or
express ideas of equality, we are put in our place.* Joshua
turned around and lifted his t-shirt up past his rib cage.

*These scars on my back are from a whipping I got
last year when I went into a department store and tried on
a pair of shoes to buy. No one was going to wait on me and
I didn't want to spend my hard-earned money buying a pair
of shoes if they didn't fit me. Because I am a large kid, the
owner didn't say much to me, but later that night, he and
some of his white-hooded friends paid a little visit to my
house. They held me down and gave me a reminder with
their whip not to ever touch the white men's goods again.
These violent beatings and in some cases, actual lynchings
where blacks are killed, make many people scared to "step
out of line." You asked my opinion about ways we can
gain more rights like the whites have, and I agree with
some of the ideas being discussed in the Civil Rights
Movement. We've got to get whites on our side. We've got
to let them know us on a personal level so they can learn
first-hand, the unequal treatment of blacks. I think your
Freedom Movement and Freedom Schools are a good
thing. When you and the other Northerners go back home,*

you can share your experiences from here with others and maybe open up their eyes a little. Because slavery has been here so long, we're not going to get any rights overnight. We've got to keep at it, though.

Samantha thought about the close call she and Marla had had last night. They could have been brutalized or killed. Joshua knew firsthand the pain of it. A good scare was all she'd endured. *My Chicago incident was even a worse scare.*

Joshua, do you have a Linnville Public Library card?

I have one to the black library, Ma'am.

How would you and one or two of your friends like to go with me after school today and apply for a library card to the white library? It may be a place to start.

Sure. I would like to check out some books about law. Our library hasn't got much on that topic. I suggest we take Beatrice and Victoria with us. Two girls and one boy—that shouldn't be too intimidating for them.

Okay. Beatrice, Victoria, and Joshua, meet me outside by the school sign right after school. I'll phone for a COFO driver to take us to the Linnville library and then drop you off at home when we're done.

Joshua looked at Beatrice and Victoria. Samantha saw three smiles.

Can you bring along a white teacher, too. That might be good for our cause.

Sure.

***

Samantha and her brother Ethan walked along Michigan Avenue. Ethan's long legs made it difficult for her to keep up with his strides. Their mother had insisted Ethan accompany her; it wasn't safe for a black teenage girl to travel to that part of town alone. They had just gotten off city bus #52 and only had three blocks to walk to get to the Chicago Institute of Art.

Samantha, let's not waste any time. Just get in and do your thing and then we'll get the bus back. There's no way we can be here after dark, that's for sure.

I do appreciate you coming with me, Ethan. All I have to do is find two of the popular paintings and answer a few questions about them. Then I need to choose one piece of art that "speaks to me."

How about the first one you come to is the one that "speaks to you?"

I can tell you are less than motivated to be here, Ethan. I don't mind rushing through the two assigned pieces of art, but I do care about the artwork that I really like. How about you walk around and scout out some pieces you like. It might help me narrow it down a little.

No way, sis. I'm not leaving you to go off on my own. Not here. We're better off sticking closely together.

You seem awfully edgy today, Ethan. What's got into you? Ethan and Samantha were climbing the last flight of stairs to the Institute of Art. *I wouldn't say I'm edgy, just on guard. Didn't you hear what happened to Yolanda Bates when she and her cousin came to the North side last month?*

Nope. Nobody told me anything. What?

To sum it up, let's just say they were followed and it didn't turn out pretty.

Samantha didn't ask for any details. As she stepped inside the main door, she looked for helpful signage. She opened her green art folder and reread the instructions her art teacher had written on the assignment. *From the following four classic artworks, select TWO to evaluate: A Sunday Afternoon on the Island of LaGrande Jatte by George Seurat, The Bedroom by Vincent Van Gogh,*

Nighthawks by Edward Hopper, and Water Lilies by
Claude Monet.

Ethan, I will make one concession. I will evaluate the first two assigned paintings we come to. That should save us some time. It really doesn't matter which of the four I check-out because they are all by famous artists. So, let's study the directory and see which two are closest to where we are.

Now, you're talking, Sis. Hey, look here. In the Impressionistic section, is George Seurat. He's one of your assigned guys.

Okay, let's head over there. I do like his work. I'm surprised it's in the impressionistic section, actually, as he developed a new technique of painting using tiny dots of paint to create his people and scenery.

Ethan spotted the painting first. Hey, let's study the plaque by the painting. It might help you fill in the blanks on your assignment.

Ah. . . it's really not a fill-in-the-blank type of assignment. Actually, there are three questions I have to answer for each painting. You can help me with some ideas I can jot down, then I'll put them into paragraph form when we get home.

Okay.

Question one says, Observe the painting closely. Describe the subject matter the artist painted.

Ethan started dictating his thoughts. *Get your pencil out fast. Seurat, the artist, used a crazy-wild bunch of people in his painting; In the front of the painting you can see a middle-aged white woman wearing a hat with a red flower on it. Her dress makes her look like she has a really big butt. And nearby are three people sitting in the grass. One man is wearing a suit and is holding a cane. The other guy is stretched out in the grass all relaxed. He's wearing a sleeveless shirt and baggy pants. A lady is sitting next to them. She's dressed in an old-fashioned way. How about the black dog sniffing the grass—he must be in this painting for a reason.*

Ethan, you are pretty good at describing art. Keep going. Samantha continued to write some of his phrases down.

Well, there are lots of other people in the background—all white people, you could conclude. I see a guy playing the trumpet, a couple of soldiers, and several other dudes. Hey, look over here; here's a monkey. There's something odd about all this, though. The people in this picture are either standing perfectly sideways or are facing us directly. Hmm. . . that's weird.

69

Samantha glanced down at the next question. She read them aloud. *What medium was used by this artist? What special art techniques?*

Hey, isn't that two questions? I don't get those teachers. They ask you to answer one question, but they give you two.

Don't worry. I already know a lot about Seurat's art techniques. He barely made it into the impressionist style because he used tiny dots of paint, called pointillism, to make the figures and scenery. If you look closely, you can tell.

Well, how about that. So, are we done with this picture?

For now, yes. The third question just asks me to connect personally with the painting. I can do that part later, too.

Good luck with that! How can you connect to a bunch of white people standing around on the riverbank? This is nothing like Chicago.

Trust me, I'll find some way to compare it to my life—maybe describing how crowded the scene is just like our neighborhood. Once I start writing, I'm sure I can think of even more to say about it.

So, on to our next painting.

Samantha decided to ask a gray-suited museum guard for directions to the Hopper painting. She liked some of his other ones, especially, Automat, so that would be her choice for the second piece of artwork.

Excuse me, Ma'am, can you direct me to Nighthawks by Edward Hopper? I'm here to do a school assignment.

The guard, a short-haired black woman, pointed to the stairway. *You'll find that piece on the next floor on the west side. Good luck with your school project.*

I'm surprised to see so many black guards here, aren't you, Ethan?

We'll not really. It's probably not a very highly paid job. That should be no surprise that our people would be doing it. At least they must figure that since all the characters in the paintings are white, they better make things fair and have a bunch of black guards.

Samantha paused as they approached Nighthawks. *You know, you're right, Ethan. Most of the paintings we've walked by this afternoon have had white people as the subjects. This Hopper one is no different. The clerk behind the food counter is white, the man and woman customers are white, and possibly, the customer with his back to the counter is black, but who can say for sure?. This picture is*

*supposed to represent New York at night and I doubt this is
really representative of reality. I do like the realism of the
figures, though. I wish my paintings of people could be
half this good.*

*So did you look at this one long enough to answer
your three questions?*

*Sure. I can finish up at home on this one, too. How
about we ask the guard over there if there are any paintings
here with black folks as subjects? Now that you mention it,
I'm curious if they do have any black artists showing their
art here.*

Stellar idea, Sis.

Samantha couldn't tell if the guard leaning against
the door jam across the room was awake or not. His head
drooped loosely. His arms were folded, *Excuse me, Sir.
I'm supposed to find some artwork that is meaningful to
me. Does this art institute have any artwork created by. . .*

*I already heard your thoughts. Yes we do. Go up
two flights of stairs and you'll find some darn good
drawings and paintings by Chicago artist Charles White.*

Did you say his last name is White?

*Ironic, ain't it. A black guy with a last name White.
Life is funny like that. White is one of our very own home-*

grown artists. I think you'll like his work. If I'm wrong, I owe you a million dollars.

His lips curled into a nice smile.

Mister, I hope you're dead wrong, Ethan said.

Go on. Go see his work—it's a mix of graphics and paintings. My favorite one is Harvest Talk. You might just like it, too.

Thanks for your help, Sir.

Was he being polite because they were black like him? Samantha wasn't sure. *Maybe that's how life is meant to be. Blacks are nice and friendly to other black folks and whites—well, some are nice, but oftentimes, many don't put much effort into it.*

Here's the one he was talking about, Ethan said. *This speaks to me. Two black guys—both strong and proud. One is sharpening a tool—I can never remember exactly the name of it—sickle or something—and the other guy is clasping his muscular hands like he's ready for work.*

I think I agree with you and the art guard. It is a good piece—looks like a charcoal drawing to me rather than a painting.

Yeah. The plaque here says it was done in 1953 and it's a charcoal and carbon pencil drawing.

You know, I think using that medium makes the art piece even better. When you're thinking of men—especially black men—working, you know they are mostly forced to have simple, very physical jobs. The grays and blacks in this picture show the starkness blacks face in the work world, don't you think?

You are turning into one great art critic, Sam.

Thanks. She glanced down at her Timex watch. *Uh, oh. It's already 3:40. We better hustle outside and hoof it to the bus stop. I'm not sure if there are any connectors after 4:30.*

On the way down the stairs, the two passed the helpful guard. Ethan gave him a friendly wave. *Guess you don't have to fork out a million bucks, Mister. My sister and I also liked the White drawing Harvest Talk. Real nice.*

Good. You kids come back again. We're starting to get more black art here. About time.

Ethan eyeballed the front door. He made a bee-line for it. Hurry, Samantha. We've got to chop, chop to the bus stop. Don't want to miss it.

The return bus stop was around the corner from the art institute and two blocks south. Samantha double-stepped to keep up with Ethan. She rechecked her watch. *Good. 4:05. We're sitting pretty for the 4:27 p.m. bus.*

Samantha didn't notice the car at first. When she did, she knew trouble was coming. She made a quick hand signal to alert her brother.

Keep looking down, Ethan said. *Open your folder and pretend you are studying your notes and don't see them.*

The driver of the red and white Dodge Dart swerved over to the curb. Almost simultaneously, the four white teenage passengers rolled down their windows. They were all male. The guys in the back seat were smoking cigarettes; their smoke rings escaped the windows.

The kid in the front passenger seat spoke first. *Well, looky here. What do we have, boys—a couple of niggers out for a stroll. Are you planning to take the bus? Maybe we could take you for a little ride—somewhere special. Huh?*

On second thought, he continued, *let's just take you, nigger girl. We know a perfect spot for you. After we're finished with you, you'll be real grateful to us for showing you a good time.*

Ethan bit his lip. His cousin had told him about the white hoods who liked to terrorize black kids who ventured into the northern suburbs. *If only Sam hadn't had this dumb art assignment.*

The driver leaned closer to the passenger's window. *What's your name, nigger girl? Come on, get inside.*

The boy seated behind the driver opened his door. *Come on over, honey. We'll make room for you in the back seat.*

Ethan thought about the odds. He had a knife in his boot, but two of the guys were pretty athletic looking. He could easily take down the overweight kid and the blonde kid in the back seat, but he doubted he could handle all four. Time to stall.

Hey, my sister isn't going anywhere with you jerks. So, beat it.

The driver revved his engine. *Well, looky. Nigger girl's brother is defending her. Ain't that just sweet. Do you go everywhere with your sister, nigger boy? What a mama's boy. Out protecting your little sister. Well, sorry, we got other plans for her.*

Samantha logged into the conversation. *Now just what would your mothers say about what you guys are doing? I doubt your mama's raised you to be so rude. Just forget it. Leave me and my brother alone. We are doing absolutely NOTHING to bother you.*

They didn't see it coming. The number 52 barreled down the bus lane. The driver was careful to slow down

76

enough so it didn't leave any dents in the Dart's fender as it pushed the car up onto the curb. The front end smashed into a large concrete planter. He opened the rear bus door. *Get in kids. Don't worry about the fare. This ride's on me.*

A black driver taking care of his own.

***

The brown four-door Ford pulled up in front of the school. Nels, the COFO driver was surprised when his after-school driving instructions had been changed. Instead of driving the Linnville teachers directly home after school, he'd been told to take two teachers and three students to the Linnville white Public Library. *Howdy, I'm Nels from the COFO headquarters. Are you the ones who want to go to the library?*

Samantha and Gina walked closer to answer.

Hello, Nels. I'm Samantha, and this is Gina. And these are the students—Joshua, Beatrice, and Victoria who are going with us today. Are you comfortable taking us there?

It's really up to all of you I'm willing to drive anywhere in Linnville.

They piled in the car, all talking to each other. As Nels turned onto Main Street, their voices quieted. The Linnville library's brick façade was impressive. Huge black shutters framed the two large front windows. A statue of General Robert E. Lee stood in front of the entrance.

It seems bigger than I remember, Beatrice said.

And just what do you remember about this library? You aren't even allowed to use it, Joshua countered.

I mean the exterior dimensions seem larger than our black library.

Samantha thought it was a good time to give the teens a dose of reality. *Well, you are right, Beatrice. It seems larger because it definitely is. The information we got from the Linnville Chamber of Commerce Directory says that the library board for the white library received $30,000 from the Andrew Carnegie Foundation in 1912 to build this white-only library. At the same time, the city got $8,000 to build our black library.*

So, Andrew Carnegie was a racist?

I'm afraid he had died by this time and the white board of his foundation didn't want to force any integration in the South. I'm sure they thought that Linnville blacks should be appreciative for their own library, no matter how

small it was. Even though blacks are over half of the
population here,

Nels put the car into park and cleared his throat to
get the group's attention. *Sorry, to interrupt, but I need to*
tell you what to expect. Institutions like this library should
be open for everyone, but don't be surprised if the staff
ignores you completely. That's one expectation. It is
minutely possible that they will let you check out a book or
two without a big hubbub, but that outcome is also unlikely.
Another possible expectation is that someone—a patron or
employee might call the sheriff and have you arrested on
some charge or other. I want you to know that if that's the
case, call this number and one of us will come bail you out.
He handed Samantha a slip of paper. *We have built up a*
large bail fund for extenuating circumstances.

As Victoria swung her body sideways and climbed
out of the car, she asked, *So, we could be arrested for going*
into the white library and checking out a book? I didn't
realize that.

Joshua smiled. *Don't worry, Victoria. We have to*
start standing up for our rights. People all over the
country are marching, going into whites-only businesses,
and testing out the system. We are part of a movement. Be
brave.

Nels turned off the ignition, but waited in his driver's seat. *May you experience success.*

Gina glanced up above the library doorway and pointed at a saying engraved into a marble. It said, *Andrew Carnegie Linnville Library—All Are Welcome.*

Yeah, right. All whites are welcome, said Joshua.

Gina held the door open for the group and they gingerly stepped inside. The set-up was similar to their black library with a box-shaped check-out counter in the center. The counter was much bigger, though, and there were hundreds of shelves of books compared to the black library's dozen or so. Each section of shelves had a sign above it. Joshua left the group to find the law section.

On the west side, were six large rectangular tables for patrons to use for reading or study. An elderly white man sat at the end of one of the tables, quietly turning pages of a newspaper. The only other patrons were a young mother and her five or six-year old son. He was paging through a picture book while she read a novel.

Go ahead and find a book to check out and we'll meet at the check out counter in fifteen minutes, Gina said. Samantha nodded in agreement.

Victoria reached for Beatrice's hand. *How about we stick together? I have a premonition that something bad's going to happen here. If it does, I'd like you to be nearby.*

I hear you, Victoria. It seems kind of peaceful in here, but they have a phone behind that counter and can call the law any time they feel like it. Let's grab a book fast and get it over with.

Here, one of these science books will work. I'll take the one about bees and you get this flower book. Sound okay?

The girls walked over to the check-out counter and waited several steps away. The librarian behind the counter was engrossed in filing cards in a card catalog drawer. She didn't seem to notice them. Gina and Samantha approached the counter and addressed the bespectacled woman.

Hello, Ma'am, can you assist us in checking out some books? Gina had spoken politely, trying to disguise her New York accent.

I do not see any books in your hands.

Samantha spoke up. *Ma'am, these are students in our class and they wish to check out the books they are holding.*

The librarian set the card catalog drawer down on her desk and walked over to Beatrice and Victoria. *There*

are books about bees and flowers in your black library.
You can check them out there. You do not have a card for
this library.

Samantha was used to her Chicago friends who
spoke up when they felt it was warranted. She continued to
challenge the librarian.

Respectfully, Ma'am, these two young women are
citizens of Linnville and are perfectly entitled to check out a
library book in this public library. Incidentally, they have
brought identification and want to get a library card now.

Do you have a birth certificate, driver's license, and
a letter from your pastor saying that you are in good
standing in your church? She asked.

The girls held up their driver's licenses.

I didn't think so.

Respectfully, Ma'am, to get a library card from a
public library, all you need is one form of identification.
You are needlessly asking for extra identification.

She walked back to her desk and resumed filing
cards.

So, are you refusing to give library cards to these
girls because they are black? Samantha asked.

As I said, there are books about bees and flowers in the black library. If you continue to harass me, I will need to call Sheriff Owens.

The woman sitting at the reading table stood up and whispered something to her little boy. He looked back down in his picture book. She walked behind the stacks of books over to the law section and whispered something to Joshua. No one saw him hand her two books. No one saw him hand her a slip of paper with his address on it.

Let's just forget it, said Samantha. *We can say we tried to get justice today, but got denied by the Linnville white library. Where's Joshua?*

Joshua walked over to the counter.

Looks like you didn't find any books to check out, Joshua, said Victoria.

He nodded. He quietly followed the others out of the library and climbed into the back seat of Nels' car.

Nels quickly turned on the ignition and sped out of the parking spot. He kept his eye on the rearview mirror to make sure no one was following him.

Well, this was a waste of your time today, said Samantha. *Gina and I are sorry about that.*

Not really, said Joshua. *Later this evening, a white woman will drop off a package on my front porch. In the*

package will be two books from the white Linnville
Library: Law in Society Today, and The Legal Profession:
How to Pursue a Career in Law. I'd say the fact that a
white woman volunteered to check out these books for me
and deliver them to me and return them for me is a major
victory in racial justice and it happened right here in
Linnville, Mississippi today.

Chapter 4

Mississippi mornings. A gentle breeze blew the top branches of a giant burr oak tree outside the bedroom where Everett Jackson was sleeping. His host family had three boys and his cot fit cozily beside the double bed where the three bunked. Some birds were having a conversation outdoors, probably about not wanting to share food with each other. *Too bad folks are like that in the South. On one side of town are houses with big, wide porches, filled with happy white families. And here on this side of town are a network of tiny cabins, barely big enough for the black folks to fit in. Maybe this was the reason for racial injustice. Rich white folks had a given path to success through inheritance, opportunity, and domination compared to black folks who could barely make ends meet because they had no network, no wealth, no opportunity. And the whites wanted to keep it this way. It had been that way in Jackson. Whites don't want to see the blacks get ahead.*

Everett had used every iota of opportunity he could find. Having grandparents in Des Moines who had started a small heating business that expanded turned out to be his key to higher education. Grandma Rose and Grandpa Ed had high education expectations for each of their grandkids, often talking to them about college. Whenever Everett's family visited Des Moines, they were expected to tell Rose and Ed about their educational accomplishments. Everett had wanted to attend college, but wondered if his segregated Jackson schooling would suffice to get him into college. Grandma Rose, a school teacher at East High School always told him that he was solely responsible for his education. His teachers could only guide his learning, but he had to read and think extensively in order to become a knowledgeable person. Grandma Rose always gave him armfuls of books when she visited him and she expected to hear a book report on each book at their next visit together.

When it comes time for you to register for college, I want you to shoot for the stars. I've heard some examples of young people being accepted into some of the Ivy League colleges. Folks in the North are more open-minded about integration and look at it like it's prestigious to have their school integrated racially and culturally. You give those Ivy League schools a shot, she urged Everett.

When the acceptance letter to Harvard came, Grandma Rose was the first to get a phone call.

Why, I never doubted that you couldn't get accepted to a fine school like that, Everett. You have always been a

fine young man with high goals and a sense of hard work.
You make my heart full.

Grandpa Ed hadn't been too keen about his decision to team up with the Freedom Summer movement, though. *Everett, there's some bad apples out there—folks who aren't respectful of blacks who want to achieve justice. I worry that you path might cross one of those folks. It would sadden me greatly if anything ever happened to you.*

Everett used the same sales tactic on his grandparents as on his parents—convince them that participating in Freedom Summer as a teacher in Linnville would be highly educational and even possibly world-changing. Fortunately, it had worked.

The boys were starting to stir in their bed. Everett stretched his arms and sat up. He wanted to get washed up and ready for the COFO driver who would be there in thirty minutes to pick him up.

***

Hey, Mr. Everett, how come you didn't sing freedom songs with us this morning?
Yeah, where were you?

Everett smiled at the students as they filed into his classroom. *I am sorry to have missed your fine singing, but I had to put the finishing touches on our lesson. See this mimeograph machine over here? This will be the focus of our new Linnville Freedom School Newspaper. I had to check it out to make sure it was in good working order.*

Joshua sat down on the bench directly in front of the mimeograph. He'd never seen one.

So, Mr. Everett, are you saying that we students are going to be reporters for a school newspaper?

Everett pointed to a name he'd chalked on the blackboard: Robert Abbott. Once everyone was seated, he began his introduction. *Here is the name of a well-known black newspaper man. Abbott was the founder of the Chicago Defender, one of the most influential Chicago newspapers. The success of his paper made him one of the nation's most prominent post-slavery millionaires. What's interesting to me, is that Abbott was the son of slaves. Abbott was taught to hate racial injustice despite encountering it throughout his life from his printing business to his time in law school, and beyond. His newspaper was sold at a modest price to blacks in Chicago and other cities in the North. Interestingly, it was banned from Mississippi because it urged blacks to move north for opportunity.*

Today, we'll be publishing our very own Linnville Freedom School newspaper and we'll distribute it free to residents in Linnville. Now, a newspaper has many sections. Who can name one section you'd see in a newspaper?

Everett knew a good teacher gave plenty of wait time for a student to answer his question. Ten seconds or so ticked by and no one responded. Finally, Joshua spoke up. *Respectfully, Mr. Everett, most of us have never seen a newspaper close up.*

For a minute Everett was taken aback. He tried to think when he'd seen his first newspaper. *Probably at my grandparents. They subscribed to the daily Des Moines Register.* His parents hadn't taken the Linnville Gazette because the annual subscription of fifteen dollars was too high for their lower middle class budget. *It wasn't until I got to Harvard, that I read the paper daily.*

I hear you, Joshua. Come to think of it, my parents didn't subscribe to the Jackson paper either. No worries. I'll just explain the sections quickly. The front section is usually national news followed by state and local news. Next comes the opinion page where you can find letters to the editor with individuals' viewpoints and editorials. Some papers even have an advice column here. Next in the paper generally is an arts and entertainment section—it can include book reviews and even original writing by contributors. A good paper has a sports section describing professional, college, and local sports.

So, in a nutshell, these are the sections of a basic city-wide paper. Of course, we can tailor our Freedom School paper to topics you would like to write about. The plan is for you to write out your stories on a piece of notebook paper. Then while you head off to your next class, I'll type the stories onto these mimeograph masters. As you can see there is ink on the inside, so my typing strokes will transfer it to the back side of the ditto. Everett stepped over to the mimeograph machine and demonstrated how to open the lip on the drum to attach the master. He gave a few turns of the handle so students could watch copies shoot out onto a metal tray. *Voila! This is how we will make multiple copies of our very own Freedom School newspaper. Incidentally, I'm open to one of you coming up with a catchy name for our paper. Share your ideas with me.*

Joshua offered the first suggestion. *How about The Freedom Times?*

I'm thinking a good name for a newspaper would be Linnville Wings—I'm thinking that because of the Greek god Mercury had wings on his feet to travel fast. Beatrice spoke fervently.

Everett started recording his students' ideas on the chalkboard.

Victoria raised her hand. *I'm suggesting the Linnville Leader. We are studying how to be leaders in our community, so this seems to be a name that sums up our purpose. Besides, it has alliteration.*

And just what is alliteration? Asked Daniel.

Victoria patiently explained it to the whole class.

Well, since alliteration is such a big deal, how about The Linnville Ledger?

These are all great ideas, Everett announced. He set the piece of chalk down in the chalk tray. *During our work time, if any others of you have an idea, go ahead and write it on the board. I want you to vote on the name you like best by writing it on a small piece of paper and putting it inside my hat over on the desk,* he said.

Daniel wrinkled his forehead. *I thought that only the teacher was supposed to write on the board. At least that's what I learned in school.*

Everett smiled. *As you know, different teachers have different rules. I want you to think of this class as an interactive one. I want all of you to have active roles in the class and that includes writing on the board. Does that make sense?*

Daniel continued. *So you are saying, Mr. Everett, that when we are in your class, we should follow your rules and when we are in someone else's class, we should follow theirs.*

That's right. Now, I've written some headings on top of these papers. I'd like you to think of a topic for an article you would like to write and then come up here and write the title of the article under the section of the newspaper it fits. For example, if you want to write an article about the new highway being built from Linnville to Jackson, that would be state news.

Beatrice raised her hand. *Excuse me, Mr. Everett. Would an article about Andrew Goodman, James Chaney, and Mickey Schwerner being lynched go under national news or state news?*

Everett cupped his hand to his forehead. *How did the students know about the disappearance of our Freedom coworkers? We teachers here agreed not to say anything* to the students even though it hurts our hearts to have them missing.

That's a really good question, Beatrice. It certainly warrants an article and it is both national and local news. In fact, the President is sending down some help to locate these three. In your article, be careful to include only the facts we know for sure. All of us are hoping they are still alive and somewhere safe, so we don't want to write that they've died.

Joshua stood up to speak. With respect, Mr. Everett, even though we don't have the evidence yet, we can conclude that the law has killed them and disposed of their bodies. We've seen their handiwork before and wouldn't put it past them again. We hope the volunteers are safe, but we fear for the worst. That's what usually happens in this state.

I'm going to write a story about how great Freedom School is, said Victoria. You teachers are really brave and dedicated to come all the way here to teach us new ways to learn and inspire us to get freedoms. I think my story should probably go on the front page even if it is my opinion. Try not to worry about the volunteers that are missing. There's still hope.

Everett rubbed his lower lip. *We teachers here at Linnville Freedom School appreciate all of you students for so many reasons. We were sent here to teach you ways to gain more freedoms, but what's also happening, is that you are teaching us about how to live life under harsh conditions, how to live it bravely and with hope. I thank you.*

Oh, I almost forgot to tell you that newspaper stories are written in inverted pyramid style. Everett grabbed the stubby piece of chalk and drew an upside-down triangle on the board. He drew a couple of horizontal lines through the triangle, dividing it into sections. *Here at the beginning of all of your articles goes the most important information. Then after that, comes the less important information—information that's interesting, but not as essential to your story. An exception to this style is the style you'd use for Letters to the Editor or a feature for the arts and entertainment section. See me one-on-one if you plan to write something for those sections.*

Who will be reading this newspaper? asked Josephia.

That's another good question. Our target audience is the citizens of Linnville.

Do you mean the white folks, too?

This morning at our before-school teacher meeting, we discussed this question, Josephia. After school, we'll ask for volunteers to go with us to your neighborhoods and drop off a copy at each house. We'll go out in teams of two teachers and two or three students. If there are any left over, we can ask some Main Street businesses if they want to put a stack of papers on their counters for those who might want one.

So, by now, I hope you've thought of a story idea. Go ahead and write your title on these section papers and start writing your article. Come see me if you need any help. And don't forget to vote for the name of our Freedom School newspaper.

***

Linnville, Mississippi Home to Freedom School

By Victoria Williams

Somehow five really nice teachers came to Linnville, Mississippi two weeks ago and set up a Freedom School for us black high school students. The five include: Samantha Bryant from Northwestern University in Chicago, Illinois; Marla Johnson from the University of Wisconsin in Madison, Wisconsin; Gina Lovic from New

York State University; Thomas Jenner II (we call him Tom) from San Jose State College in San Jose, California, and Everett Jackson who attends Harvard University in New York but is one of us Mississippians.

The five teachers fixed up a run-down community center by giving it a fresh coat of paint. They even built some benches and stools for us students to sit on.

The Freedom School has an interesting curriculum. Instead of just the regular Reading, Writing, and Math classes like we are used to taking in our schools, we are also learning here how to get more freedoms. The teachers are reminding us that there are many great black Americans and they are getting us to think about what we cannot do because we are black and ways we can work to gain more freedoms. So far, it has been interesting, especially how we start each day with freedom songs while Miss Marla plays her guitar and Hector accompanies her on the harmonica. In fact, this newspaper you are reading right now is one of our school projects.

The teachers are risking their lives to come here to Linnville, Mississippi because they are changing the way we do things here. Not too many citizens are in favor of changes like that. I can speak for all of the students here, though, that we are sure glad these teachers--some of them only got a few weeks to prepare for this-- came here and we are grateful for what they are doing. (I know this is an opinion, Mr. Everett, but it also is the truth).

Three Freedom Summer Staff Missing

By Beatrice Anderson

Three civil rights leaders from the Council of Federated Organizations (COFO) have gone missing right here in Mississippi. They are Andrew Goodman, James Chaney, and Mickey Schwerner. They are connected to the Freedom Summer movement because they had been trying to register blacks in Mississippi to vote.

James Chaney is from Meridan, Missippi, and Andrew Goodman and Michael Schwerner are both from New York City.

Here's what we know for sure. These three men had traveled from Meridian to Longdale to talk with some congregation members at a black church that had been burned. The law arrested them in Philadelphia, Mississippi for speeding. They were taken to the local jail and kept for several hours. Then, as they pulled out of town in their car, the law and some others followed them. From here, it isn't certain what happened next. All we know for sure is they went "missing."

Then three days after they went missing, the FBI found their burnt up car. No bodies were found in or near the car. It remains a mystery about what exactly happened, but those who grew up in Mississippi, can make a pretty good guess about what has happened to them.

We hope that this bad action does not affect all the brave northern civil rights leaders who came to our state this summer. It has been a valuable experience for us black young people. (And some of the old people who are hosting the Freedom teachers, are liking it, too).

Justice in Society

By Joshua Arnot

(Mr. Everett, this should probably go in the Opinion Section)

Throughout history, people have formed social groups for the sake of preserving their members. As social groups expand in size, there is usually a need to establish ground rules that govern the interaction between members in the social groups and interaction between social groups. These ground rules are referred to as justice. Social groups that have a high level of justice in their group and between other groups are deemed to be successful. What are the specific tenets of justice? Why is it difficult for some groups to achieve justice?

Experts in sociology say that justice depends on two major principles. One important principle of justice is that each person is guaranteed to have the most extensive liberty compatible with the liberty of others. Liberty refers to ease in moving about society, ease in obtaining education, and ease in voting. The second principle of justice says that social and economic positions are to be to everyone's advantage and open to all.

In today's society, especially in the southern states of the United States, there is an uneven distribution of justice. This is evidenced in both principles of justice. In Mississippi, for example, blacks are often stopped by the law just because they might be traveling from home to a neighbor's house at night. Many southern schools remain segregated, although there have been a few attempts to integrate some in the south. And then there is the disparity in voting. Local voting is controlled by all-white boards who impose nearly impossible tasks for blacks to complete in order to qualify for voting registration. The current Mississippi registration process requires applicants to interpret an on-the-spot hand-selected section of the Constitution. Needless to say, the interpretations never seem to be acceptable to the white interviewers. Looking at premise two—a fair path to social and economic position also shows injustice. There is widespread documentation that blacks in the South are prevented by intentional and systemic racism from attaining social and economic equality.

What can be done so that all in the United States of America have an equal chance at justice? This remains a difficult-to-answer question. People like Martin Luther King Jr. and other civil rights leaders are leading non-violent activities throughout the country to bring an awareness to the disparity between blacks and whites. King recently said, "Injustice anywhere is a threat to justice everywhere." I applaud the work of King and others, but I believe that justice will only come when whites open up their hearts and see blacks not as lower-valued human beings, but rather as equals that deserve the principles of social justice.

Everett finished typing the sixteen articles onto mimeograph masters. Their writing filled seven pages. Not bad for Issue number 1 of the *Linnville Leader*. *Linnville Leader, now there's a good name for a student newspaper. I'm glad that name won.*

***

Beatrice walked over to the group of students and teachers. *I'm glad I'm on your newspaper team, Miss Samantha and Miss Marla. You are cool.*

Samantha began handing out stacks of twenty-or-so class newspapers to Joshua, Victoria, Beatrice, and Daniel. *And I'm glad, too. You can thank Everett. He set up our Linnville Leader distribution team. Is everybody ready for a little walking this afternoon?*

Joshua and Daniel walked ahead. Samantha double-stepped to catch up with them. Marla walked between Victoria and Beatrice. *Hey, you guys, slow down. This isn't a race.*

Marla thought about how excited the students were to share the newspaper with their families. Their faces beamed with pride as they walked along together.

This will be the first time my family has ever seen a newspaper, Beatrice announced.

And they're not the only ones. The concept of a free newspaper is a novelty for all folks here, added Victoria.

When they got to the corner of Beehive Street and NW Oak Streets, Joshua and Daniel stopped until the others caught up. *How about Daniel, Joshua, and I take the north side and you three the south side?*

Marla agreed. *Good plan, Samantha. Let's meet here when you're done and we'll all head back to the school together.*

***

Marla checked her Timex. Distributing the papers had only taken an hour and a-half. Of course, the number of black-owned houses in town was low compared to those living outside of town. Those living in the country were out-of-luck when it came to reading the *Linnville Leader. Maybe they could stop by school for a copy.*

Joshua, Victoria, Beatrice, and Daniel gave the teachers their extra papers before walking home.

Before the COFO driver shows up to give us a lift home, how about we take a few stacks of papers to the diner and the bank?

That works for me, Samantha. Everett said he wanted a couple of outlets for whites to see the paper.

I'm really proud of the work the kids did, aren't you?

Yes, I glanced at the articles while I was waiting for you to finish your last class. I can't believe Everett taught them so much about journalism in one class.

I agree. He gave them a big challenge and they met it.

The white diner had a few of its regular customers enjoying an afternoon cup of coffee and piece of pie. The one waitress who was working the shift didn't pay any attention to the girls as they set a stack of papers on the counter by the register. Samantha walked over to her and announced that the papers on the counter were for free distribution. Marla and Samantha exited quickly.

The Bank of Linnvile was directly across the street from the diner. Loretta had told Samantha and Marla that it was the only bank in town and the place where she kept her savings—except for what she had buried in a jar in her vegetable garden. To keep the whites happy, the bankers had set up different hours for blacks and whites. Blacks were allowed to bank there between 8:00-9:00 a.m. and 5:00-6:00 p.m. on weekdays. Whites had the best times: 10:00-5:00 on weekdays and 9:00-noon on Saturdays. Sometimes there were two tellers on duty, but today, just one.

So, Marla, what are you thinking? Samantha asked. *Since it's 4:30, should I go in with the papers?*

Nonsense! We are a team. I'm going in with you.

Samantha gingerly pulled the brass door handle open and held the door for Marla to walk in with her. A thin woman was sitting on a tall stool behind the counter. She twirled a curl of her auburn hair with her right forefinger. She addressed Marla. I'm May Burns. *How may I help you today?*

Oh, this is my friend Samantha. We're teachers at the Freedom School and we wanted to ask you if you would allow us to leave a stack of student newspapers here at the bank for customers to pick up if they wished.

The woman pointed to a metal cart by the entrance. *Over there. You can put the stuff on that shelf. There's other junk and advertising flyers for people to pick up if they want.*

Samantha estimated there were thirty to forty newspapers left to put on the shelf. She removed the string around the stack and placed them on the shelf. *Thank you, Ma'am,* she said.

Whatever. May Burns looked down at her outstretched fingernails *I need a fresh coat of polish on these nails,* she said to herself.

At least we left some papers at two white businesses today, even though no one seemed eager to get them, Samantha said. Engaged in conversation, neither teacher saw the sheriff's car motor slowly down Main Street. Neither saw him get out of the car and walk over behind them. *Ladies, you will need to come with me. He grasped their shoulders firmly.* They felt the handcuffs pinch their skin and they felt their shoulders slam into the hot upholstery in the back seat of his car.

Chapter 5

Loretta Mays leaned back in her chair by the window. She watched a June bug slowly waddle along the worn window-sill. She'd wait here for the driver to bring the girls home. Time. She had plenty of it.

A warm Mississippi breeze rustled the curtain. *Actually, it's down-right hot today. I'm wondering what stories the girls will share with me tonight. There is always some excitement happening at their Freedom School. I'm thinking wrong. The school is just as much mine as it is theirs. Whoever dreamed up ideas like that school ought to get a big piece of my peach cobbler. Why, the lessons they can teach the kids nowadays. . . so full of action and interesting material. Nothing like ours. And Samantha and Marla are so confident for it being their first year teaching.* . .

Loretta felt a little twitch in her right shoulder. *Might be 'Arthur' speaking to me. Whoever said the Golden Years were good is dead wrong—there's nothing golden about 'em.*

Loretta thought back to her first year teaching at Brushy Hill school, two miles northwest of town. *Lord, that was a year of learning for me and the students. I recall I had eighteen students that year. It was a full house in that little school and preparing for three grade levels was a lot of work. I barely got any help from the county, either.*

Loretta remembered the books the white county supervisor dropped off each year before school started. Even though she knew, she checked each one anyway. The books were discarded from the white teachers and each one had a sign-in sticker in the front of the book with the name of the student who'd used it that year. When the ten lines of the sticker filled up, the white teachers would box up the books and write 'discard' on top of the box. Loretta recalled cutting squares out of construction paper to glue over the signed stickers. She'd use a ruler to carefully draw new lines for her students. *I know the students were smart enough to know the books were old ones, but how about the look on their faces when they discovered they were the first to sign the book lists in the 'new' books.*

Sure do miss my students. That first year, Yolanda was my favorite. I never let on, but I always asked her to help out with some responsibility or other. And she loved helping the younger ones read. My first graders were good readers thanks to her help. I'm glad she went on to a college in Atlanta. It was a big move for her, but the day I got her note saying she had earned her Mississippi black teaching certificate was a day I'll always remember. She must be a wonderful teacher and I'm sure her students are very good readers.

Of course, there were a few 'live wires' that year. The Franklin boys for sure. They never could get to school on time and when they did come, they didn't take it seriously. The youngest one, Weldon, always liked to poke the girls sitting in front of him. He did it so sneakily that I could never catch him in action. I think he got tired of scrubbing the blackboard so much and he finally cut it out.

. .

Loretta woke with a start. Something was wrong. It was pitch dark outside. The frogs were croaking and mosquitoes were buzzing around the window screen. Mississippi night. *The girls. Where were they? Had they come home and found me sleeping and fixed their own dinner? Maybe they are chatting in their room.*

Loretta got up slowly from her chair. Her right knee ached pretty badly. She straightened it out and bent it back and forth a few times. *There, now it's stable enough to walk on.* She looked down the hallway and saw no light underneath the bedroom door. Tiny beads of perspiration formed on her forehead. The grandfather clock chimed nine times. *Nine o'clock already. There's trouble. I can feel it throughout my body.*

Loretta knew better than to drive her car at night. Often the good-olds were out just looking for sport. The law could be out, too, checking the back roads for a black person to make a mistake. She grabbed her flashlight from the front porch and walked to her shed just west of the house. Reginald had built the shed himself when they were first married. *At the time, I thought it was a foolish decision. We could have saved that money for our children. Then, after none came along, I was rather glad he thought to build it as a protection for our car. The less that whites saw we owned, the better. Some who kept their automobiles right out in the open often woke up in the mornings finding windows broken out, flat tires, or dents bashed into the bodies.*

She shone her flashlight along the east wall until she found the nail and removed the key from the nail. The tank was half-full and that would be plenty to get her to Perry's place and back. *Here I go, ready or not.* She put the key in the ignition and slid the shift stick to reverse. Loretta always backed up just a little before turning the car. She wanted to face the road instead of back out on it. *I might*

*have to go a different direction at the last minute so it's
good to be prepared.*

*Perry and his wife Mila will have the latest news
about what's going on. His neighbor, Hannah, is the cook
for the jail and she will tell him if there's been an incident.*
Loretta had to drive by two houses before reaching Perry's.
Both owners were whites. They seemed like okay folks,
but one couldn't be sure. Loretta shifted into first gear and
reduced her speed to ten miles an hour. The low speed
wouldn't kick up as much gravel or gravel dust. To be
even safer, she turned off her headlights. She knew the
road by heart. *Straight past the first house, then around a
curve and past the second one. Perry's will be a mile or so
up the road from there.*

She turned her headlights back on as she pulled into
Perry's yard. She flashed them three times—the signal that
she was black. That was important.

Perry saw her coming and met her out on his porch.
*Why, hello, Loretta. Come on in. There's a special guest
you'll want to see.*

*I'm really in a hurry to get back, Perry, if you know
what I mean. I just came to see if you've heard any news
about my girls. They didn't come home after school. I just
know there's been trouble.*

Perry walked over to the driver's door. *Turn your car off, Loretta. I do have some news for you. But you should come inside to hear it.* He opened the door and helped her out. She walked up the three porch steps and past the screen door as Perry held it open for her. Perry's front door opened up into his small, rectangular living room. Marla was lying on her side on a cot in the room's center. Perry's wife Mila was standing beside Marla, fluffing a feather pillow.

Loretta couldn't help it. She walked over quickly and put her arms around Marla. Oh, my goodness. You are alive. I am so happy.

Loretta looked into Marla's eyes and knew. She'd been punished. She knew Perry's wife was tending to her. *When she's ready, she can tell me.*

Perry helped Loretta into a chair. *Yes, it is good that Marla is safe. It's best if she spends the night here, just to keep things in check. Mila can tend to her if she needs it. If she feels up to teaching tomorrow, you can tell the driver to pick her up here. If not, we can keep her 'till she does. The school folk will understand. Now about the other girl, Samantha. Owens arrested her and kept her. Hannah fed her supper and sang a song to her. We passed word to the freedom office that she was jailed and they are going over tomorrow to try to bail her out. Remember her in your prayers, Loretta, because the judge is in Owens' pocket and just might like to deny bail. Well, that's enough for you to worry about. You better get back home. Do you want me to follow you?*

Thank you Perry, but that's not necessary. And thank you too, Mila. You are good people. You are right that it's smart for Marla to stay here overnight. Marla, you try to get some rest. On behalf of the law department, we apologize. They've got a lot to learn about justice.

Marla balanced her weight on her forearms and slowly stood up. *Bless you, Miss Loretta, you are so sweet to have come over here looking for me. I will always remember your kind heart.*

Loretta kept the headlights off on the way back.

***

You ladies will need to come with me, Sheriff Owens growled as he pushed them into the back seat of the car.

The sheriff drove his car around to the jail's back door. A high fence made the back yard of the jail secluded from view. Sheriff Owens got out of the car and walked up

112

to the back door, giving it two taps. Like it was planned, his deputy shoved the door open and walked over to the car.

Look, Deputy Glen. We got ourselves a couple of lawbreakers. You take one and I'll take the other.

Each officer guided a girl out of the car and into the back entrance. Inside the small foyer, the officers uncuffed the girls and took their names and addresses down. They roughly pressed their thumbs and forefingers onto an inked pad and then onto some forms.

Sheriff Owens, will you please tell us why we are being arrested? Samantha asked.

Owens whispered something to his deputy. Then he turned and faced Samantha. *We have a special plan for each of you girls.* Facing Samantha, he said, *You, you nigger agitator, are being arrested for inciting riots, disturbing the peace, and jaywalking. Deputy Glen will escort you to one of Linnville's finest jail cells.*

Samantha was speechless. *Why was she really being arrested? Oh, that's right. Not only am I black, but I'm a Northern black here in Mississippi and they want to put a monkey wrench into Freedom Summer plans.*

The deputy pulled out a stick from his belt and gave her a shove down the hallway. *Get that black ass of yours moving. . .*

Now, we have a different punishment for you, Marla Johnson from Wisconsin. You should know better than to come down here and stick your nose in our business. I have the pleasure of giving you a little reminder to pack up your bags and get on the next bus going North. If you don't have enough bus fare, call your mommy and daddy, and I'm sure they will wire you the money. I don't want to see your face in Linnville after today. Get out of town. Do you get my drift?

Marla said nothing. His eyes, though blue, had an eerie. villainous sheen. He grabbed her arm with one hand and pushed her through the door.

Owens shoved her over to a section of the brick where aa coiled garden hose was attached to the foundation. He held her against the wall as he pulled a two-foot section of the hose from its metal coil box. *Hope you like this souvenir.*

He pulled the hose back and struck the backs of her bare legs with monstrous force. The grooved metal end of the nozzle cut into her skin.

Marla screamed in pain. Again, and again, he whipped the hose across the backs of her upper and lower legs. Her blood-soaked skirt clung to her thighs. She focused on something to escape the pain—sunlight sparkling on the water of Lake Monona in her home town. Her screams subsided. She closed her eyes. Finally, it stopped.

Owens dragged her to the gate and shoved her through it onto the sidewalk. Then he walked back inside the jail.

She wasn't sure how long she had lain on the ground. Marla opened her eyes, and recognized the faces of her students. Beatrice was kneeling over her and Joshua, and Daniel were standing a few feet away. *Miss Marla, here, take a sip of this.* Beatrice handed her a bottle. *This has some crushed medicine in water that will take away your pain. Here, drink up. The jail cook was just here and gave me this medicine to give you. She put some cool cloths on your cuts to stop the bleeding.*

Marla tipped her head back. The cool liquid felt good on her throat, but it left a medicine taste in her mouth. She drank it willingly. *How did you know I was here?*

Joshua spoke first. On our way home from delivering the papers, we saw you and Samantha go into the white part of town. We circled back, fearing that something bad would happen to you teachers. When we saw his car follow you, we were a hundred percent sure that something bad would occur. We kept following the car at a distance, hiding in bushes and such. We suspected Owens would arrest both of you. Guess his plan was just to beat you up.

Samantha. We've got to get her out. She's been put in jail by the deputy. Marla tried to stand up, but fell back down.

Miss Marla, that's good of you to worry about Samantha, but there's nothing we can do right now. While you were resting here, Daniel ran to the COFO office and reported what happened. They are going to send a car over soon and take you to a safe place. They will also try to bail her out of jail tomorrow.

But she's never been in jail before. I'm so worried.

She'll be okay. We know that Owens and his sidekick will be leaving the jail right at five o'clock because they like to go home for a big supper meal. The night shift isn't as mean. In fact, one of our townsfolk who does the cooking for the jail will come over and spend a little time with Samantha. So, don't waste your energy worrying about her. She'll be okay. Put your energy into recovering.

Joshua, Daniel, and Beatrice, thank you so much. You have taken some risks to help me and I appreciate it.

The COFO red and white Dodge Dart skidded to a halt beside Marla. Nels got out and rushed over to her. *Marla, are you okay? We heard what happened.*

Yes, I'm okay, thanks to these great kids. Daniel and Joshua, will you help me get up and walk to the car?

Like trained medics on a battlefield, the two put Marla's arms over their shoulders and propped her walk to the car. Nels held the backseat door open so she could slide in.

Do you want me to go with you to show you where Perry's house is? Beatrice said.

Thanks, but I know his place. You just head home.

And who is Perry? Marla asked. *Why am I going there? Miss Loretta will be worried.*

It's best for now that you don't stay with Miss Loretta. They know that's where you are boarding, so it's not safe right now. Perry is a good guy and he and his wife will take you in. Somehow, they'll get word to Loretta. Don't worry. We've got a good communication network

even though some of the folks don't have phones. We have
ways to get the word around.

***

The deputy grabbed the ring of jail cell keys from the hook above Sheriff Owens' desk. He unlocked cell four and pulled back the bar-door. *Inside you go, Samantha Bryant. This should be a great hotel room for a Chicago tramp like you* He gave her a little push into the sparse cell and locked the door behind her.

She glanced around. *Not much here. A cot, a toilet, sink, and one small shelf.* A small window made of translucent blocks let in some light. Samantha sat down on the cot. Her eyelids felt heavy. Soon she was in a deep sleep.

In her subconscious, she heard someone unlocking the jail cell door. Startled, she sat up and realized she was in a cell. *Who was the older black woman standing beside her?*

Shh, child. Don't fret. I'm Hannah. I'm the jailhouse cook and I brought you some supper. Sit up now, and I'll tell you this evening's fine menu.

Hello, Ma'am. Thank you, but I'm not very hungry right now.

I'm sure that all you've been through has clouded your appetite, but I'm telling you that it's very important you eat well. You will need energy in the next few days and you will need to think clearly. Eating a healthy meal will help you make the right decisions. Now, let me show you what I've brought and remember, it's all my home cooking.

Hannah lifted a cloth towel from the tray. *Here in this bowl are some nice warm butter beans. They are flavored with a little bacon and will be a good source of protein. Here is a bowl of fresh lettuce salad—the greens come from my garden, too. I've made the salad tasty by chopping some fresh radishes, crab apples, and sprinkling in a few pecans. It's a real healthy salad. You won't want to refuse these two fluffy biscuits, either. Now, the last item in this fine menu is a big apple turnover. My suggestion is to save a little milk back from your drinking and when you get done eating the beans and salad, just put the turnover in the salad bowl and pour a little milk over it. There's nothing like the sweetness of cinnamon, apples, and pie crust mixing with some fresh milk.*

Samantha looked at the food. The aromas tempted her. She'd read books about the jail staff starving the prisoners. *How do the officials let you give me such good food? Will they take it from me as soon as you leave?*

No, dear. I'll share a little secret with you. Before I brought you your tray, I set a tray heaping full of beans, salad, biscuits, and apple turnovers in front of the night jailer. He's appreciative of my culinary skills and likes to dig right into the generous portions I serve him. Gives the prisoners plenty of time to eat their own food. Now, let me see you start eating this nourishing food. While you eat, I want to sing you a little song. Maybe it will calm you and help you not to worry. It's a familiar tune. 'Swing Low, Sweet Chariot.' She leaned close to Samantha and whispered, *But, listen closely to the words—they are new.* Hannah glanced behind her to make sure the night jailer wasn't peeking in at her. From a pocket in her apron, she withdrew a small book and an old battered flashlight. She loosened a hair tie and wrapped the cloth strap around the book and flashlight. She reached under the cot and pressed the tied bundle into the cross-wood pieces. She did it so quickly, that Samantha couldn't figure out how she was successful in securing the book and flashlight to the underside of the cot. No one could see the items from the open side of the cell.

This is my family Bible and a flashlight so you can read and study it by night. As soon as the jailer fills his fat belly with my good food, he takes a nap for a couple of hours. I give him a little sleeping powder in his food—that assures you he will not be bothering you for at least that amount of time. That will give you time to do some careful Bible study. The Bible as you know, is filled with stories of folks who had trials and tribulations, but with faith and perseverance, were able to move ahead in life. That's what you need to do, study and have faith. My people and I will be praying for you to do that.

Hannah began to sing softly in a rich alto voice, *Swing low, sweet chariot, your good friend Marla is safe. Swing low, sweet chariot, coming for to carry me home."*

Samantha wrinkled her forehead. *Wait a minute. These aren't the words to this spiritual. Hannah's sending me some kind of message.* She concentrated on the words. *She's telling me that Marla is safe somewhere.*

Hannah added some additional verses. *I looked over Linnville and what did I see, coming for to carry me home, COFO knows that you are in jail, coming for to carry me home. Swing low, sweet chariot, they will come to bail you out. Swing low, sweet chariot, coming for to carry me home.*

The night jail keeper finished his last bite. *What's going on in there, woman? I don't want to hear any more of that sad singing.*

Hannah stopped. She had made her main points. *I have to go now. Wait a few minutes. When you hear the snoring, you'll know the coast is clear to start you Bible study. When the snoring stops, tie up the flashlight and Bible under the cot. Get a good night's rest. Tomorrow will be a busy day here at the Linnville Jail. I will be bringing you breakfast. Good night, dear.*

Thank you Hannah. You are a good woman. I will keep you in my heart.

Hannah was right. In a few minutes, the snoring began. Samantha turned on the tiny flashlight and opened the Bible to the inside cover. Someone had written Hannah's name in beautiful cursive writing. *I can't believe she trusts me with her personal Bible.* A poem taped to the page caught her attention. She read it through.I t was a short poem titled "Today" by a poet Thomas Carlyle and challenged the reader to focus on each new day.

I recall reading this somewhere—maybe English lit my freshman year. It has a message for me right now. Time is something we can never get back. It should be used purposefully. Once it's gone, it's gone. Even though I'm locked up here, it must be for a purpose and I've got to be strong. I can't let any day slip away without accomplishing something, even if it's a small thought or action. I know Martin Luther King Jr. willingly went to jail in Birmingham last year and his published letter from jail that we read on the bus on the way down here, inspired many civil rights participants including me.

Marla reflected more about how King had urged people participating in the movement to use nonviolent action. *He is constantly criticized for doing the direct-action events like sit-ins and marches. Even ministers ask him why he just didn't negotiate with the governments. What was it he'd said about this?* She stared at the ceiling in her cell for a minute to ponder the question. *Oh, yeah. He said that nonviolent direct action creates a crisis and fosters tension so that a community which has constantly refused to negotiate is forced to confront the issue.* She slapped a mosquito biting her ankle.

The sheriff had taken her Timex when he fingerprinted her, so Marla wasn't exactly certain what time it was. She guessed about one hour had passed since the night jailer dozed off. *I better crack open this Bible. Hanna is sure to ask me tomorrow what I read about.* She opened to the next page which listed the books of the Bible in order. She'd studied it some in her church Bible study group. But her mind had always seemed to wander during the Bible lessons. Lots of people in the Bible suffered. *There was Job—he faced some bad times. Seems like he thought God forgot about him. There has to be someone or some group that faced challenges in a positive way. . .*

She remembered something about David. *Wasn't he chosen to be King, but forced to run and hide from King Saul. Didn't that last for several years?* She flipped the Bible open to the Book of Samuel and started reading. David had to hide in caves and often subsist on only what his men could find.

The message comforted her. In every psalm where David pours out his heart to God during his pain, grief, and struggles, David concludes the psalm with praising God and giving Him glory. *This story speaks to me now.*

Chapter 6

Tom knew how to push his father's buttons. He'd always gotten what he wanted—if he could prove there was an educational connection. That had worked when he wanted to come to the Freedom project. *All I had to do was rationalize why it would benefit me to participate in this historical movement, and he was all ears.*

Thomas dialed his father's work number. It didn't matter that dozens of volunteers were gathered around the headquarters' office in Linnville.

Jenner, Ryden and Finline. How may I help you?

Ah. . . . I'm Thomas Jenner's son. Is he there?

Yes, Mr. Jenner is in. Let me see if he is available to take your call. Please hold.

Tom was nervous. Whether or not his dad would get involved was a toss-up. He had his limits sometimes. Maybe he should have just waited until COFO located a local attorney. *I sure hope my old man comes through and helps.*

The phone connection wasn't the best, but Tom recognized his father's voice on the other end. He held tightly to the receiver, rehearsing his conversation in his mind.

Thomas, are you okay? When Cynthia told me you were on the line, the first thing I thought about was the Chaney-Schwerner-Goodman deal. What a shocker. So, tell me what's going on.

Tom knew his father well enough to conclude that his father would not expect him to call during work time unless it was serious. *Dad, good to hear your voice. I want to thank you again for agreeing to let me come. This has been a life-changing experience being here. Every day is full of teaching and adventure. The reason I'm calling, though, is that one of my co-teachers got arrested yesterday. The sheriff has filed a bunch of charges against her and they're not going to let her out on bail. Apparently, the judge is just as crooked as the sheriff. I know how busy you are with your high-profile cases, but I wondered if you could help Samantha in some way, maybe even if you could give us a little advice.*

Thomas Sr. listened without interrupting. He valued his son's involvement in racial justice. *Lord knows we are woefully behind in civil rights in this country.*

How about I fly out there this afternoon and take on her case? I could use a change of pace.

Tom was stunned. His father only took on cases that proved to be showy and financially lucrative. *I can't*

126

believe he'd instantly decide to come without studying the case. Tom turned his head away from the receiver. He gave the volunteers who were eavesdropping a heads-up nod. Kirk, the head of the office signaled that he wanted to talk to Tom's father. Tom handed him the phone.

Hello, Mr. Jenner. I'm Kirk, the senior volunteer here at COFO headquarters in Linnville. I've been standing by your son and he just indicated that you might be willing to come here and give us some legal advice about one of our volunteers who was arrested. Her name is Samantha Jackson from Chicago.

Hello, Kirk. Yes, that's right. I like a challenge and I suspect that getting the young woman a good outcome will be just that challenge. And here's more good news: several years ago, I needed to try a case in Mississippi, so I took the state bar there. Not only can I give you some advice, but I can represent her as her attorney. Can you briefly tell me what charges were levied against the woman?

Thank you, Sir, for agreeing to represent her— that's great news!. Yes. She's been charged with jaywalking, disturbing the peace, and inciting unrest. That's what we know for sure. Unfortunately, I went over today to bail her out and was denied as she is according to them, a flight risk. Another young teacher from Madison—her name is Marla Johnson was taken in at the same time. They released her, but gave her a good whipping with a garden hose before they let her go. She was told to get out of town.

Who-ee! I knew that the law there was suspect, but I didn't realize it was inhumane. Here's what I want you to do. Get some word to the two women. I will be Samantha's defense attorney. Tell her not to answer any questions to the local sheriff. I'll be there later this afternoon and meet with her. Also, tell the other woman, Marla, that I will represent her in a law suit. We are going to sue the Linnville Sheriff's Department for all they've got and more. See if anyone there has a camera and can take a few pictures of her injuries—you know, some close-ups. It needs to be done discreetly.

Tom reached for the phone. He wanted to give his dad some tips. *Thanks again, Dad. I'm really touched that you are coming out here. I wanted to tell you to bring some mosquito repellant—the bugs here in Mississippi are really hungry. Also, be prepared for a high level of poverty. It took me a couple of days to adjust myself. I'll ask my host family if you can also bunk with them. It will be pretty rough, though.*

Thomas, I'm ready for whatever I come upon. You don't know this, but my father, your grandfather, grew up dirt-poor. And by this, I mean the floor of his house was dirt—no running water, no indoor plumbing. He worked hard and got a few breaks so that I had a better life. And I've passed that on to you. So, don't worry about me not liking it when I arrive. I'm proud of you for stepping out in the world, and I'm going to do my darndest to get those girls some justice. I'll meet you at this headquarters about three o'clock.

Dad, how do you know you can get a flight that quickly?

I'm heading out of the office as soon as we're done talking. Our firm now has a private jet. Time for me to have a turn using it. I keep a suitcase packed in my trunk, so I'll call your mother, request the pilot, and be on my way. See you soon, Son.

Right, Dad. See you soon.

Tom put the receiver down. Suddenly, he felt nervous. *The law here is crooked. I hope they don't hurt my dad.*

Thomas Jenner Sr. drove to the airport and parked his car near the hangar. He opened the trunk of his BMW and unzipped his suitcase. He removed the Colt 45 from his concealed holster and placed it inside a secret compartment in the suitcase. That was one advantage of having a private jet. No security checks.

***

Miss Marla, you're here!

Beatrice was sitting in the Freedom School auditorium with the other students. It was time for the freedom singing to start the day, and Beatrice had thought that they would have to sing without Marla's guitar accompaniment. Hector mostly played descant with his harmonica.

Joshua started it. He stood up and clapped for Marla. Then the others did. Thunderous applause filled the Freedom School Auditorium. Applause for a white teacher who had taken risks to come to their town and teach them about freedom. Applause for a young woman who had played her guitar each morning, leading songs about freedom. Applause for a person who had been physically beaten the previous day and stood straight and tall before them now, ready to continue with life. Applause for Marla Johnson from Madison, Wisconsin, now standing proudly before them in the Linnville Freedom School.

Marla smiled. She was touched that the students were saluting her today. The physical pain had subsided thanks to several applications of aloe plant salve that Mila had applied throughout the night. With soft hands, Mila had washed each cut, patted them dry, and applied a thin coat of aloe from her windowsill collection of aloe vera plants. By morning, Marla felt better. She felt like getting back to the Freedom School so classes could continue as planned. Mila urged her to stay home a day or two and rest, but once she recognized Marla's determination, she focused on ways to help her feel comfortable going back. *You take this goose-down pillow and sit on it every now and then. Take one of these aspirins every hour and that will help, too.*

Marla knew that Samantha would be missed at school. Samantha had planned lessons about black culture and was scheduled to lead a culture fair in each of her classes throughout the day. The students were planning small-group presentations to share with each other, presentations that reflected black culture in general, or their family's own culture. The students had been looking forward to it and Marla was worried that there would be a lot of disappointment not to have the fairs. *Loretta—she will carry things on.*

Marla strummed the guitar and the applause quieted. *Thanks, students. You are most kind. You can't imagine how much your recognition means to me. I know you all know by now that I took a whipping at the hands of Sheriff Owens. But I've had some time to think about the experience and I've forgiven him.*

Hector spoke up. *Respectfullly, Miss Marla. What he did to you was terrible. I don't know how you could forgive that piece of trash.* Several others echoed Hector's thoughts.

I see what you are saying, Hector, but if we are to advance the civil rights movement, we need to understand the hearts of those who oppose it. When I looked into Sheriff Owens' eyes before he beat me, I saw eyes full of hatred. He doesn't really hate me. He hates that his way of life, white domination, is coming to an end. He hates that his ignorance will soon be evident throughout the country. He hates that he will have to change. At some deep level in his heart, he knows what he did is wrong, but he doesn't have the tools to build a new view—a view where all people are equal, no matter the color of their skin. I forgive Sheriff Owens because I see him for who he is, a hollow man whose heart is small and jaded. I have decided to forgive him so that I can move forward. Please support me by also forgiving him.

Now, I have a surprise for you. As you know, one of our teachers and my friend, Samantha, was arrested yesterday on some trumped-up charges. She really wanted to be here today to guide the black culture fair in her classes. I know she will miss your presentations. So, I have a surprise for you. Today, we have a special guest substitute teacher who will fill in for Samantha. She is a teacher that taught many of your parents. She is a little on the old side, but she tells me that her years of teaching were the happiest years of her life. Her students were her life. She agreed to come today to sub for Samantha. Please listen to her and follow her lead today. Marla gave a little shout out. *Come on in the aud, Loretta!*

Students, will you welcome Miss Loretta E. Mays to our Linnville Freedom School.

Marla couldn't believe it. The students stood and shouted her name. They applauded wildly.

Loretta walked over and stood by Marla. She parted her lips in a wide grin. She looked from side to side. *Why, thank you, boys and girls. I know I'm going to have a very good day at Freedom School.*

Marla knew it didn't really matter which freedom song they started with. The students were fully charged and ready to learn. *She strummed the G chord. Let's put our hearts into singing a popular civil rights song.* She didn't have to name the song, they joined in with her voice after two notes: *We shall overcome, we shall overcome, we shall overcome some day-ay-ay-ay-ay, oh-oh, deep in my heart, I do believe, we shall overcome some day. . .*

***

Why did the phone always ring when Sheriff Owens was out of the office? Glen picked up the receiver and listened. It was the message they had hoped for. The local judge was denying bail for Bryant. *Good. Keeping her here in jail will send a stronger message to the rabble rousers.*

Hanna pretended to ignore the call. She looked down at the floor as she pushed the breakfast cart over to the deputy's desk. She'd deliver his before going to Samantha's cell.

Samantha had slept fitfully through the night. Finally, she saw some rays of light penetrating the glass block window in her cell. She sat up on the edge of her cot and stretched her arms. She used the crude toilet in the corner of her cell and washed her hands and face in the sink. Her legs felt stiff. *Probably because I spent so much time stretched out on my cot.* She decided to begin her day by walking laps around her cell. She counted four paces along the door side, three paces along the side wall, another four paces along the back wall and then three paces to her starting spot. There—fourteen paces per lap. *I'll try to walk several laps in the morning, noon, and evening. Even though I'm really cooped up in here, if I exercise, I think I'll feel better.*

Samantha's third lap was interrupted. The deputy unlocked the door to let Hannah enter with a breakfast tray. *Get her set up fast, Hannah. I'm not feeling very patient today.*

Now, you go dig into that pile of hotcakes and sizzling bacon I brought you, Deputy Glen. While you are chowing down, I'm going to meet with Samantha, here, and explain some of our jail rules It will help her get along better. Don't you worry. I won't be long.

Good food. That was Hannah's strategy to get power. It seemed to work. The deputy turned the key, locking Hannah in for her mission, then left to go eat his breakfast.

Good to see you, Samantha.

Nice to see you, too. Thank you for your gift. I enjoyed it. David brings me inspiration.

I'm so glad. I'm also glad to see you are speaking generally. It's best not to say too much. I do have another song for you I'd like to sing. It's another verse to Swing Low Sweet Chariot. Are you ready?

Samantha nodded.

Swing low, sweet chariot, you won't be getting bailed out of jail. Swing low, sweet chariot, a lawyer's coming to represent you. If you get questioned by Sheriff Owens, coming for to carry me home, Don't say nothing without your lawyer present, coming for to carry me home.

Samantha smiled. *That's a lovely song. Thank you, Hanna.*

Hannah leaned down and pretended to arrange Samantha's hair. She whispered a quick message. *Marla got beat up by the sheriff, but she's okay. Back at school today. She took Miss Loretta to be your substitute. Wanted to let you know so you wouldn't worry about your students not getting to share their projects. The lawyer will be here this afternoon.*

Get over here, Hannah. The deputy was unlocking the door.

Yes, sir. My, you devoured your breakfast mighty fast. I'm going to have to bring you more flapjacks tomorrow for breakfast. You are a fine eater. Your mother must be proud of you.

Samantha heard a strange voice speaking with Sheriff Owens by the sheriff's desk. The man's accent reminded her of the unique pronunciation Gina had. That New York way of speaking. *I wonder what he's here for.*

The stranger seemed to shout at Sheriff Owens. *Listen, Sheriff. I'm only going to say this once. You better listen because your job is at stake. The Federal Bureau of Investigation is our country's top level of law enforcement. Your piddling level of law enforcement is down here.* He reached down and drew his hand along the floor. *We are busy looking for the three volunteers who your state says are missing, but we know better. Our men will be watching every county sheriff closely until we solve that case. We got a call yesterday saying you have arrested one of the teachers from Chicago. I'm warning you to treat her decently in jail until her trial comes up. If I find out you've mistreated her in any way, agents will personally escort you to the statehouse for your own criminal trial. Do you hear me?*

We always take good care of our Linnville prisoners, Sir. You can rest assured that she will be fed and housed with our finest Linnville hospitality. You stop by anytime and we'll show you the same great hospitality.

***

Loretta recalled the Christmas pageant she had her students perform at Brushy Creek School in December 1954. It was a reenactment of the Birth of Jesus. *Probably shouldn't have done something with a religious meaning, but that was back in the days when we incorporated the Good Word into our classes. Who was it I had play Mary that year?* She thought for a moment. *Oh, it was Marabelle Watkins, a pretty girl with good acting skills.* Then, she remembered the scene that brought the house down—the audience laughing uproariously. She had asked one of the more athletic boys to impersonate a donkey—*Jeremiah, I think.* When it came time for Mary to ride to Bethlehem on the donkey, Jeremiah forgot he was supposed to be a slow-plodding donkey, and instead reared up on his hind legs like a bucking bronco and tore like a flash of lightning across the stage causing Mary to fall off backwards onto the floor. The crowd tried to stifle their laughter, after all, it was a serious scene. First, a few covered their mouths to stifle their snickering. Then the snickering turned into widespread laughing, followed by some slapping their legs with uproarious laughter. *Memories.*

Loretta focused on a good introduction for the first group of students in her classroom. *I'm glad to be here today to listen to your projects. Your projects about black culture.* She wanted to set a few ground rules. *I understand that some of you are giving individual presentations today and others of you are giving small group dramas. Regardless, remember your good presenting skills. Be sure to articulate your words clearly and speak up with good volume. A good presenter looks at the audience from corner to corner in the room. And don't forget to use gestures with your hands. It makes a fine presentation excellent. And most importantly, we will dignify each presentation by sharing polite applause at the end.*

So does anyone want to go first? She waited a few seconds before seeing two students in the back row raise their hand. *Yes, good. Come on up here to the front. Tell me your names and your topic.* They carried some stools to the front of the room and sat down on them across from each other.

Hello, everyone. Joshua did their introduction. *Miss Loretta, I'm Joshua and this is Daniel. We have a special treat for all you folks here at Freedom School. Today, I am going to impersonate the new civil rights leader, Dr. Martin Luther King, Jr., and my partner is going to be a journalist asking me questions about my involvement in the civil rights movement. We hope you like it.*

Hello, folks. I'm Sam Barnett, a journalist from the New York Times. Today, you are in for a treat. My special guest is Martin Luther King Jr. and he is taking a few minutes to answer my questions about his involvement in the civil rights movement.

I'm glad to be here, Mr. Barnett.

Feel free to call me Sam. Here's my first question, for you Dr. King, just how did you get started in the civil rights movement?

Well, Sam, you see I come from a long line of preachers. Through their ministry, they brought a lot of changes to the people in Atlanta. After college, I also wanted to enter the ministry where I felt I could make a difference.

Thank you for that fine answer. My next question is: Besides college, where else did you get ideas for ways to improve racial justice?

I've always felt that it's necessary to have events to draw attention to injustice. If people around the country become more aware of our lack of freedoms and equality, then they might be more likely to help make changes. In 1959 I traveled to India and studied under Mahatma Gandhi, a leader who convinced the British to exit his country. He held sit-ins and marches that convinced the British to return rule to the Indians. Because his strategies involved nonviolence, they drew support of the British. When I returned, I helped organize many nonviolent events in the South and these events have gained awareness by whites of the injustices their black brothers and sisters face daily.

Can you tell us about some of these specific events you organized here?

Well, one was the Montgomery bus boycott. You recall that Rosa Parks, a fine seamstress, was arrested because she refused to give her bus seat to a white man. This was in 1955. I helped the good people of Montgomery organize a bus boycott as we advanced Rosa's case all the way to the Supreme Court. The city bus system depended on the fares from the thousands of blacks who rode the buses each day, so when blacks started walking or carpooling instead of riding city buses, it made an

economic impact on the city. The case failed the first time,
but on December 20, 1956, the Supreme Court upheld the
district court ruling that segregation on public buses is
unconstitutional.

Dr. King, do you feel your nonviolent events are
working?

There have been many boycotts, sit-ins and marches
designed to demolish segregationist policies and I think
people around the country are beginning to understand the
systematic racism in our society. So, yes, I think they are
working. We have many more hearts to change, though.

You gave a big speech in 1963 in Washington, D.C.
Why do you think that speech was so popular?

That is a really good question, Samuel. I think it
resonated because it is a message for all time—that we
should judge people not by their skin color, but rather by
the content of their character. I think people heard familiar
words from the constitution—all men are created equal—
and began to realize that some in society were not being
treated equally.

My last question is about the reaction the law has
when we blacks stage nonviolent events. We have a teacher
from this school—her name is Samantha Bryant—and she
was arrested the other day just for coming her to Linnville

*to be a Freedom Teacher. What can we do to help her and
to keep the cause of racial justice going on?*

*As you all know, there is injustice in every segment
of society: education, jobs, voting, housing, law, just to
name a few. While I am saddened to learn about this
teacher's arrest, I know that for her to join in the Freedom
Teacher movement took bravery and insight. These
qualities will propel her to keep her chin up during her
incarceration. I was arrested in Birmingham, as you
probably know, and while I was in jail, some criticized me
for not tackling racial injustice through the court system
instead of in the streets. They criticized me for being an
outsider, causing trouble in the streets of Birmingham.
They called me out for creating tension. Didn't I know, my
accusers said, that we should wait until a better time to call
for racial changes? But here's what we know: we have no
alternative because freedom is never voluntarily given by
the oppressor; it must be demanded by the oppressed. So,
today, I leave you with this message: the institution of
slavery in this country has continued to impact our lives. It
was the impetus for white supremacy and continues to be
with us in the form of segregation. Until every one of you
in this room has the same rights as every white teen in*

America, we need to work together to call out injustices and work toward justice.

Loretta was the first to stand and applaud. The other students followed. When the applause softened, she spoke. *My, my. I have been a teacher for more years than the two of your ages put together, Joshua and Daniel. You did a very fine job researching the accomplishments of this great leader. And you did a very fine job of reaching my heart. God bless you as you continue to learn and share your learning with others. Now, who will be next to share their culture project?*

***

Owens decided to skip Hannah's lunch. He'd go over to the corner diner and talk shop with the locals. *See what they're thinking.*

He sat down at the long community table in the middle of the room. *Always the same crowd here. The movers and shakers of Linnille: Billy Rae Jones, Burt Nemick, George McGrath, and Hunter. Radley.*

Howdy, boys. Owens greeted them as he pulled out a chair. *Nice to see all of you. Fine day.*

Theresa, a regular waitress reached over his shoulder and poured him a cup of steaming coffee. *What can I get you today, Sheriff?*

Owens wasn't too hungry, but he did like the hot beef sandwiches they served. *Fix me up one of those good beef sandwiches, Theresa. And a piece of your fresh cherry pie.*

Whatever you say, Sheriff.

Owens wanted to get right to the subject. *So, men, what's the latest news around town?*

Billy Rae Jones seemed to be abreast of not only the comings and goings in Linnville, but also in the county. *These are truly crazy times we're living in, Sheriff, aren't they? There's good news, like the sale price of cattle is way up. Then there's bad news like the interference by the Northern interlopers. Why, they are interfering in a big way.*

Owens wanted details. He feigned ignorance. *Now just what do you mean by interfering, Billy?*

Well, in case you haven't heard, they are going around trying to register voters. And I don't mean white voters. My kid drove by that school yesterday and said there are close to a hundred of our city's finest attending it. They are teaching the students how to upset the apple cart.

145

Now I don't know what you others think about it, but there's no way we can tolerate something so subversive here.

The door to the Linnville Downtown Diner opened and a stranger entered. It was Jenner, disguised as a rancher with a long-sleeved plaid shirt and leather chaps over his jeans. Mabel was at the counter making change for a customer, and he looked at her to get her attention. He spoke in a loud, raspy voice. *I'm a cattle buyer from Omaha. Do you know of anyone in town I can talk to?*

Mister, right over there is George McGrath. The one in the gray shirt. He runs our area cattle barn and he'll help you.

Jenner strode over to the table. He looked directly at McGrath. *You the manager of the sale barn? I'm Ned Springer, a cattle buyer from Omaha.*

Pull up a chair, Springer. We were just having a friendly conversation about some troubles here in Linnville. Oh, let me introduce you to some of our illustrious town leaders. Here on my left is Billy Rae Jones, next to his left is Burt Nemick, then Hunter Radley, and last but not least, our illustrious sheriff Riley Owens.

Jenner was a wizard at memorizing visual clues. He quickly rehearsed the appearances of the crew sitting before

146

him. *McGrath—lean with big biceps, Jones—scrawny build and face has pot marks, Nemick—stocky with greasy black hair, Radley—short but slightly balding, Owens—big with a pot gut.*

Jenner wanted to squeeze the men for more information. *What do you mean by having troubles here?*

Radley spoke up. *Seems some locals are getting a little too big for their britches. Some Yankees have come down here and started trouble.*

Owens couldn't resist joining in. *I've got me a Nigger teacher from Chicago in my jail right now. She needs a little lesson herself.*

Springer wrinkled his forehead. *I don't get it. Aren't there enough teachers here in Mississippi? Why are they coming all the way from the North?*

Owens talked more. *It's what they call the civil rights movement. It's like a plague that's moving all through the South. Martin Luther King and his people are stirring up our local folks. Trying to get them agitated so they take over what we whites have earned fair and square. That Chicago teacher is the first one I've arrested. These fine men you see at the table are going to be some fine jury members. When she gets her death penalty, it will be sure to get the locals back under control.*

147

Springer slid over to his right so Theresa could fill his coffee cup. He chuckled. *Well, good luck with that.*

Owens couldn't stop. *We've got plans to torch that school of theirs, for another thing. It's been a fire hazard for years. Any volunteers? Does tonight work for anyone?*

Hunter and I will be honored. What do you think, Hunter, does tonight work for you? Burt Nemick waited for his nod. *Good, meet at my place at ten. We'll grab a little kerosene and head out.*

Owens grinned. *I know you two can handle it so I won't be needed. Got to keep my fingerprints off the deed—if you read me.*

Burt nodded. *Yeah, Sheriff. You can rest easy that me and Hunter will complete the task satisfactorily.*

Springson rejoined the conversation. *So, sorry to change the topic, but McGrath, is there any way I can buy some cattle from you? I'd like to fatten them up here in the area before I drive them North. Think I can get a good deal from your operation?*

Let's talk. Stop by the sale barn office this afternoon and we'll negotiate. I think we can work something out.

Springson stood up. *Nice to meet you all. Sorry I've got to run. Have a few other errands to attend to.*

The tablemates chorused goodbyes as he walked to the door.

Once he was out of eyesight of the diner, and into his rental car, Thomas Jenner removed the hot black wig and leather chaps. He drove over to COFO headquarters. Once inside, he introduced himself and updated the other volunteers about the plans to torch the school. *I'm sleeping there tonight with my son. We'll have a little surprise for Hunter Radley and Burt Nemick.*

He walked outdoors and around to the back of the building. It was quiet. There, Thomas Jennner Sr. changed into a beige suit, brushed his blonde hair, and slipped a pair of lifts into his dress shoes. *I want to look a little taller so he doesn't recognize me from the diner.* He drove back to Main Street to the Linnville Jail. His client would be waiting for him.

Chapter 7

Thomas Jenner Sr. adjusted his tie. He doubted the sheriff would recognize him. Having been a ventriloquist during his college days, he was a master of voice. Time to use a California accent. There really wasn't a distinct California accent, but he would meet the sheriff in a very different voice than Ned Springer had used. The one he selected was a deep bass—a commanding type of voice. Owens was sitting at his desk as he entered. Just like in the movies, he had his ankles crossed, feet on his desk.

Ned approached the sheriff's desk. *Hello, I'm Thomas Jenner, attorney for Samantha Bryant.* I *would like to meet my client now in a private room.*

Owens rolled his eyes. He kept his feet on the desk. *Right. And I would like to have a million dollars. You can meet her for fifteen minutes in her cell. That's the best I can do.*

Look, Sheriff. My brother-in-law is head of the Southern Sheriff's Association. If you don't provide me a private room within five minutes, I'll tell him about your unethical behavior and he can have you ousted from your little fiefdom here. If you doubt me, go ahead and look up his name—it's Gene Grimson.

Owens slowly slid his feet to the floor. *Alright, I'll let you have the back supply room. But don't take much time.* He reached up and removed the cell key ring from the nail. He gave them a toss to Glen. *My deputy will get the woman and show you were the room is. No funny stuff allowed.*

Samantha overheard the conversation. Hannah had been right on target with her message. A lawyer was here to see her. She stood up and smoothed her hair. It surprised her to see a well-dressed white man standing before her.

Hello, Miss Bryant, I'm Thomas Jenner, your defense attorney. Please come with me so we can get acquainted and discuss your case. The deputy said nothing as he unlocked the door.

Sheriff Owens has graciously arranged for us to meet in a private room. She followed him to a back room where two chairs had been placed amid boxes of supplies.

The expression on your face, Miss Bryant, showed me you are surprised. Can you explain why? His voice quickly changed to a higher faster-paced one.

Well, I'm surprised for a couple of reasons. I did know an attorney would be coming to see me this afternoon, but frankly, I'm surprised that you are so well-dressed.

And by that, I'm guessing that you are surprised to see a white attorney. Am I right?

Respectfully, Mr. Jenner, I'm from Chicago. Not many white attorneys would represent a black woman.

Jenner smiled. *I think we are going to get along just fine.*

Sir, you have the same name as one of my fellow teachers at the Freedom School. Is that a coincidence?

Ah, you are very perceptive. Yes, I am Thomas Jenner Sr., and your colleague Thomas Jenner Jr. is my very own son. He gave me a call saying you were in a bit of a pickle, and I volunteered to fly out here to give you a hand.

All the way from California? I can't believe it.

The way I see it--may I call you Samantha—it's time to take on the racism in the southern legal system. In short, you and I are going to collaborate to show the folks of Linnville that they cannot run roughshod over justice.

Yes, please call me Samantha.

Thomas opened his briefcase and took out a lined tablet. He took a ball point pen out of his inner jacket pocket and removed the top. He drew a doodle on the top of the pad as he continued talking. *I have a few questions to discuss with you. I already know about the charges they've levied against you, and I know that they denied you bail, so we can talk about the next step I'm going to take: apply to the judge for a change of venue. This will force us to give him a reason why we think we cannot get justice in his courtroom, and likely aggravate him before he denies the change. We'll continue to keep them procedural hopping so they can't figure out our specific defense. Be prepared for the sheriff to try to weasel out our strategy from you, and because of that, I'm not going to tell you much. You need to trust me, Samantha, to guide the case without telling you each step. Can you agree to that?*

Yes. I understand.

So, if the sheriff or deputy or anyone else asks you questions about our witnesses or strategy, just make up some answers. The more creative, the better. In fact, if you can steer them on the wrong course by spilling the beans— something you've made up—at the opportune time, it would be great. We want them to be running around in circles in their minds. Does that make sense?

Samantha liked this man. He was clearly on her side. He was going to expect her to do her part , too. *Mr. Jenner, I was on my drama team in high school, and one of the drama activities I loved the most was improvisation. Trust me, I can make up stories.*

Good. Just so you know, there are FBI agents in the area. One stopped by to tell the sheriff and his crew to treat you with kid gloves. You let me know during my visits if they step out of line.

I did overhear that conversation this morning. The agent was very forceful and I'm hopeful he put a scare into the sheriff. I will keep you posted about what's happening.

Good, one last thing. I am also going to represent your colleague Marla Johnson. We are going to file a civil lawsuit against the sheriff's department for their mistreatment of her. I want to leverage the two cases against each other. Any questions?

Thank you for representing Marla, too. It's just awful what happened to her. I just have one question. When do you think my trial will start?

Good question. The request for a venue change will just set the case back a day or two. I'd guess that we'll go to court next week. So, you hang in there and stay positive. I'm going to demand that you get paper and pencil so you can keep a journal. Disguise it as a story between some poems, or something. In your journal, record all your reasons for wanting to become a Freedom Teacher. Incidentally, my son told me you are a great teacher.

And so is he. I wish you could see how well he works with the students.

Thomas glanced down at his watch. *Actually, I'm headed over to your school in a few minutes. I'll pop in on my son and see if what you say about his teaching is true.* He stood up to signal their time had ended. He reached out his hand to shake hers.

Thank you so much, Mr. Jenner. Your presence reassures me. I know this process will be challenging, but knowing you are helping me makes me feel better.

Samantha, you are experiencing a movement—the civil rights movement in America. Through your trial, you will make a big difference to those needing freedoms. I only hope by representing you that I can also make a difference.

When the deputy locked her back in her cell, Samantha didn't hear the key click. She was absorbed in her conversation with Mr. Jenner. *I can't think of a time when a white man reached out his hand to shake mine.*

Jenner was secretly betting that Owens would be too lazy to check his claim that his brother-in-law was head of the Southern Sheriff's Association. He did have a brother, but not in the legal profession—a marine biologist.

***

Tom was winding down his last afternoon lesson. The idea for the lesson had come to him before school when he was looking through a black history book Gina had on her desk. He had randomly flipped through the pages, landing on a section about George Washington Carver and a list of all the products made from peanuts, a crop he'd introduced to southern farmers. *I'll teach about this guy with a little rhythm activity. The kids can shout 'From peanuts ,George Washington Carver invented. . .' then I'll shout out one example of a peanut use. Then they can clap and start the chant over again. I wonder how many examples I can go through before they get tired of this activity.*

Tom had already shouted out fifty-three peanut uses and the claps were getting louder and louder. Clearly, they enjoyed the activity and showed no signs of boredom. *Should we stop yet, he yelled?*

No!

From peanuts, George Washington Carver invented. . .

Laundry soap—CLAP!

From peanuts, George Washington Carver invented. . .

Baby massage cream—CLAP!

From peanuts, George Washington Carver invented. . .

Medicine—CLAP!

From peanuts, George Washington Carver invented. . .

Paint—CLAP!

From peanuts, George Washington Carver invented. . .

Rubber—CLAP!

From peanuts, George Washington Carver invented. . .

Paper—CLAP!!

From peanuts, George Washington Carver invented. . .

Gas—CLAP!

From peanuts, George Washington Carver invented. . .

Insulating board—CLAP!!

Thomas Senior walked into the Linnville Freedom School. He recognized the unmistakable voice of his son leading the noisy activity. *Yep, a chip off the old block.* He followed the noise to Thomas' classroom where the young teacher was standing on his desk, directing the chant like a choir director.

Have you mentioned candy bars yet? The senior shouted. The students clapped and Tom stopped, surprised to see his father in his classroom.

He climbed down from his desk. *Hey, everybody, this is my dad. He's a lawyer in California and is here to represent Miss Samantha.*

The students started cheering and clapping. The noise they made was even louder than for the peanut chants.

Beatrice waved both hands to get his attention. When will you get her out of jail?

Thomas rested his chin in his right hand. He looked thoughtfully at the students. *Your question is a very good one. I met with Samantha just now and she is in good spirits. I've asked her to write some notes about the Freedom School project and her reasons for teaching here. I've got a strategy in mind, so I'll be ready to present her case in a couple of days. No telling whether the sheriff will try to stall the trial. If he does, I've got a few tricks up my sleeve to get the trial moving. It's a common tactic for law to try to drag out the start of a case and intentionally cause people to lose interest in it. Then, they follow-up with a very bad verdict, knowing people are not paying much attention. So, rest assured, we will be pushing to get Samantha's case in the court room as soon as possible. Say, while I have the floor, would any of you be willing to testify on Samantha or Marla's behalf.*

But Miss Marla is here today.

Thomas realized he hadn't told the students about the civil law suit on Marla's behalf. *Gee whiz, I haven't talked to Marla about it even. That's got to happen next.* He gave a brief explanation. *When the sheriff and his deputy picked up Samantha and Marla, they arrested Samantha and beat Marla. Both of those actions need to be contested. I'm going to talk to Marla right now.*

Tom, will you get the names of any students here at the school who would be good witnesses—you know, their names and why they could help the case. I really need to go speak with Marla. Would one of you volunteer to take me to Marla's classroom?

Beatrice stood up and walked over to Thomas Sr. *I will show you sir, and I would also be a good witness because I was one of the students who helped her after the sheriff beat her and threw her out on the sidewalk. Joshua and Daniel both saw the beating.*

Get their names down, Tom. Let's go, Beatrice.

Thomas Jenner felt exhilarated. He had always enjoyed challenges, especially those related to his legal career. Most people thought he took on the high-profile cases because they brought in the big money settlements. *Really, it's the challenge of outthinking my opponents that allow me to love this career. And these will be the epitome of cases. I'll be taking on a complete system of unjust law. To outsmart the sheriff and townspeople will be an exciting challenge.*

Marla was sitting on Mila's goose down pillow at her desk. She had already dismissed her last class for the day and was looking at her lesson plan for the next day. Beatrice interrupted her thoughts. *Miss Marla, this gentleman is Thomas Renner Sr. He's Tom's dad and a lawyer. He's going to be Miss Samantha's attorney.*

Marla's eyebrows lifted. *Come sit down, both of you, please. So nice to meet you, Mr. Jenner. I know*

Samantha will be so appreciative of your representation. And thanks, Beatrice, for bringing him here to see me.

Nice to meet you too, Marla. My son tells me you are quite the teacher—and song leader.

He's too kind. I love to sing and because I know a few basic guitar chords, I'm able to lead our morning freedom singing. The students seem to enjoy sharing their feelings via music, don't you agree, Beatrice?

Absolutely!

Jenner continued. *Let me share that I met with Samantha today and she is in a good mental state. I gave her a little homework assignment of my own. I want her to mislead the sheriff about where her case is going. Sort of steer him down the wrong road. She seemed ready to meet the challenge. I also arranged for her to get some writing materials to summarize her experiences at Freedom School—not just her arrest, but all of the positive reasons she's chosen to participate in Freedom School. That will help us with the case, too.*

That sounds like a good strategy.

Now, what I'd like to talk to you about is very important. My overall plan is to keep the sheriff's office hopping with work. If we can keep them coming and going, they might make some legal snafus that would be to our advantage. Here's where you come in. What Sheriff Owens did to you was not only mean-spirited, but it was highly illegal. I'd like to file a civil lawsuit on your behalf, suing the Linnville Sheriff's Department for the beating they gave you. Can I get you to support this, Marla?

I'm not sure what to say. I'd like to forget about it if possible, so I'm thinking a law suit might just keep the horrible experience in my mind and make it more difficult to do that.

I understand. Another reason I'm asking you to agree to be the plaintiff in this case is that this case might positively influence the outcome of Samantha's case. Kind of like piggybacking on it to get more effect.

I will do anything to help Samantha, even if it means revisiting that awful experience. So, yes. I agree to help you.

Thank you, Marla. You are a brave young woman to stand up to the Linnville law. Or should I say, lack of law. Your case will be a civil law suit. I will need you to testify and I will need evidence. I know this is difficult, but I will need a photo showing the extent of your injuries. Jenner opened his briefcase and removed a Polaroid camera. *Would you be willing to have one of the women teachers take a close-up picture of your injuries? It could be done privately.*

Marla stood up slowly. *Beatrice, you treated me and have already seen the wounds. Would you be willing to take the pictures?*

Sure, Ma'am. If Mr. Jenner shows me how the camera works.

Jenner motioned for Beatrice to approach closer. *You'll do fine, Beatrice. I'll show you how to load the film. Just peel back the paper here and insert the film in this slot. Then point the camera like this and press this button. In a few seconds, the film will appear here. It takes a couple more seconds to get a clear image. Here's three packets of film. Marla, if I leave the room, do you feel comfortable for Beatrice to take your picture right now.*

Let's get it done. Of course.

I'll step out of the room and stand by the door to keep anyone from popping in. Beatrice, you come get me when you're done.

Jenner walked outside the classroom and closed the door. He leaned against the door jam. *She was easy to convince. Her case will send the sheriff in a tailspin.*

Tom saw his father leaning against the door and walked over. *Hey, Dad, are you going to bunk with me at my host family's tonight? I know they'd love to meet you and they sure could use the four dollars. My host mother is a great cook.*

Four bucks for a dinner and bed? That's a great price.

Actually, we're supposed to pay them four dollars for the whole week.

Somehow get word to them that I will stay there starting tomorrow night. You and I have a special place that we are going to bunk tonight.

And where might that be?

Keep it quiet, but we are staying right here in the Linnville Freedom School. We have a lesson to teach two Linnville good-old-boys.

Dad, here we call them the 'good-olds' because they definitely aren't boys.

Ah, clever.

Why are we staying here, Dad?

Let's go to town and get a bite and I'll explain. We'll stop at your host family on the way and say some hellos. Are you ready to hit the bricks?

Sure, Dad.

Go wait in the rental car for me. I need to touch bases with Marla and I'll be out.

Tom ventured down the hallway and said goodbye to Gina, Everett, and Miss Loretta. They were waiting for the COFO car to take them home.

Beatrice opened the classroom door. Here are the pictures I took, Mr. Jenner. Take a look and see if they are what you want. Marla didn't want to see them, but she wanted you to take a real close look. She said she'd be glad to take them over if you wanted.

Jenner stepped back into the room and flipped through the pictures. One of them showed a close-up of the back of Marla's upper thighs Jenner counted fourteen long cuts. Another was a shot taken of her calves. Jenner couldn't count the exact number of cuts—maybe twenty. And around each cut which was starting to heal, were dark black bruises emerging. *My God! That man is a monster and I plan to straighten him out.*

These pictures will be just the evidence we need. Thanks to both of you for this.

Marla stood up and walked to the door with the pillow. Well, I better get out to the front to catch the COFO car. It looks like Miss Loretta is already in it. Nice to meet you, Mr. Jenner, and thanks, Beatrice, for helping us out.

I better get going home, too. It was a special day here at Freedom School. Thank you, Miss Marla. Thank you, Mr. Jenner.

Tom waved to the Freedom Teachers as they drove off with Nels. Soon his dad emerged from the school. Tom jumped in the rental car with his father. *So, son, tell me how to get to your host family—now what is their name?*

It's not far. Just go straight ahead and I'll tell you where to turn. The family's name is Claude and Maybelle Woods. They have some cute kids. You'll like them all. Just be ready, their place is small and we'll have limited accommodations.

Son, that's of no importance to me. I don't care if I have to sleep outside on the ground. I'm here—and you, too—to change the status in the South. The people I've met so far are limited in their understanding of justice. We are going to give them a wake-up call.

Dad, turn left here. Their place is the second one we'll come to.

Jenner pulled into the dirt driveway. The cabin was unpainted and the boards worn. Two young boys were playfully wrestling in the dirt front yard. Tom waved his arm out the passenger window. *Hey, Willy and Wayne— who's winning?*

Both boys ran over to Tom. Willie was out of breath. *I'd be winning the wrestling match if my brother wasn't cheating.*

Hey, I wasn't the one cheating. You were.

Guys, I'd like you to meet my dad. His name is Thomas.

I didn't know you had a dad, Wayne said.

Yep. He's going to stay here with me if it's all right with your parents.

My parents will agree 'cause they like you, Tom.

Well, can you go get them and ask them to come out and meet my dad?

Both boys tore across the yard, jumped on the porch, and competed to open the screen door. Soon, Claude and Mabelle emerged onto the porch, wide-eyed.

Jenner and Tom climbed out of the rental car and sauntered over to the porch. *Maybelle and Claude, this is my father, Thomas.*

Nice to meet you, Claude said. *You have a real nice son. He's been good to our boys and I know the students at the school think he's a fine teacher. My nephew Daniel told me that.*

Jenner reached out his hand to shake theirs. *Nice to hear that. Seeing your boys wrestling in the yard took me back to the time when Tom was that age. He liked to wrestle his brother, too.*

Tom asked the question. *Mabel, and Claude, would it be okay if my dad bunked here while he was in town. He's going to need a place to stay for the trial—he's representing one of the Freedom Teachers.*

We heard about Samantha. Please know that we are behind justice one-hundred percent. Of course, you can stay here. We will make room.

Jenner explained his itinerary. *Actually, there's another place Tom and I need to be tonight, but we'd like to stay here starting tomorrow, if that would work.*

Maybelle stepped forward. *That will be just fine. It will give me time to pick the peaches and make you a nice peach pie.*

I do have one request before we head downtown. Would you have a couple of digging shovels we could borrow for a bit of time?

Claude nodded. *They are in the shed. I'll get them.*

He returned with the two shovels balanced on his left shoulder. *These should be very good digging shovels. I just sharpened the edges yesterday.*

Thanks, I'll get them back to you tomorrow. Sorry to have to rush off, but Tom and I have some work to do. Thanks for your nice welcome. See you tomorrow.

Both Jenner and Tom gave the couple friendly waves as the car backed out. Mabelle kept waving even after they had pulled out onto the gravel road.

So, Dad. Mind telling me what this mysterious plan involving shovels is all about?

It will make sense once we get to our destination. Now, one last stop for some bedding and rope. Where's the department store?

Off highway 67. Now, I'm really intrigued. Shovels? Bedding? Rope?

Is that it—Wright's Dry Goods?

Pretty sure. I haven't had a need to buy any bedding while I've been here.

I'm thinking it would be a good idea for you to just wait in the car while I shop, Tom

Sure.

The store was small and had a very limited selection of goods. Jenner walked to the counter and asked for bedding. *I need some bedding—do you have any to sell?*

The gray-haired clerk stared at Jenner. *How much bedding do you need?*

Two sets will be just fine. He took out his billfold and pulled out a twenty-dollar bill. *Will this cover it?*

You are a smart customer. I just don't know how you knew each set was exactly ten dollars. The rope is five.

I just guessed. I must be good at estimating. Jenner waited for the clerk to put the bedding in a paper sack; he handed the clerk the bills and walked out the door.

Let's grab a quick bite at the diner, then I'll explain what we'll be doing for the next couple hours.

***

Mississippi dusk. Jenner and Tom leaned against the trunk of a burly oak tree, seated on the ground with their feet extended. They had finished using the shovels which were now stowed in the trunk. Jenner had driven the car behind the school and parked it there. Now, the orange hues of the setting sun were barely visible as the sky began to darken. *Dad, I think the Spanish word to describe this scene is 'el anochecer.'*

I'm glad you are putting your education to good use.

So when do you think they'll be coming?

As a somewhat expert in human behavior, I'm guessing around ten p.m. Are you up to this, Son?

Dad, you have added an element of excitement and danger to my life. How could a kid not enjoy something like this. Of course, I'm ready for the action.

Good. I'm glad you found a pair of scissors in the school. They helped us put the finishing touches on our costumes.

Jenner put his pocket knife in his left pocket. It had been awhile since he'd made a lariat. His summer college ranching job had taught him the skill. He handed one to Tom. *Let's do a little roping practice until our guests arrive.* He stood up and swung his lariat three times before landing the loop around Tom. He tightened it, then quickly removed it. *Now, you try roping me.*

Tom imitated his father's actions, but the loop missed. His second throw was successful.

Whoopie! You are a true cowboy! Try one more throw just to make sure you've got it.

Tom put a little more elbow grease into his rope rotation and the loop quickly encircled his father. For dramatic effect, he pulled the loop a little tighter this time. Jenner wriggled free. *My son, the roper!*

You never cease to amaze me with all the skills you've learned throughout your life, Dad.

Well, I'm certainly drawing on some of them here in Linnville. Tonight I'll use my voice-throwing to let Burt Nemick and Hunter Radley think that they are surrounded by dozens of people. Can't wait.

Jenner and Tom resumed their relaxed position under the oak tree. Gradually, darkness descended in the valley and the crescent moon barely illuminated the sky. A discussion of constellations ping-ponged until it was time.

Truck headlights approached the school. Jenner and Tom donned their white-hooded robes. The truck slowed in front of Freedom School and stopped in the driveway. Peeking from behind a tree, Jenner and Tom observed one of the two men climb out of the truck and walk to the truck bed to pick up a metal can. Both men walked slowly toward the school.

The interlopers walked across the lawn which was covered in pine branches. Suddenly, the branches gave way and they plunged downward into a deep pit, taking the branches down with them. The grown men screamed like flighty teenage girls.

Instantly, Jenner and Tom stepped forward. They each swung a lariat and roped their prey. Jenner flicked on

172

a flashlight and shined it back and forth between Tom and himself. The light revealed that the two were wearing the unmistakable white robes of the Klu Klux Klan. Jenner disguised his voice. It came out loud and mean-spirited. *So, what do you know. Here are little Hunter Radley and his sidekick Burt Nemick. What's in that can you brought? A little juice to torch down the school?* Jenner used his ventriloquist skills to make several other voices so it sounded like others were standing nearby. *Now, I'm only going to tell you numbskulls once: I'm the official kleagle of this county and you are interfering in my klavern. I have something better than a little fire to show the school folk that they aren't wanted. So I'm keeping your kerosene. You are lucky that I'm going to let you drive away without a reminder of your trespassing. Now my colleague and I are going to pull you out of the pit and escort you to your poor excuse of a truck. You better move full speed down the road and get on home. Take your teddy bears to bed with you tonight. You might need them in case I call in some of my men to revisit you.*

Jenner and Tom pulled the men out of the pit and led them to the truck. They unloosened the lariats and opened the truck doors, giving each man a shove. Jenner repeated the loud crowd sound with his voice.

Nemick was the driver. He didn't remember how he got home. He just knew he would not mess with the Linnville Freedom School again.

Nice job, Dad. You scared the heck out of those bums.

Let's have a little contest. See if we can shovel the dirt back into the pit in less than an hour. Ready?

Chapter 8

Lydia Struck pulled back the middle desk drawer and took out her finger nail file. Things had been low this morning at the Linnville Court House, so she finally had some time to do a little personal grooming. Besides, her boss, Mr. Granger, always left about now for his daily coffee break at the diner. Not that he ever checked up on her work progress anyway. Her spicy pink fingernail polish was in the outside compartment of her purse and she'd get that out when she was done with the nail filing.

Lydia had been the clerk of court for twenty-seven years and knew everything backwards and forwards—staff, procedures, forms—every detail about every minute aspect of county law. Sometimes lawyers tried to fool her, but she just pulled out the county procedures manual and took them to task. She'd written the manual, so it didn't take her long to find the answer to a disputed procedure.

She gave each nail two coats of the polish, and blew lightly on them to make sure they were thoroughly dry before returning the jar of polish to her purse. Continuing her grooming regimen, she removed a hair pick and small mirror from the inner compartment of her purse. *This*

Mississippi humidity can wreak havoc with my hairstyle, that's for sure. Looks flat as a pancake. Keeping her eyes focused on the small mirror, Lydia fluffed the top and sides of her short blonde hairstyle. *Thank goodness, the sunshine yellow dye keeps my gray patches covered.*

The door opened and a man strode over to her desk. He wore a linen suit, nice shoes and a red striped tie. *Not from around here, that's for sure.*

The man spoke first. *Hello, Ma'am, I'm Thomas Jenner Sr., an attorney and I have a legal case to file with you.*

Lydia focused on his dreamy blue eyes. They seemed to magnetically attract hers. And his hair was wavy and dense. *As thick as a twenty year-old's.* After several seconds, she gained her composure. *Hello, Sir. I am Lydia Struck, the Linnville Clerk of Court. I will be happy to help you. Come over here and sit down.*

Lydia turned her right hand palm-up and gestured from her desk to a leather chair opposite her desk. *Just put your paperwork here on my desk and I'll look it over. Sit down and make yourself comfortable.*

Jenner expected the woman to read through his documents word-by-word and make some changes in the case procedures, so he leaned back against the chair

176

prepared to lose himself in some daydream or other while she combed it for discrepancies.

When Jenner placed his paperwork in front of her, a scent of manly aftershave wafted by her nose. *It's rather musky.* She noticed how the skin on his neck was so taut and how his shoulders were broad. *Tell me about yourself, Mr. Jenner. You must be from out-of-town. What brings you to our county?*

Lydia didn't give Jenner time to answer. She glued her eyes to his and continued to ramble. *Well, if you are staying in town for a while, I highly recommend you stay at the Geraud Hotel. It's one of Linnville's finest. Was built over a hundred years ago, but has been magnificently restored. It even has a dining room with the best pecan pie you've ever tasted. I certainly would be happy to walk you over there and introduce you to the manager. He'd want to give you one of his best rooms, I'm sure.*

Jenner folded his hands in his lap. He was right that it would take some time to get his paperwork registered, but he'd been wrong about the reason. This woman was giddy about him. He'd let her keep gushing. Maybe she'd overlook a few things.

And if you have time while you're here, be sure to drive up Nob Hill. It has a very scenic view of the area.

177

You'll see some fine plantations. My brother is the proud owner of the John B. Struck Plantation. It's been in our family for hundreds of years. I can give you the directions if you want to drive by. Also, we have some fine pecan farms where you can buy treats made from pecans—bread, pie, and cookies. Of course, there are no calories in any of those things.

Jenner gave her a polite smile. He'd let her babble on a few more minutes before redirecting her.

My brother and I are the only two surviving Strucks in the county. For some reason or other, our cousins have migrated North. Some moved to Chicago, some to Pittsburgh. John and I love Mississippi, though. It is such a great state to live in. The people here are so friendly to everyone.

Time up. *So, thank you Lydia, for that fine narrative about this area. I do believe you've helped me to gain even a deeper appreciation of it. I don't mean to interrupt your wonderful commentary, but I'm running behind a little this morning, and I wondered if you would please look over my case.*

Lydia opened her right desk drawer and got out her clerk of court seal. She stamped the top sheet and put the stamp back in the drawer. She placed the stamped documents in the "Processed" bin on her desk. *There's no need for me to take up any more of your valuable time-- I'm sure these papers are in fine order. I'll be glad to process your case, Mr. Jenner.*

Lydia stood up and reached out to shake Jenner's hand. *Thank you, Mr. Jenner for the privilege of working with you this morning. If you have any further questions, feel free to stop back and talk with me. I'm here every workday from nine to five.*

Jenner stood up. He could hardly believe what had happened. *I'm filing a civil lawsuit against the Linnville Sheriff's Department for one million dollars and this woman hasn't even read my summary page. And she didn't even notice the change of venue request form for the Bryant case, either.*

Thank YOU, Miss Struck for your fine attention. I'll be on my way.

Jenner gave her a small wave and walked out the Linnville County Courthouse. *If she opens my case proposal, she'll find out she's just agreed to have Marla Johnson's case heard before a federal judge of my choice. My choice is to have the Dane County Wisconsin Federal Circuit Judge in Madison, Wisconsin—Marla's hometown-- process the case and to have the judge rule on the case without requiring a jury trial or in-person defense. I'll just present my evidence to the judge in Madison personally so Marla won't have to relive the trauma. A liberal northern judge will be appalled to see one of his constituents physically beaten by a southern sheriff. This is my lucky day.*

Jenner speed-walked down the sidewalk to his rental car. Time to work on Samantha's case. *Unlike Marla's case, Samantha's will be a full-blown jury case. The showier, the better.* Jenner sat behind the steering wheel mentally listing what he'd need to do to reach his goals. *First thing I better do is interview my witnesses.* He put the key in the ignition, shifted into reverse gear, and steered the car in the direction of the Freedom School.

***

Gina carried a stack of worn clipboards down the Freedom School hallway. She walked into Everett's classroom and placed them on his desk. The students were busy working in small discussion groups and barely noticed Gina's presence.

Everett was jotting some notes down on a pad. He looked up when Gina came in. *Thanks, Gina. These came just in time for my students to use for our voting interviews.*

Good, I'm glad. It will make the kids look professional when they step out into the community. When are you going out?

'Time waits for no man.' We're going to go out in five or ten minutes. I've already set up groups.

Oh, one other thing. Tom's dad just got here. He wants to interview Joshua, Daniel, and Beatrice. Since they are in your class, will it be okay with you if they stay back for interviews?

Yeah. He needs to talk to them soon while their memories are freshest. I'll let them know.

Thanks, Everett. You are the best.

Not really, but thanks for the compliment.

Everett hustled around the classroom, whispering to the three about the interviews. *Jenner can probably just use my room as soon as we get out of here.*

Everett raised his hand as a signal for the kids to stop their group work and listen to him for an announcement. *Everybody, you've done a masterful job role-playing your interviews. Remember to be sure and ask some questions of interest at the beginning of your interview. You want to establish a connection with the person you are speaking with. Now, a few of you—you know who you are—will be staying back to be interviewed for Samantha's case. The rest of you grab a clipboard, piece of paper, and pencil off my desk and meet me outside the front door. We're ready to interview our first batch of future voters. They're waiting for us at Louie's Diner. Let's head out.*

Everett, his dozen students in tow, filed out of the classroom, down the hallway, and out the door of Freedom School.

Joshua, Beatrice, and Daniel moved together and sat down on a bench near the front of the classroom. Jenner walked in and sat down at Everett's desk.

Hello, kids. Actually, I shouldn't call you kids— you're young adults. It's just that you seem so young to me. I'd give anything to go back in time and be your age.

Beatrice frowned. *Respectfully, Mr. Jenner, you wouldn't be too thrilled to be our age if you were black.*

I hear you, Beatrice. I'm just so proud of you and the teachers for trying to establish racial justice here in the South. I know it's got to be tough with what you're dealing with each day—the fears and worries of what could happen, but I'm inspired by what you are trying to accomplish and I wish it were me here instead of my son.

Joshua chimed in the conversation. *Look at it this way, Sir. Each of us has certain talents that we can apply to the civil rights movement. You, as a white attorney, can guide the laws around the arrests of civil rights workers.*

Good point, Joshua. That hits the nail on the head. So, incidentally, what motivated each of you to participate in Freedom School?

I'll tackle that question first, Joshua said. *Speaking for myself, it's all about one word: opportunity. I think a lot about what makes some people have a better life than others, and in my opinion, it all boils down to looking for opportunity. It's not something that begs you to find it. Often, opportunity is hidden behind other things and can't be seen. But when you discover even a tiny glimpse of opportunity, you've got to reach out and grab it. That's me and Freedom School. I saw a poster this spring at Louie's Diner saying that volunteers would be coming down here to teach us lessons about freedom. Needless to say, I was very curious about what those lessons would entail, so I walked over to the COFO headquarters and signed up. I've never been so challenged to think about justice before. When the classes started, I was blown away be the fact that black and*

183

white people were teaming up together to teach. The lessons have challenged my thinking and helped me to learn that I deserve to have the same basic rights as others. When I worked together on a class presentation about Martin Luther King Jr. not only did I learn about his leadership, but I learned a new way of teaching—a way I've never been taught before: project learning. Much of my learning in the black school was good, I'm not criticizing it, but as you probably know, our black schools here are overcrowded and lack resources. Why, we learn from the old textbooks the white teachers throw away. And you can be sure that there are no black individuals featured in those history books. The Freedom Teachers are teaching us to be proud of our heritage. I hope I haven't taken too much of your time with this answer.

Not at all. You've answered the question well. How about you, Beatrice?

I agree with what Joshua said, mostly. For me it's a little different. I've learned that white people have good hearts. Why would they come down here and pay their own money for lodging and teaching supplies? I wrestled with this question when I first started coming to classes here. I guess I've never known any white people before, so I didn't trust the white teachers—Miss Marla, Miss Gina, and Tom at first. When I saw that they had the strong desire to help us be proud about our black heritage, even when they were white, then I opened my eyes. They are the epitome of goodness, that's for sure! I wish that other black people could get to know white people better. It would help further the cause of racial freedom, I think.

And what are you thinking about the Freedom School project, Daniel?

I don't want to sound ungrateful, but white people have more of everything than blacks. It started with the domination of slavery when masters treated their slaves more like animals than people. They were forced to live in shacks and eat simple foods. They often weren't allowed to stay together as a family unit, children being separated to go to different plantations. They were often physically mistreated, beaten or even killed if they spoke up about injustice. Sometimes they were lynched just as an example to other blacks not to challenge the white power structure. And the early education had to be done secretly because the slave masters didn't want their "property" to become educated. We're talking about the institution of slavery that was in place about a hundred years ago. What makes me really disgusted, is that not much has changed for blacks in those hundred years. Look at our economic status. Look at voting. Look at our schools. Look at job opportunities. Look at discrimination. Even though it may not be as obvious as a hundred years ago, in just about every area of society. My family is poor, Mr. Jenner, but we are like every other American family—we have hopes and dreams. It's near impossible for black people here in this state to ever accomplish their dreams. It's certainly not because they don't try, or because as some white people say, they're lazy, but it's because all the systems are rigged against them. Our only way out of poverty, is for a young person from the area to be invited North by a relative and encouraged to attend a northern college. Now, that sounds easy on the surface, but even getting a ride to Chicago, Boston, or Madison isn't easy. Because we're paid little more than subsistence wages, we even find it difficult to reimburse our relatives for food and lodging while we take college classes. And even though there's no blatant racism up North like there is here, there is a lot of subtle racism. People get jobs through the white network, leaving blacks with limited opportunities. You see, Mr. Jenner, it's such a web of white supremacy here, that we can hardly escape and even if we do, the spider is always hunting us, looking for ways to catch us.

Jenner glanced down at his notepad. He wrote the name of each student and one brief summary statement. He glanced up and looked directly into each set of eyes. *I can't thank the three of you enough for articulating these viewpoints. I can use your testimony not only in Marla's case, but also in the jury trial.* He saw the figure of Loretta Mays in the doorway.

Excuse me, Mr. Jenner, I need to get a book from the shelf in this room. Would that be interrupting you too much if I scooted in and got it and scooted right back out?

Come right in, Miss Mays. He scooted his chair closer to the desk so she could pass by him without getting crowded. *These fine Freedom School students have been telling me about their reasons for attending Freedom School and we are finished with our discussion. You aren't interrupting at all.*

Loretta's eyes spotted the history book on the left side of the small shelf. She had never seen such a book until the young teacher Gina had shown her before the lessons started. Loretta's knowledge about strong African-American historical figures had come from oral stories she'd heard, passed down from her ancestors or shared orally by other neighbors or by black preachers. To have the accomplishments of her people written down in books was an amazing feat. Gina had said she was welcome to take the book home and read it that evening. *Even if I only get to leaf through it, I'm thrilled.*

Perry will be here to pick me up shortly, and I really want to take this book home to study. Thank you again, Mr. Jenner, for allowing me to interrupt you to get it.

Beatrice looked at Jenner wide-eyed. *But, respectfully, Sir, we've just told you our inner thoughts about justice and this Freedom School. We didn't tell you anything about seeing the sheriff haul off Miss Samantha or beat Miss Marla. Don't you want to hear about what we saw?*

Jenner stood up. Actually, the three of you have shared exactly what I hoped for. Your teacher, Samantha, is really not the only one that's on trial. Freedom School is the defendant. In this trial, I'll be sharing parts of the messages you just shared with me. Not only do we hope to free Samantha from jail, but we hope to free the South from its racist ways. When the public learns about how dire the opportunities are here for blacks, they will be shamed. Fortunately, some who learn will take action and work towards racial justice. Your stories pieced together, will form the basis of an awareness that will placed before not

188

only Sheriff Owens and the white jury of Linnville, but the whole country will get to learn the intricacies of your lives and challenges.

Joshua wrinkled his forehead. *And just how do you plan to inform the whole country about all of this, Sir?*

Let me remind you that I come from California and as you probably don't know, I have represented a significant number of clients in the film industry. It's time for them to shall we say, do a little 'pay back.' Now, 'mum's the word,' until I have them on the hook.

Daniel interrupted. *Sir, I'm not understanding the fishing expression you just used. What do you mean?*

Jenner sat on the corner of the desk and crossed his ankles. *Ah, forgive me. I often fill my messages with idioms and expressions that may sound confusing. What I'm saying today, is that I envision the Bryant case to be bigger than just freeing one nice person from a lousy jail. Her trial is going to be a dramatic event, captured on film and broadcast over major television networks. Who knows, it may even become a stand-alone full-length movie—it certainly has all the elements: rising action, climax, denouement. . .*

What I meant when I said, 'mum's the word,' is that I haven't phoned anyone yet to specifically ask them to help, so please don't tell anyone about this plan yet. I'll let you know when you can spill the beans—I mean share this information with others.

Beatrice needed an answer. *Back to my earlier question, Mr. Jenner. Why don't you need us to tell you more about Miss Samantha's arrest and Miss Marla's beating?*

I still may need a couple of your reactions to the events, but we know the date of the incidents and I want you to keep your memories of seeing the arrests and beatings fresh in your minds. That's all. You'll see.

Jenner called out to Loretta as she was about to exit the classroom. *Oh, Miss Mays, I wonder if you would also be willing to give me some historic background about teaching here in Mississippi-- from your point of view.*

You want me to talk about teaching?

Yes, some of your best memories of the profession. Some of your star pupils. Some of the challenges you faced teaching—all teachers have challenges, don't they?

Why, I'm sure you are right, Mr. Jenner. Of course. I'll start reminiscing about my teaching days and jot down a few notes. Anything if it will help with the case.

My son tells me you did a great job substituting today for Miss Samantha and I don't doubt it one bit.

I did have a delightful day, Mr. Jenner. Why this nice group of students seated before you gave some above average presentations in class. You should have heard them. If only those who didn't make it could have heard them, they could have held on longer.

And by 'those who didn't make it,' do you mean black people who whites have lynched.

Sadly, people here have been kept in place by whites who go around with their lynching ways.

Miss Loretta, do you know of anyone around here who was lynched, but survived?

Loretta squinted. After a couple seconds she looked at Mr. Jenner. *There is someone you could talk to. His name is Ebidiah Green. He was left in a bad way, but his wife can interpret his mumblings for you if you want to meet him.*

I'd like that very much.

***

Owens sat down at his large oak desk and opened the brown envelope centered on his desk. Probably the clerk of court office runner had dropped it off while he was out for coffee. *Now what? That office is always sending more paperwork over. Don't they know that I'm too busy to read all the garbage they send my way?*

This packet was thicker than most. He unfastened the back envelope clasp and removed the stapled mass of paper. His eyes bulged out. There on the face of the packet was typed: *Notice to the Linnville Sheriff's office: the civil lawsuit of Marla Johnson of Wisconsin vs. the Linnville, Mississippi Sheriff's Department will be heard by a federal judge in Dane County, Wisconsin on or about the fifteenth of July, 1964.*

There was a smaller typed message at the bottom of page one: *Plaintiff Marla Johnson of Madison Wisconsin is suing Defendant Sheriff Leroy Owens and his department for one million dollars damages.*

The Defendant is required to return this signed form showing receipt of document to Clerk of Court Linnville and written evidence countering the charges herein the enclosed document by the tenth of July, 1964.

Owens closed his eyes and put his head down on his desk. *How could this have happened? Lydia Struck always takes care of me. What was she thinking to let an upstart out-of-state-attorney push her around .*

He shoved himself up and reached for his hat. He didn't remember if he told anyone in the office where he was going or not.

Chapter 9

Dean Jedemiah Roanoke pushed himself away from the table. His wife had gone overboard tonight. The buttery mashed potatoes and the brown sugar-topped carrots had tasted ever so good, but he'd have to loosen his belt at least one notch and take a momentary break before dessert. Of course, he hadn't needed to have had two large servings. *But I never want to hurt Irma's feelings. She goes to such lengths to prepare the foods I like for supper that I take those extra helpings.*

Dean, I've been thinking I need to go visit my sister. She called today and said she was feeling very lonesome. You know I haven't been to see her in over a year.

I thought you didn't like driving to Alabama. It's over a three-hour drive.

You read my mind, Dear. I don't like driving that far myself. I thought I might take Georgette and her brother Thomas. Thomas could help me with some of the driving. You know, we could spell each other a bit from time to time.

Do I translate what you are saying to: you want me to pay Thomas to do all of the driving there and he and his sister also have some relatives to visit in Huntsville?

How did I ever marry such a smart man? Why, Dear, you know how special it would be for me not to have to be alone in the car worrying about what to do if I got a flat tire or low oil pressure. Thomas has been working for us for nineteen years and he's been such a dependable gardener. When Georgette dropped off our clean laundry this morning, she reminded me that their ailing mother lived on the outskirts of Huntsville. If you think it's been a long time since I've seen Sis, it's been even longer—some four years—since the two of them have been together with their mother

Since when have you been so engrossed in the social needs of our family's part-time employees?

You told me yourself that a happy worker is a dedicated one.

So the fifteen dollars I pay Thomas each month isn't enough to keep him happy? I know for a fact that I'm one of the better paying employers here in Linnville. I suppose you want me to start a trend to not only be the best paying employer, but also to give the most lavish vacations.

Irma rotated the earring on her right ear. She blinked her eyelashes and smiled flirtingly. *So, I take that as a 'yes' that you approve of my well-laid out plan, Dear.*

I think I'm being hoodwinked, Irma, but who am I to thwart the social plans of you and your two friends. Yes, I give you permission to take the Packard. I'll speak to Thomas tomorrow about the financial arrangements. You go and have a nice little visit with your sister. Who knows, you may bring me back some fresh pecans.

Irma stood up and blew Dean a kiss. *You are simply the most wonderful husband a woman could have. Now you'll need to make a really big decision. I baked two desserts this afternoon. Would you like a piece of sweet potato pie or a slice of caramel cake?*

Dean didn't want to hurt his wife's feelings. *Guess I better have a piece of each, Dear.*

Irma pushed herself up from her chair. *That's a very good choice, Dear.*

She set two china dessert plates in front of Dean. He kept his gaze squarely on them and alternately took forkfuls of pie and cake until both had been consumed. *I can't tell which I like better, Irma. It's a good thing I asked for each.*

Irma smiled. *Dear, you know you like all my desserts. You've been such a good eater of my cooking. I'll make sure to put up some desserts for you before I leave for Sis's. Maybe we can get someone to come in and cook for you while I'm gone. What do you think?*

Not a bad idea, Irma. You always seem to be a step ahead of me. Say, I feel pretty full from supper. I think I'll walk over to the office for an hour or so. I can work off a few calories that way. I never got a chance to open my mail today—too many interruptions. You won't mind, will you?

Dean knew she wouldn't. She'd just scored a major marital victory: his blessing to take a chauffeured trip out-of-state to visit her sister. *She isn't going to care about my comings or goings at all after I granted her that wish.*

You go right ahead and walk over to your office, Dear. I need to call Sis with the good news that I'm coming for sure. We might be on the phone a bit, so don't worry about hurrying back.

Irma cleared her dessert plate and coffee cup from the table. She'd return after the phone call and do the rest of the clean-up work. *A few dirty plates can wait until after the call.*

Dean's office would be a nice quiet place to make her call. She gave Dean a little half-wave and walked into his dark-paneled office. She sat down in his brown swivel chair and reached for the phone. She dialed *Cherry 222-3073.* Her sister picked up after one ring.

I just knew you'd be calling me any second, Irma. And I can tell from the timeliness of your call that you got your way on the trip. I'm thrilled you are coming.

That old saying, 'The way to a man's heart is through his stomach,' is one-hundred percent true. Once again, the two 'P's' did it—potatoes and pie. Works every time. Dean will pay Thomas to drive me to your place, Sis. We'll bring his sister, Georgette along

Oh, I agree. There are so many things we can do when you're here, Irma. We can have some nice parties and maybe some small day trips. . . .

Dean overheard the first part of his wife's conversation as he walked down the hall and out the door. She was mighty happy. *Dad always said to let the women think they got things over on you and your life would be happy. He was right.*

Dean was glad he'd decided to walk. Grant Avenue was real pretty this time of year. The magnolia trees bloomed along both sides of the street and there was a black wrought iron fence that showcased the lines of Victorian homes along both sides of the avenue. Thanks to Thomas and the other black gardeners, there wasn't a blade of grass out of place and all the shrubs and flower gardens were perky.

Dean noticed a pair of bluebirds flitting about on the ground. He passed them noticing how much more colorful the feathers were on the male compared to the female. *Kind of the opposite in the human species. The women are the colorful ones—just think about their clothes they wear—reds, pinks, bright blues. . . and we men—we don the browns and blacks of the color spectrum. Must be a hidden message here somewhere. . .*

The Linnville County Courthouse was a majestic building. Even eight blocks away, the sturdy marble pillars could be seen supporting the structure. Statues depicting the state's history stood proudly along the front of the building. Dean always reviewed them left-to-right before going inside. First, as Dean referred to them, *the clump of colonizers*—generic figures of a Frenchman, a Spaniard, and an Englishman. Dean recognized the statues were to honor the European explorers who represented the colonization of the land, especially its rich delta bottomland. *Let's see, if I remember my high school state*

199

history lessons, that time period began in the 1540s. These not-so-popular rulers oversaw settlers who held enslaved Africans. Dean mused how the rulers had their black mistresses and often freed them and their multiracial children. *Now that's something that was never in our history books.*

Of course, the first statue—obviously missing from this lineup—should be one of the Choctaw and Chickasaw natives. They were here first and built a rich culture full of traditions. But like much of the country's indigenous peoples, these people were driven west of the river so the whites could get on with their business. The Linnville city fathers chose to omit any tribute to them.

Last in the lineup of statues. was a planter. *That next statue of a planter should really be of a slave. The Euro-Americans brought slaves here to support their cotton empires. All the rich farmland along the Yazoo and Mississippi Rivers was controlled by the few, wealthy planters. It's no wonder that in addition to controlling the richest land, they also controlled the wealth, and the politics of the state.* Dean's favorite subject in school had been history and he relished revisiting it.

Count on the Linnville City Council to omit all the negative history in our state—slavery, the disfranchising constitution which took the lands and political power of blacks, the Indian Removal Act, the Civil War, the depression, and the continued suppression of the rights of blacks.

Dean's friends and colleagues were more conservative, so he kept his libertarian views mostly to himself and to Irma. Her father had been a minister with a big heart and didn't think people had the right to dominate others. He agreed. He and Irma often had discussions about ways they could make life more opportunistic for the blacks they knew. Only Irma knew about the loans he gave to blacks he noticed had potential. *I would have been a better Yankee than Confederate.* He had built his career in the South, and for all its imperfections, it offered a slow-paced way of life that suited him.

His history review finished, Dean unlocked the door and entered the foyer. The city fathers had spared no expense to decorate the interior either. A large portrait of William Claiborne hung on the west wall. Dean had some respect for the guy. Although he was on record for acquiring some land from the Choctaw and Chickasaw, Claiborne was recognized as being sympathetic toward them. *He was more of a nationalist, than a localist, I'd say.*

Dean placed his hand on the golden oak handrail and began ascending the marble steps to the second floor where his and other official offices were located. *Maybe if I walk double-time, I can work off a few calories from that big dinner.*

He fumbled through his key ring until he found the skeleton key for Office 121. His eyes were magnetically attracted to the stack of mail on the upper right corner of his desk. *I think I can gnaw through that pile in a half hour or so.*

On top was a no-brainer: a renewal form for his county law license. He took out his checkbook and cut a check for a hundred. Then, several pieces of junk mail. The last envelope was a copy of a document Lydia Struck had sent over. He used his brass letter opener to slit the envelope. He removed the single sheet of notarized paper and read the message: *In the case of Linnville Circuit Court vs. Samantha Bryant, the attorney for the defendant, Thomas Jenner Sr., is requesting a change of venue.*

What? How could an attorney not get justice in my court? Dean jumped up from his chair and paced back and forth. He had heard about the Bryant girl getting arrested. He wasn't surprised that Owens had arrested someone from the Freedom Summer Movement. They were stirring up the status quo and that had led to concern by Owens and several local leaders.

But wait a minute, with a name like this, this attorney is no local; he's come in from the outside and is probably wanting to prove a point about racial justice. He doesn't know that unofficially, I like the dynamic energy of the young people who've come down here trying to change things. Hmm . . . I'm going to lead him on a bit—pretend to be irate that he claims he can't get justice here. I want the case here, though; It will be entertaining to see how he handles Owens and the boys.

Dean slid out his middle desk drawer and removed his fountain pen. In the space at the bottom of the document, he wrote: *Defense must explain why he believes he cannot get justice in my court. Signed, Judge Dean Jedemiah Roanoke*

He replaced it in the envelope. Tomorrow, he'd drop it off to Lydia.

Chapter 10

Gina Lovick gathered the notes her students had written to Samantha. She couldn't imagine how her friend and colleague could keep her spirits up being stuck in the local jail. Gina imagined herself being confined in a small, barren room with no books, no TV, no human contact. *Maybe I'm just a wimp, though. Or maybe it's my claustrophobia that makes me reel to think of being confined in a very small area. I hope they are letting Samantha out for some walks now and then.*

Gina had no idea whether the jailer would let her give Samantha the notes or not. It was worth a try at least. She had an hour before her next class at Freedom School, so enough time to walk over to the jail and present the notes. The students had folded paper in half and used some colored pencils to draw a design or figure on the front and then written some cheery messages inside. The messages were short, but heartfelt. Beatrice had drawn a picture of an ant carrying a large cookie on its back on the cover of hers and her inside message said, "Carry that load of yours, Girl!" Gina thought the symbolism of carrying the responsibility of serving jail time with optimism was inspirational—*at least I hope cards like Beatrice's will inspire her.*

Gina thought back to her own reason for becoming a Freedom Teacher. It started back in her junior high Girl Scout troop when she was working on a badge. Her leader had suggested she volunteer at a local center for behaviorally disabled kids. Somehow her leader knew the activities director there and recommended it as an opportunity that would be helpful to the kids housed at the center as well as for Gina. So every Saturday morning—*seems it must have been for three months*—she hopped on the New York Subway and got off in front of the Center for Educational and Behavioral Growth to do her one-hour craft-time with the kids. Gina had taken all the art classes she could in school and loved working with every art medium. Her art teacher often taped her sketchbook drawings on the classroom bulletin board as examples of good drawing skills. *I knew the volunteering would be more craft work than art work, but I wanted to give working with the kids a shot—even though I knew they would have behavior challenges.*

Her first time there, Gina had waited patiently while the center's receptionist unlocked the door and looked over her volunteer paperwork. *She told me to go down the hallway to the second door where the art room was located and I remember being a little surprised to see that the teacher there was not only male, but black. My parents were always open with me about race, but I just didn't have much opportunity to cross paths with people of different races. Mr. Colbert—he told me to call him Bob—was really nice. He explained the project goals for the lessons and told me to just be myself and walk around and help kids with their projects. Mostly, he wanted me to compliment them as they worked on task and compliment their skills. I was fine with that, though I remember being nervous about what to do if one of the kids flipped out. Fortunately, they related to me and seemed to enjoy having me sit near them and talk to them softly. Only once, did a kid have a behavior fit—was his name Tommy? I can't quite remember. What I do remember clearly is the message that Bob said to me every time before I left the center—'You shared your talents today, Gina, with some children who were not as blessed as you.' Mr Colbert was right. I grew up an upper middle class white girl in Manhattan who had two loving parents—two parents who loved and nurtured me and gave me every opportunity you could ask for. I went to a great private school, participated in music lessons, went on trips abroad with my family, and experienced every benefit from a white upper class family. Bob never told me about his personal life, and I got the notion that it didn't matter what economic level he was, his heart was dedicated to making a difference to these kids through art.*

When I heard about the Freedom School Project, I thought about how many of the kids in the South didn't have the opportunities I did. While I wanted to come down here to teach, I had wished I would teach younger kids, not high school ones. I had my doubts about being successful with older students. But now, thanks to the training I got and the way the schools were set up with supportive co-teachers, I'm so thankful I'm working with these high school students. They have accepted me and helped me learn more about myself as well.

Gina had reached the Linnville Jail. She opened the outer door which led to a small entry room with a phone on a desk. She walked behind the desk to a door and pulled on the handle. *I must need to speak into the phone.* Cautiously, she picked up the receiver and introduced herself. Her hand tightened around the envelope containing the student-designed cards. She hadn't met the sheriff in person and didn't relish talking to him.

A woman's voice spoke to her. *Hello, this is the sheriff's office. Hannah here. Who are you?*

Gina relaxed her grip on the card envelope. *I'm Gina, a teacher friend of Samantha. I have some cards her students made that I'd like to drop off for her.*

The phone went silent. Gina wondered if she should leave the envelope on the desk. Maybe the jail matron would come out into the entry room and pick them up after she left. The door to the entry room quickly opened and a woman leaned around it. *Hurry, now, and you can come in and give those cards to your friend yourself.*

You mean I can talk to Samantha?

The woman's hand rested on Gina's shoulder. *Why of course. Something's going on and both the sheriff and deputy are out of the jail. It's just me and the janitor. You come on in and visit with your friend for a few minutes. I'll be watching out the window for when they are coming back. You can leave out the back door if they come.*

Hannah led Gina past the desks and into the cell area. She gestured to Samantha's cell.

Samantha! I'm so glad to see you! How are you doing?

Samantha put down a notebook on the edge of her cot and stood up. She rushed over to the bars and reached out her hands. Gina pulled her forward for an awkward hug.

Gina, you can't imagine how happy I am to see you today. It's been an awful experience being cooped up here, but I'm encouraged that I have a lawyer who is going to represent me and he says my court case will be starting soon.

I'm glad about that, Sam. You know he's Tom's dad, don't you?

Yes. From the minute I met him, I sensed he would do a good job representing me. I sure hope so as this is a place I don't want to have to spend one minute more time in than essential.

Gina loosened her grip on the envelope with student cards. *Here, Samantha. The freedom kids made some cards for you. They really miss you.* She handed her the card packet through an opening in the bars.

Gee, thanks. She took the envelope from Gina's outstretched hand. She opened the envelope and pulled out the thick wad of cards.

I didn't know if I could get them to you or not, but I knew it was worth a try. We all really miss you, Sam.

I know. How's Loretta holding up? I'm glad that she is subbing for me.

You know, I have to say that she's doing a great job. Marla says It seems like coming back to teaching has given her a new lease on life. She's having your students share their cultural projects. I heard that they all are doing a great job.

I'm so glad. I knew they would. To be able to showcase notable blacks in history is important an essential for them. They sure have accomplished a lot in the short time we've been teaching them, haven't they?

Right on, Sister.

Please tell everyone at school 'hi' for me, will you?

Will do, friend.

Samantha reached under her cot and felt for some half-sheets of paper. She pulled the thin paper packet out and handed it to Gina. *So, Gina, these are some haiku poems I wrote about racial justice—would you share them with the students—maybe read them aloud after the morning freedom song time?*

Wow! That's great! I don't know how you manage to keep staying so positive while being stuck here in jail. You amaze me, girl. The students will love these. Incidentally, I overheard Everett talking with Nels and

some at COFO think we should bring the students to watch
the trial. The lawyer wants to make a big deal about how
racial justice is what's on trial, not just you.

Samantha grinned. *Actually, it is.*

Hannah tapped Gina on the shoulder.. *Hurry, Gina.*
You need to follow me out the back door. The deputy is on
his way back here and he won't appreciate Samantha
having any visitors. Come fast. She grabbed Gina's wrist
and pulled her along.

Bye, Samantha. Take care.

I will. And you, too. Samantha stuffed the cards
back into the envelope and placed the envelope under the
edge of her cot. The cloth tie held it in place above the
floor. *I'll read these later tonight.*

Hannah pressed hard against the steel door. She
opened it just wide enough for Gina to squeeze through.

Hannah took a cloth out of her pocket and pretended
to dust the floorboards as Deputy Dan walked in through
the entrance way. *I don't know how so much Mississippi*
dust can end up here in this jail.

Glen took off his hat and set it on his desk. He
plopped down in his desk chair and rolled his eyes. *Don't*
trouble me about any dust, Woman. We've got bigger
things than that to be worrying about. Sheriff Owens is in

a tizzy. Even worse than that. Seems that hot shot lawyer is filing a case against our office and besides that, he's messing with the Bryant court case. We're knee-deep in alligators!

Well, that is certainly troubling news, Deputy. I better be getting home and cooking supper for you and the others. Maybe I need to bake up a special dessert for you. How about my pecan caramel cake?

Yeah. Pecan caramel cake. Glen closed his eyes and leaned forward, resting his head in his hands. Hanna couldn't tell if the noise he was making was moaning or crying. She slipped out the back door.

***

Gina felt mobbed. The word had gotten around the school that she'd left to take the student cards over to Samantha.

Did you see her? Beatrice asked. She knew that visitors were never allowed to see the Linnville inmates, but she couldn't help asking.

Yes, I did get to talk with her for a few minutes. The officials were gone for a bit and Hannah let me in. Please don't spread the word.

Loretta walked into the discussion. *Tell me, how does Samantha look. Is she all right?*

Samantha eyeballed the ten-or-so students and teachers gathered around her. She wanted to reassure them. She raised her voice and shared, *Samantha said to tell you all hello and to thank you for the cards. I couldn't stay long, so she plans to open them up later.*

Later when Owens isn't around, blurted Adam.

Samantha was so glad to hear that you are continuing to share your history projects under Miss Loretta's supervision. Gina noticed that Loretta's smile stretched across her face. *Samantha wishes you to keep doing your best in school and in life.*

Gina sensed someone was standing beside her. She looked over her right shoulder and recognized Tom's father. She turned toward Jenner and in a lower voice, addressed him. *Hello, Sir. Samantha is so glad you are representing her.*

Jenner nodded. He walked over to Loretta and whispered a message to her. *Can you go with me for a short visit to the man you told me about who'd been lynched? I'd like to meet him.*

Ebidiah Green? Yes. I will do that. If we go now, we won't interrupt his supper. His wife Bea will be grateful for our visit, I'm sure.

Are you sure you want to ask a teacher to give you instructions? She chuckled. She turned to Everett. *Son, will you tell Perry when he comes to pick me up, that I am with Attorney Jenner. I suspect he will drop me off at my house when we are finished visiting Mr. Green. Is that right, Mr. Jenner?*

Yes. I will definitely take you back home after our visit, Loretta.

Jenner extended his forearm to guide Loretta out of the school.

Why, Mr. Jenner, I do believe you are going to spoil me with your gentlemanliness.

It's the least I can do, Loretta, for your assistance. You are taking a big personal risk just to house the Freedom School kids, not to mention helping out at school, and taking me to see Mr. Green. I'm most appreciative. I think I will have to take you out to dinner some night to show my appreciation.

Loretta wasn't sure how to respond. The fine restaurants like he'd want to dine in would certainly not welcome him with a black woman as his guest. The only

214

place they would be allowed to eat at would be Louie'ss diner, the black restaurant.

That is a lovely invitation, Mr. Jenner. I hope to take you up on it.

Jenner opened the passenger door and patiently waited while Loretta stepped in, seated herself, and arranged her dress to cover her knees.

So, is Mr. Green's place far from here? Jenner backed out onto the gravel road.

Not really. Just follow this road and when you come to the "T", bear to the right. You'll come to Ebidiah and Bea's place in about a mile or so. They live just a half-mile east of me. Oh, and be ready for a visit that pulls on your heart strings. Ebidiah was left in a bad way from the lynching. His face and body got pretty burned, and Bea has to do the talking for him. Mr. Jenner, since we go right by my house on the way, would you mind pulling in my driveway and allowing me to fetch some chicken and noodles and pecan cake for the Greens?

Nope. Be happy to stop.

Jenner was going too fast for the sharp turn into Loretta's driveway. Gravel scattered every which way. He flung his driver door open and walked around to open Loretta's.

You just wait here, Mr. Jenner. I'll just be a minute getting some provisions to take to the Greens.

Loretta climbed up her porch steps one at a time and pulled her screen door open. She hurried as quickly as she could into the house. The previous night, she'd prepared a large casserole pan of chicken and noodles and quite a bit was left over. She rummaged in a cupboard until she found a small glass pan with a lid. She scooped chicken and noodles into the smaller pan until it was nicely filled. Opening the pie cupboard, she removed a pan of pecan cake, still quite moist. She cut two generous portions and placed them in in a smaller glass container which she covered with a cloth. *Ebidiah won't be able to eat this cake, but Belle can sure enjoy it.* Both containers fit well into her carrying picnic basket. She opened the back passenger door and placed the basket on the seat. Jenner was holding the front passenger door open for her and she climbed in gingerly.

You were mighty fast filling that picnic basket, Miss Loretta.

I have my ways of hurrying when necessary, Mr. Jenner.

Jenner had seen some bad physical disfigured bodies when he'd visited the Great Lakes Naval Hospital in

216

Chicago. He'd gone to see one of his high school buddies who'd been injured in a land mine explosion during the early days of the Vietnam War. His buddy, Ray, had lost three toes on his right foot and that was one of the lesser injuries he'd seen that day. Ray's ward mates' injuries ranged from lost eyesight to missing limbs, to paralyzed bodies. Jenner had geared up for a somber mood and was surprised to see the bandaged soldiers laughing and cheering as they held wheel-chair races in the hallway. *After I left, I realized that while all of them were injured, they knew they didn't have to go back into battle and their joy was probably a feeling of relief and happiness just to be alive.*

Loretta led Jenner up the worn wooden steps and onto the porch. She knocked on the door and waited. A soft voice said, *Come on in. Loretta set the picnic basket on the kitchen table.*

Jenner's Chicago hospital visit had in no way prepared him for what he saw in the living room. A single cot was positioned in the center of the room and atop it lay a badly scarred body. Jenner saw the fingers on each hand fused together—probably a result of heat. Jenner forced himself to look at Ebidiah's face, sunken eyes and scarred masses of tissue where a mouth should have been.

217

Jenner nodded toward Ebidiah and then Bea. *Hello, Ebidiah and Bea. I'm Thomas Jenner, and I'm glad to meet you.*

Ebidiah made a soft gurgling sound which Bea translated. *Hello, Mr. Jenner. My man says he's really pleased to meet you.*

Likewise. I thank you for allowing me to talk with you. Miss Loretta says that you were lynched, Mr. Green. When did that happen?

Jenner kept his eyes focused on Green's sunken eyes out of respect.

Ebidiah slurred some sounds and Bea spoke. *It was five years ago, Sir. Ebidiah was asleep in bed when a carload of white men pulled into the driveway. He went out on the porch to see what was going on. Two of the men jumped out of the back seat of the car and grabbed him, tying his hands behind his back. The others pounded a big cross in the dirt, then tied Elijah to the cross. They poured some gas on it and the cross started burning with my man tied to it. They got in their car and drove off. By the time I got a bucket of water to pour on him, he was pretty burned up. Doc said he wouldn't pull through, but somehow, he's managed to live.*

Jenner was appalled. He didn't know what to say next. A question slowly formed in his mind. *Did either of you see who any of the men were that did this?*

Ebidiah mumbled something indecipherable. Bea waited and then said, *Even though the men had their white hoods on, I recognized the voices of a couple of the men: Burton Nemick and Billy Rae Jones.*

Bea looked directly at Jenner. *Mr. Jenner, I was standing right inside the screen door and I clearly heard the voice of Sheriff Owens. He was yelling at the men to hurry and get in the car.*

I don't doubt your recollection one bit, Bea, but how are you so sure it was his voice?

Well, Sir, before Hannah cooked and cleaned at the jailhouse, it was my job. Mr Owens had a habit of saying a certain expression when he was nervous: 'Gol dang bolwevils,' he often said it. I heard him shout that evening, 'Gol dang bolwevils, get in the car!'

Jenner didn't want to stress out Ebidiah any longer with memory of the event. *Mr. and Mrs. Green, I thank you for sharing your memories of the lynching with me, though I know it was painful. I hope to get you some justice for what's been dealt your way. I will keep in touch with you.*

Do you need me to stay and help with Ebidiah's feeding? Loretta asked Bea.

No, Dear. I can manage just fine. You go on home now.

Loretta walked over to the kitchen table and removed the two food containers. *Here's some chicken and noodles and pecan cake for you two. You enjoy it.* She picked up the empty picnic basket and walked back to Ebidiah's cot.

God loves you, Ebidiah. Loretta put her hand on his mangled arm. You take care, now.

Bea followed them to the door. *Thank you so much for coming and for the food. You are good people.*

Out in the car, Jenner wiped some tears from his eyes. How people could be so inhumane simply escaped him. *Loretta, tell me, just how does Ebidiah eat. It appears his mouth is scarred shut.*

Well, on the left side of his mouth is a tiny opening—so small you can hardly see it. Belle puts a straw in that opening. Before she does that, she props Elijah up on some pillows so he doesn't choke. She cooks down all his food into a liquid form and when it's cool, she puts drops of it down the straw into his mouth. Sometimes it gets stuck here and there so she has to massage his back to

220

help the digestive process. It takes a lot of time to get through a meal, that's for sure. Every now and then, I stop by and help her. She's very appreciative of that as well as the money folks drop off so she can pay her bills without working.

You know, Loretta, the longer I stay around here, the more impressed I become with the kindness your people show to one another. And Ebidiah could easily harbor anger toward me, a white man, for the injustices some white men did to him, yet he doesn't. What a lesson in forgiveness.

We all know that there are some wonderful white people and there are some very evil ones. We also know that when the wonderful white people start speaking out more, that the injustices will decline. That's why it's good for us to have you here, Mr. Jenner. You in your position as an attorney can make a difference in a big way.

I only hope so.

Chapter 11

'*Gol darn bolwevils*. Owens slumped down in his desk chair.

Deputy Glen looked up from reading the sports section of the weekly *Linnville Sentinel*. He knew why the sheriff was worried. The legal cases were mushrooming out of hand.

Tom, you need to get focused. We have the power and can knock down their cases. Want me to help you start working on them?

You're right. Glen. We have two separate things going on here, the Samantha Bryant case and the Marla Johnson one. I'm going to set up two manilla folders and start taking notes for each case. Let's start on the Bryant case.

Just my suggestion, but why don't you sort of interview the girl and find out a little information about how her attorney is going to argue the case. She impresses me as pretty intelligent for a black girl and maybe she would spill the beans if she knew she could get some privileges.

What do you mean by 'privileges?'

You know, just lead her on thinking she could get a lighter sentence if she shared some information with us.

And another suggestion: better call up Hector Smith and get him updated. He'll need to know everything to represent us.

Glen, you are a genius. I knew there was a reason I had you here as my deputy.

Owens picked up the receiver and dialed the courthouse. He wasn't exactly certain who had answered— probably a new secretary. *Sheriff Owens here. Can you connect me with Hector Smith?*

One minute please.

Hey, Sheriff. Hector here. What's up?

Smith, I need your legal advice. A hot shot lawyer from California is slapping a law suit on me for a little incident I had with a lippy white intruder. Can you come over for a little pow-wow?

Hmm. You know I'm buried in preparation for the Bryant case. You didn't give me much context for the case, you know. Now that you mention it, I did see a paper circulating through the office about a law suit. They've got to be kidding if they think they can squeeze a million out of our county.

Well, do whatever you can to shut up those Yankees and their Freedom propaganda. I've had just about all I can take of them here in Linnville messing with our state of the union.

I hear you, Owens, but we've got to tread lightly. The Feds are circling around our state looking for the three missing civil rights workers. We can't just do anything blatant right now. I've been working on witnesses for the case and so far I've narrowed it down to Nemick, Radley, McGrath, and Jones. We'll need to get together sometime soon—maybe this weekend—and go over the particulars.

I pretty much agree, but we better keep Nemick and McGrath for the jury And McGrath would be a good jury foreman.

Yeah, that sounds good. Say, would it help if I tried to squeeze out a little information from Bryant about what direction her attorney's going? I'll offer her a sweet deal or two and get her to loosen her tongue. What do you think?

Not a bad idea. Be careful, though. We don't want her telling her attorney what we're up to. See if you can find out a few things. As far as the Johnson lawsuit goes, I think I read that the attorney is going to present his case in front of a judge in Wisconsin and we just get to submit some written statements. I'll put something together soon and mail it to the judge. Don't know why we can't present our argument in person—must be the lawyer has some ties with that judge. We're hoping the judge knows that the million dollar request is just pie in the sky—no small county in any state has that kind of dough.

Okay, so let me get this straight. You'll be taking care of the Johnson case and doing the write-up for it. I'll sniff out some information from the Bryant girl and get that to you. Then you, Jones, Radley, and I will get together this weekend to prepare our case

Yeah. That sounds about right. Unless we can come up with some stall tactics, the case is scheduled to come before the judge next week.

Maybe it's a good tactic to get it going—the more time we give that hot shot lawyer, the more he might come up with against us.

Owens, just so you know, the general sentiment around the country is changing. Our way of keeping the blacks subservient is losing popularity. Be ready for a slight adjustment in your attitude and deportment.

If that means letting the blacks have their way in things, then I'm holding firm. There's no way blacks are going to take the lead in Linn County—not on my watch.

Just sayin'.

So, I'll be getting on with my interview. I'll get
back to you Smith

Right. Bye.

Owens put the receiver down on the hook. He
walked over to the refrigerator and took out a can of
lemonade. *Glen, would you deliver this to the Bryant girl.*
Tell her we want to have a friendly chat in five minutes.
This should put her in a good mood.

How about adding a bag of Fritos?

Owens opened his large lower right desk where he
stashed dozens of bags of salty snacks. *I hate to give up*
these Fritos. He rummaged through the myriad supply of
snack bags and pulled out a bag of Wavy Chips. *I guess I*
can spare one of these. They usually are a little too greasy
even for me. He handed the bag off.

Let her drink and eat in peace. Then fetch her and
bring her over to the work table.

Samantha was reading Hannah's Bible when she
heard footsteps. She quickly closed it and set it under the
cot. She sat up and pretended she'd been sitting
daydreaming. *Oh, hello, Deputy.*

Here's a couple of treats for you to enjoy. I'll be back in a short time. The sheriff wants to have a friendly chat with you about how things are going.

Glen extended his right hand through the bars and gave Samantha the lemonade and chips. He turned and walked back down the short corridor.

What could be going on? Why would they bring me a treat? Oh—I know. . . they hope to get some information from me about the case. I guess this is my chance to use my improv skills.

Samantha popped the tab on the lemonade can. The tart beverage felt cool against her dry throat. She opened the chips and munched on a few. *I'm going to just eat a few of these at a time.*

Samantha was just half-way through the can of lemonade when the deputy reappeared. He unlocked her cell door and gestured for her to follow him. *You can bring the can with you to finish.*

He led her to a small, metal table and pulled out a heavy oak chair for her to be seated in. As soon as she was seated, Owens walked over to the table, and sat down. She noticed his farcical smile. *Howdy, Miss Bryant. Did you enjoy your little snack, courtesy of the Linnville Jail?*

Yes, I did. Samantha looked directly at him, ready to respond to his questions.

Well, your lawyer probably told you that your case should come to trial next week. You know you are facing some pretty big charges with some pretty big penalties. The deputy and I were just discussing how it would be helpful for you and us if we worked together to solve some of these problems.

And what do you mean by that, Sir?

Well, basically, I'm wondering what you and your attorney are planning to do at the trial—you met with him the other day and surely he told you something. If you could share that with us, we would personally dismiss one or two of the charges against you. Of course, that would be dependent on you not telling your lawyer about our 'little deal.'

Which charges would you dismiss?

Well, we'd keep the inciting unrest, but we'd consider dropping the disturbing peace and jaywalking charges.

What guarantee would I have that you would really dismiss those two charges?

I see your point. Well, let's just take out a drop charges form from this drawer and fill it out. We'll make a

228

carbon copy so if I don't get mine to the courthouse, you'll have a back-up copy for your lawyer to take over. Sound fair?

Owens placed a piece of carbon paper between the two forms and started filling in Samantha's name and arrest details. I'll write in the two dropped charges after you answer my two questions satisfactorily.

Now, a good answer to my first question gets the jaywalking charge dropped. Can you tell me what witnesses your lawyer plans to call?

Jenner hadn't told her, so she didn't have to even think she was lying to Owens. In case Owens had a plan to threaten or injure any of the potential witnesses, she didn't want to name anyone local. *As of our last meeting, he plans to call me as the main witness as well as some important civil rights figures—I think Martin Luther King Jr. and Dick Gregory.*

Oh, so the guy's going to get some big shots to say you shouldn't be arrested. Interesting. . . It doesn't make a lick of sense to me, but that's city slicker lawyers for you— they get way off the subject.

Jenner lifted his pen an wrote in 'jaywalking' under the charges dropped section of the form. *I'm real happy with your first answer, so we are going to drop the jaywalking charge. Now here's a bigger question—let's see how you answer this one. What general tactic is your lawyer going to take in his counter argument? You know, the things he will say that might make our sheriff's department look negative?*

Again, Jenner hadn't told her his exact line of questioning. *What can I say to mislead him?*

I'm not really sure I should tell you what he plans to say. But then, I would like that second charge dropped. . . Oh, alright, I guess I can tell you if you promise not to tell him I told you.

You have my word.

Okay, then. I know that the reason he's going to have really big figures testify is because he wants the judge to focus on how bad they are and you might focus on arresting them instead of lower profile people like me.

Me arrest King and Gregory?

Yes, they plan to criss-cross through Mississippi in the next few weeks and my attorney has the dates they will be in this state and county—he's going to criticize you for being lazy and not arresting the kingpins of the movement, rather than small fry like me. But on the side, he will offer a plea deal that in exchange for releasing me from all charges, he will give you the dates and locations of King's and Gregory's visits. Samantha pretended to look worried. *You promise you won't tell my attorney this?*

Who-eee! That is the craziest plan I've ever heard. But then I've never dealt with any California lawyers. My attorney will find this plan plum crazy. But, no, I won't give up this little secret.

Owens picked up the pen again and wrote 'disturbing peace' under the charges-to-be-dropped form section. *This answer has been more than satisfactory. In fact, not only will we be dropping the two charges, I'll be seeing to it that you have a nice little treat every day before the trial. Do you like Fritos?* He stood up and handed her the copy of the original drop charges paper.

Samantha wasn't sure if it was a trick question or not. *I do like them better than potato chips, Sir.*

Deputy, please take Miss Bryant back to her cell. She has been real cooperative.

He walked over to his desk and took out a bag of Fritos. He handed it to Samantha and motioned to Glen to escort her back to her cell.

Glen sat down at his desk. He turned to Owens and said, *I overheard her answers, Tom. Can you believe a lawyer would take such a crazy line of defense? Where is he coming from?*

It is bizarre if you think about it. Wait 'till Smith hears about this. Owens picked up the receiver and dialed the courthouse. He didn't remember if he was telling Hector Smith the plan or maybe it was the secretary who answered the phone. Regardless, he felt somewhat upbeat about the whole situation now.

Chapter 12

Mississippi had been Everett Jackson's home forever. His keen memory could recall all the way back in time to his fourth birthday. *The sad birthday.* Why he was focusing on it right now, he wasn't really sure. *Taking the Linnville Freedom School students to Louie's Diner to interview some old timers and convince them to take risks for the right to vote might just be another action in futility.*

Mother was the best cleaning woman in Linnville. Her reputation was so solid that the white residents competed to get her to be their cleaning woman. She left their homes spotless and often did something a little bit extra for each client. There was the time she noticed the Grangers had a broken figurine on the top of their piano. She went home and mixed up a special batch of porcelain glue and stayed a little later than usual expertly gluing the three broken figurine pieces back together. When Mrs. Granger showed her husband the beautiful restoration, he was likewise impressed and gave Mother an extra dollar tip.

Mother knew how to act around her white clients. She knew that it was important for her to be able to do her cleaning work while not getting in their way. She called herself "The Invisible Woman" and prided herself in working hard and fast in a stealth-like manner. While her eyes never directly faced those of her customers, she took in all their behaviors. She learned that Mrs. Granger would often go off into her bedroom and have some crying spells. Mother would have a fresh glass of lemonade waiting for her when she emerged red-eyed and sorrowful. Mother had a hard time understanding why someone with so many material goods could be sad for no obvious reason. I overheard her telling my father about it one evening, suggesting that Mrs. Grnger's marriage must be a bad one. Father cut her off rather abruptly, saying she shouldn't worry about the state of their marriage—if something was amiss, it was their own fault..

Mostly, I remember Mondays when I was little. Granny couldn't watch me on Mondays while Mother worked, so she got permission from her Monday clients for me to accompany her to their homes. I usually took along an activity bag with paper, a drawing pencil and a couple of worn books. My mother gave me strict instructions to be quiet as a mouse and not get in her way or the way of the clients. Mostly, I sat in a corner of the room she was cleaning and drew pictures of my imaginary world, Honan.

My drawings of dragons and castles even impressed her clients and some would pay me a nickel to keep one.

My favorite Monday stop with Mother was her last one. We arrived after lunch at the Jamison's large two-story home. Mr. and Mrs. Jamison were quite wealthy and in my five-year-old viewpoint, quite important. Mr. Jamison was usually walking down the front marble steps on his way back to work after lunch, as Mother and I arrived for work. Mr. Jamison never said anything to us, but he did tip his hat to acknowledge our presence. What I liked most about the Jamisons, was their son Jimmy. Jimmy had been born with only one good leg. The other one was missing from his knee on down. Probably because of his disability, he was kept home and had a home school teacher come every morning. By the time I arrived with my mother, Jimmy was ready to get active. His grandfather had crafted a wooden peg-leg for him and Jimmy had become pretty skillful at maneuvering on it. I think Mrs. Jamison was glad for me to play with Jimmy because not many white boys took the time to stop by their house and include Jimmy in activities. Somehow Mother had convinced Mrs. Jamison that it would be advantageous for both of us to play together, and she willingly agreed.

Our favorite pastime was to hike down to the creek behind their house and wade across it. We'd used some scrap wood my dad gave us to build a castle. Here, we set up headquarters for Honan and here we defended the territory from attacking dragons and evil knights. It didn't take long for me to awaken Jimmy's imagination, and soon he got involved in pretending fallen sticks were our shiny swords and the bubbling creek was the alligator-filled moat around our castle. It always seemed impossible that it was time to go home with my mother as the time just flew by playing with Jimmy.

I will always remember the fall Monday afternoon a week before my birthday. My mother asked Mrs. Jamison if she could bring a little cake with her the next Monday for Jimmy and me to share. My mother thought Mrs. Jamison showed approval, so on the day of my birthday, she carried a basket up the marble steps with a double-layer chocolate cake inside. After tipping his hat to my mother, Mr. Jamison saw the basket and asked my mother what was inside. After her explanation, Mr. Jamison did an about-face and went inside to confer with his wife.

Mrs. Jamison greeted my mother and me at the door. *I'm so sorry, but Jimmy isn't able to play outdoors with your son today. He's in his room. I guess Everett will*

have to sit at the porch table while you do your work. She
turned quickly and disappeared down the hallway.

'Do you think Jimmy is sick?' I asked my mother. I
couldn't imagine him not wanting to play outside in Honan.

'Must be,' was all she said. *'Why don't you draw*
Jimmy a special picture of castles and dragons and we can
leave it for him before we go home.'

I saw my mother set the basket with the cake by the
front door. I sat quietly at the porch table, but I had a hard
time focusing on my drawing. My eyes kept gazing west
toward the creek where I had hoped to celebrate my
birthday by slaying three fierce dragons. I had hoped
Jimmy would warn me before each one attacked.

Mother finished her cleaning faster than usual that
day. Before we left, she took my drawing upstairs and slid
it under Jimmy's door. Mrs. Jamison never came out of her
room to wish us good-bye that day. Looking back, I realize
that Mr. Jamison was a cruel man. His intent upon
learning that I wanted to celebrate my birthday with his
son, was to deny me that pleasure. In the course of his
inhumanity, he took away fun from his own son. That's
what racism is like. Sometimes it just makes a person sad.

Everett brought his thoughts back to the present.
He'd had the students practice interviewing skills and

hoped the seven students he'd brought with him were ready to complete the interviews at Louie's Diner. When he opened the diner door, he grinned. Seated around scattered tables were a dozen or more black men waiting for their voting conversations with the Linnville students.

Louis, the octogenarian owner, wiped his hands on his makeshift apron, and walked over to Everett. *You the teacher of this group? he asked. I'm Louis.*

Hello, Sir. Yes. I'm Everett Jackson. The students continued to file into the diner, forming a group by the check-out counter.

I heard that you are one of us.

Yes, I was born in Jacksonville, and am glad to be back in my home state.

Are you funnin' me, son? Most folks don't have very good memories of living here in this state.

Well, I hear you, Sir. But I do have some good family memories from my past here. Now, did COFO tell you what these students wanted to do?

Yes, one of their people said you wanted to speak to some folks and talk to them about why they should vote and convince them to sign the registration card.

Yes, that's about right.

Everett faced the group of students. *Okay, kids. Everybody sit down by one of the customers here in the diner and complete your interviews. A few of you might have to interview two people. Come get a registration card from me when you need one. Hop to it.*

Everett heard the diner door open. He turned and saw Joshua, Beatrice, and Daniel coming in. *They must have finished their interview with Mr. Jenner pretty fast.*

Joshua took a couple of long strides over to a table and sat down next to a middle-aged man who was sipping a cup of coffee. He reached out his right hand to shake as he introduced himself. *Hello, Sir, my name is Joshua Arnot. I'm from. . .*

I know who you are, the man interrupted. *You are Willie Arnot's boy. I know you come from good stock. My name is Pete Jenkins. I knew your dad and mom when you were just a pipsqueak of a lad. My wife and I moved away from Linnville for a time and we just came back. Louis told me you kids needed some volunteers to register to vote, so here I am.*

Well, the fact that you know my parents is good. But there is one big difference between my dad and me: my dad is very cautious—as for me, I'm more adventurous.

Are you saying that your dad wouldn't be rocking the raciall justice boat, but you are?

Sort of like that. To be prepared for my future, I want to get all the education I can. That's why I'm coming to this Freedom School—the learning we're provided here is far different than what we get in our black schools.

Are you saying that the out-of-state teachers are better quality than ours?

Not at all, Mr. Jenkins. It's just that in our schools, we use the discarded white school text books. There's not a word in them about famous black individuals who achieved greatness.

It' always been that way, you know. Seems we just have to get our black history from another source. We should feel blessed to have family, a home, and a job.

Respectfully, Sir, as a people, we should be able to give our families more opportunities, we should have better homes, and certainly we should have more job opportunities. White people out-earn us two-to-one in most areas—and that's assuming a black person can even get hired.

You know what—you are a chip off the old block. I used to have this same discussion with your father and he had a similar viewpoint as yours, Joshua. I don't disagree

240

with you that black folks should have more, but you've got to admit that we came here as slaves. It takes a long time for white folks who brought us here as slaves to see us as equals in their hearts. Some do, but many can't overlook their own prejudice towards us. Now, we could carry on this line of discussion all day, but I'm thinking you came here to talk to me about voting, so carry on.

I agree with you that this is a good discussion topic. I do have a few questions I'd like to discuss with you.

Joshua reached in his left jeans pocket and removed a folded paper and a stubby pencil. He'd memorized the questions Everett wanted him to ask his interviewee and his photographic memory wouldn't require him to write down Jenkins' s answers. He'd do it anyway, so Jenkins would think he was recording their session.

Now before we start talking about the questions on that paper of yours, I insist you call me Pete during the rest of our conversation.

Yes, Sir, Pete. My first question is: Have you ever voted in an American election?

Pete grinned. *I assume that's just a warm-up question—one you already know the answer to. Here's my answer, anyway. NO! I wish I had the right to vote, but there's no way the whites here in Linnville would stand for that.*

You're right, I do know the answer, but I'm just following the questions my teachers told me to ask.

Joshua jotted down a few words on his paper. *Thanks for that answer. My next question is: Why haven't you ever voted?*

Pete took a sip from his coffee and looked Joshua directly in the eyes. *There is one main reason that I've never voted and that is the voting process is crooked—for blacks, that is. I did try interpreting the constitution three times and I failed three times. Actually, I don't consider myself failing because I did a mighty fine job of interpreting the constitution passages I was given—if I have to say so myself. When I was leaving the courthouse after the third time, the voting commissioner squinted at me and said, 'Boy, this is your third time; it better be your last time. Your kind is not fit to engage in voting in this country. You should let my people vote on your behalf. And besides, if I see you here one more time, your wife might find herself the victim of a hit-and-run car accident sometime. Some of the voting commissioners aren't as nice as me and I'd hate for that to happen to her.'*

Pete, I'm upset to hear that the voting commissioner threatened you to keep you from voting. It's unacceptable. I don't know if you've heard about our plan to have black folks sign a voting registration card and vote in a parallel Democratic primary election—we'll call ourselves the Mississippi Freedom Democratic Party. We can use your registration to help us get a delegation at the next Presidential convention in New Jersey. Some of the openminded whites from the North may take issue with the fact that blacks can't officially vote here in the South.

If you would be willing to sign that card, you would help our cause. Delegates will present the total list of names to the body of the next Democratic convention and the delegates will decide if they want the names listed as real registered voters.

So where can I get a card?

Joshua stood up. *Let me grab one from my teacher, Everett. I'll be right back.*

You do that, Son.

Joshua glanced around the room. Most of the other students were standing together by the counter chatting with each other. Everett reached out and gave Joshua one of the cards and a pen. *So, Joshua, it looks like you are engaged in a deep conversation with your interviewee. How is it going?*

Gee, I'm embarrassed, Mr. Everett. It looks like everyone is finished interviewing and I'm the last one.

No worries, Joshua. I could tell just from watching you, that you were full of passion in your conversation. You were successful in getting Mr. Jenkins to sign a card

Thank you. I'll get him to fill it out quickly.

Joshua guided Pete Jenkins in filling out the voter registration card. He gathered the card and pen and stood up to signal their session was over.

Pete reached out his hand to shake Joshua's. *Thank you, Joshua, for trying to forward democracy for us blacks. We need young people like you to step out and make the world better.*

Thank YOU, Pete, for your time today. I will remember your dedication to the voting process.

And I will remember your passion for justice, Young Man. May you have a rosy future. And just what are your plans?

With the Lord's blessing, I hope to be an attorney one day.

You will be a mighty fine one-- of that I'm certain. Thank you, Pete.

244

Pete sat back down at the table. He took another sip of his coffee.

On the walk back to the Freedom School, Joshua couldn't help think about how Pete's wife had been threatened so he wouldn't reapply for voting. *When I'm an attorney, I'm going to make sure that all people will have the right to vote. Anyone who interferes with the voting process will have to answer to a higher force: ME!*

Chapter 13

The Linnville Downtown Diner had a back room
that could be rented for special occasions. Of course,
Sheriff Owens didn't have to pay a penny to meet there
with whoever he needed to conference with. A simple call
to Mabel that he needed to meet there with so-and-so was
all he had to do.

He'd told Jones, and Radley to meet him and Hector
Smith there Saturday at 3:00 p.m. Smith, apparently,
wouldn't need much time to prep them for their witness
roles in the trial.

The diner's waitress, Theresa, was on duty. Owens
fancied her, but being a family man, tried not to flirt much
with her. *Mornin' Theresa. Your blue eyes are very
sparkly today, if you don't mind me saying so.*

*Hello, Sheriff. It's good to see you, too. Did you
come here hungry as a bear? I hope so, Mel's spent a lot
of time cooking up a batch of biscuits and gravy. Not to
mention baking a blueberry cobbler and three peach pies.*

*Theresa, you know I have to keep an eye on my
waist line. But a small serving of his biscuits and gravy
and a thin slice of pie might be okay. Count on me to be a*

paying customer, that's for sure. Oh, I don't know if you know this or not, but I'm meeting in the back room with Billy, Hunter, and Hector.

Oh? You must have something big going down the pike. Do you mean Herman Smith or Herman Brown?

Smith. He's going to enlighten us a little about law and order.

I see. Sure. You head on back there and I'll be back for a round of coffee in just a few minutes. Who's footin' the bill for this big pow-wow, or are you all payin' your own bills—I'm just askin'.

Now, don't you worry, Theresa. I'll cover the whole bill. And I will leave you a nice, generous tip.

That would be mighty nice, Sheriff. My mother's in the hospital and I could use a few extra dollars.

Owens glanced one more time at Theresa's face before turning and walking down the tiled hallway to the back room. He flipped on the light switch and saw several cockroaches scamper behind the paneling. *I'll sit facing the door so I can greet the guys as they come in.*

Hunter Radley and Billy Jones walked in together. *Howdy, guys,* he said. *Pull up a chair.*

Billy spoke first. *Howdy yourself, Owens. Thanks for inviting us to this little get-together. Not that I'd rather be out at my favorite fishin' hole or nothin'.*

You've never caught a fish big enough to keep, Jones.

And I suppose you have, Owens?

Yeah. My trophy-winning bass was a sixteen-pounder.

That's nothing to sneeze at, Hunter Radley said.

So what exactly went wrong the other night at the school? Sheriff Owens asked.

Hunter dropped his face and started explaining. *Well, Sheriff, it seems that our fellow KKKers are alive and well throughout the state. The other night when me and Bart decided to give the Freedom School a friendly burst of flame, there were a couple of KKKers already there, warning us to get off their territory.*

Owens wrinkled his forehead. *Gosh. I didn't think there were any other groups working our area right now. I'll have to double-check with the guys at the top and see what's going on. Seems our organization is bigger than I realized. Thanks for giving it a try, though. You didn't get hurt, did you?*

Naw. No worries. The two of them did give us a little scare, though.

The conversation stopped as Herman Smith walked over to the table. *Hello, gentlemen. Are you ready to talk shop about the upcoming trial.*

Just as soon as we have a bit of biscuits and gravy, Smith.

Hmmm. . . that does sound good. Don't mind if I join you in a helping or two, do you?

Heads nodded in agreement. Theresa came in carrying a coffee pot in one hand and a tray of cups in the other. She served up a round of coffee before taking out her order pad. *I suppose Sheriff Owens already told you our feature today is biscuits and gravy. If you know what's good for you, you'll order this.*

Owens grinned. *Now, Theresa, we don't want any of that good home-cooked food to go to waste, so you bring us each a heaping big plate of it.* He swept his hand around the table to show her he was ordering for the group.

I'll be right back with your order, men. Let me know if you need more coffee or anything else.

I'll take some of your 'anything else,' Jones said. Laughter erupted.

Theresa ignored his remark and headed back to the kitchen to turn in her order.

Herman stood up to get the group's attention. *Men, I have a busy schedule today, so while we're waiting for our food, I'd like to brief you on the Bryant court case.* When they quieted, he sat back down.

The case should come up soon—I've spoken with Judge Roanoke and he wants to get right on it. I can't tell you the exact day we'll start, but I'll keep you posted as soon as I hear. I need to call each of you as witnesses. Radley, you will need to testify that there have been problems since the Freedom School started here—you know, say that Bryant came into our town and used subversive techniques to interfere with the law and order in our community. Like stealing wood to build the school. Jones, I want you to testify that you saw Bryant interfering with the constitution by distributing her communist newspaper. Owens, you focus on the librarian harassment. McGrath's not here, but as soon as deliberations start, he'll serve as foreman of the jury. No one will want to do the job, so he can just volunteer in the jury room as soon as the case is done.

Looks like you've put plenty of thought into this, Smith. I'm glad I'm Sheriff of such a well-oiled town, that's for sure.

Thanks, Owens, for the compliment. Now all of you do some thinking about what you're going to say. If you get stuck, just give me a call. I'm sure the trial will go as smooth as clockwork, so don't worry. The defense has a kook of a lawyer, so you won't have to worry about any tough questions.

Theresa carried a large oval tray over to the table. She placed it on a food serving cart where the men observed clouds of steam rising from the plates of food. She served the men clockwise, starting with Sheriff Owens. The conversation waned as the men dug into their generous portions of biscuits and gravy.

Anything else I can get you?

Owens spoke up. *Yep. Don't forget to bring each of us a big slab of peach pie when we're done. And write up the bill for all of this.* He reached in his pants pocket and took out a worn leather billfold. Owens quickly extracted a ten-dollar bill and handed it to Theresa. *Here you go, Theresa—a nice big tip for this finely served meal.* As Theresa reached out her hand to accept the bill Owens whispered, *Let's keep this little gathering a secret, Theresa. You can do that, can't you?*

    Absolutely, Sheriff Owens. Mum's the word.

***

Owens unloosened his belt a notch as he walked into the sheriff's office. *I should have known better than to have that second piece of pie.*

    Glen met him inside the doorway. *Sheriff. We've got a little situation here. Bryant's lawyer is here demanding she be allowed to make a phone call to her parents.*

    Owens walked over to the bench by his desk. Jenner was reading some document from his opened briefcase.

    What brings you here, now, Jenner?

    Hello, Sheriff. I recently communicated with Samantha Bryant's parents and explained that she was being held here in jail. I want her to phone her parents and let them know she is doing okay. Please release her and let her use your phone to make the call.

    And just why should I do that?

For two reasons. One: because it's the right thing. Two: because there are federal agents in the neighboring county right now who would rather enjoy giving you a lesson in human compassion. I have their number right here and can easily go across the street to the hotel to call them to come over.

You are a horse thief, Jenner. Wanting this and wanting that. When will this badgering of yours stop?

Owens rubbed his thumb and forefinger along the tip of his chin. *Well, I guess I have no choice. Deputy, go fetch the girl and bring her here. The call better be under fifteen minutes.*

When Samantha heard the deputy's footsteps approaching her jail cell, she hurriedly stuffed Hanna's Bible under the cot. She sat up and pretended to be daydreaming.

Come with me, Miss. Your lawyer is here and you're going to be making a short phone call to your parents. Be sure to tell them about the fine hospitality we're giving you here at the Linnville Jail.

The deputy unlocked her cell and waited for her to exit into the hallway. He turned and walked back to the main room.

Hello, Mr. Jenner. It's good to see you today.

And the same to you, Samantha. I'm going to dial you family's home phone and you have yourself a nice chat with your mother. I called her the other day and of course she was worried when I explained the situation here. It would be reassuring for her to hear your voice.

Jenner dialed the number and handed the black receiver to Samantha.

Hello, Bryant residence.

Hi, Mom. It's so good to hear your voice.

Jenner sat on the edge of Owens' desk and could easily hear both voices.

I've been so worried about you Samantha. Ever since you left for Mississippi, I've been on edge, afraid that something bad like this might happen. Are you okay, dear?

Yes, Mother. Tell me how are Dad and Ethan doing?

Well, just fine. Your father just got a promotion at work and I'm so proud of him. And Ethan is doing well in school. He just took the college entrance exam and scored very high. He's planning to go to Chicago Institute of Technology next fall, so the scores should help him get in. You know how Ethan has always enjoyed assembling and disassembling things—he's sure to make a fine engineer.

That's great news, Mom. Oh, incidentally, I don't want you to worry about me. I'm having a wonderful time here in Linnville. The kids at school are such eager learners—I hope I have students just like these when I get my first real teaching assignment.

Your lawyer said all your fellow teachers really think highly of you. How's Marla doing?

Samantha avoided telling her about Marla's mistreatment. *She's having the time of her life, Mom. You know what a great student she is; well, she really teaches the kids so well about their African American heritage. You'd really enjoy seeing her in action.*

Do you have any idea when they will release you, dear?

Not exactly. But don't worry. I'm okay here. I have a pad of paper and a pencil. I've been writing lots of haiku poems about civil rights. It keeps me plenty busy. Mr. Jenner might be able to answer your question, though. I'll hand the phone to him.

Jenner grasped the receiver. *Hello, Mrs. Bryant, I'm sure you're curious about when Samantha will be released. You need to know that there will be a jury trial coming up soon—I'll call you about the exact date.*

You mean she's going to be on trial? I thought we could just send down some bail money so she could be released.

I wish that were true, Mrs. Bryant. Unfortunately, the sheriff has blocked her release on bail and we need to go through the trial process.

Oh, dear.

But don't let this news discourage you, Ma'am. I will represent her at the trial and there should be a positive outcome.

Jenner thought he detected some soft sobbing in the background. He handed the receiver back to Samantha.

Mom, it's me back. I want you to know that the nice lady who is our home host, Miss Loretta, is subbing for me while I'm out. From what Gina told me, she's doing a great job.

Who's Gina?

She's a teacher on our team—from New York. Samantha reminded herself to stop sharing information about Marla's recent visit to the jail. She didn't want Hannah to get in trouble for letting Marla in.

Oh, that's nice. Dear, is there anything we can send you?

Thanks, Mom, but I've got everything I need. The food here is pretty good, too. I better sign off as they don't want my call to be too long. I love you. Mom.

I love you, Dear. You take care. I hope to talk with you again soon.

Samantha set the receiver down on the phone. She saw the deputy walking back toward her cell and knew that was a signal for her to follow.

Samantha, I'll be back tomorrow to visit with you about the trial. You stay safe and sound 'till then.

She turned and gave a half-wave. *Thanks, Mr. Jenner, for setting up this phone call. Thank you, too, Mr. Owens and Deputy Glen. It was good talking with my mom.*

Samantha sat back down on her cot. *Cards from the Freedom School kids and a phone call from my mother. Life is good.*

Chapter 14

I'm so happy, Miss Loretta.

And I'm happier than you, Marla. I'm so glad that COFO decided to let you stay with me again. Besides being fun, I will enjoy planning lessons with you.

Marla reached across the table and picked up Loretta's empty dinner plate, stacking on top of hers. *No arguing with me, Miss Loretta. I'm going to wash the dishes tonight. That's final. Especially after that dee-licious meal. I've never had cornbread so moist and beans and ham so tasty. You are an excellent cook. I sure wish my mother could come down and meet you.*

You just keep that thought, Marla. Maybe one day we can all get together.

That would be super.

Marla filled the dish pan with water from the storage jar on the counter. She gave a small squirt of dish soap into the water and swished it in circles until bubbles formed.

Loretta opened her end counter drawer and took out a cotton dish towel. You just hand me the dishes as you rinse them, and I'll quickly dry them. *We'll be a dishwashing team—the best in Mississippi.*

I'm so glad you and all the volunteers came down here, Loretta continued. *We do need increase our voting registration here. My widowed husband dreamed of being a registered voter and voting, but unfortunately, he passed before this wonderful mission. Now, it's up to me to get registered. Even if my registration just goes for the Mississippi Freedom Democratic Party, it's important to do this. Why, tomorrow, I'm going to ask Everett for one of the sign-up cards.*

That's super, Miss Loretta. Marla finished rinsing the cast-iron skillet and handed it to Loretta.

It's too bad that our Freedom School students are too young to register to vote, don't you think?

Maybe we should plan a lesson for tomorrow based around voting. What do you think about that idea, Miss Loretta?

Why, that's a fine idea for a lesson, Marla. I'll get out a tablet of paper and we can start writing our objectives right now.

Marla sat beside Loretta at the cleared table. *I just love teaching—the planning is almost as exciting as the teaching, don't you agree?*

259

Absolutely.

How about we set up a voting process for a mock Linnville city council? We could have nominations and voting for council members, and actually have the council meet to discuss hypothetical issues. We can pattern the council after city councils in the North, with students not on the council representing interested citizens who come before the council to discuss their side of the issue.

Marla, that is a wonderful idea. I've never attended a city council meeting, but I can imagine how we might want to structure our pretend ones based on democracy.

Loretta picked up her yellow number two pencil and wrote:

Objective #1: Students will learn how a mayor conducts a city-wide meeting with elected council members.

Wait a minute—I thought you didn't know how a city council worked. . .

I know the janitor who cleans city hall—he always fills me in about the comings and goings of our local government and that's how I know how the mayor works with the council.

Why, you are a sly, fox, Miss Loretta! You know more than you let on!

Two teachers, engaged in planning, didn't notice the Mississippi sun set nor the Mississippi moon rise. As they headed to their respective bedrooms, their souls were full of anticipation. Anticipation that the Freedom School students would learn what it meant to vote, to be a civic leader. As Marla drifted off to sleep, she couldn't help but wonder what Gina had meant when she announced a secret surprise would be shared the next day. *I wonder what that surprise is. . . . .*

***

Good morning, Gina. Why are you looking so happy today?

Hey, Everett, good friend. Don't I always look happy?

Yeah, but you look exceptionally happy today.

Well, don't tell anyone, but I have two surprises for our students today.

Two? Can I have a hint.

Well, since you are such a good egg, I'll let you in on the scoop. You might not know, but I sent a request home to my dad's Lions club for some typewriters.

I think I recall you mentioning it.

Well, the Upper Manhattan Lions Club came through with a donation—quite a sizeable one and my dad used it to purchase some manual typewriters for our school. That means I can teach them how to type!

I'm floored. That was the number one request on the students' wish list they filled out on day one. Looks like I'll be taking over your Algebra 1 classes in the morning so you can help them learn this valuable skill. But, Gina, how will you do it since we don't have any typing books?

It's easy. I took every letter of the alphabet and every punctuation mark and used them in words and sentences. I took my original copy to COFO and they made multiple typing instruction booklets the students can use. Everett, you are not only looking at a typing teacher, but also a typing book author.

Where are the typewriters?

If you'd come a little earlier today, you would have seen them proudly distributed in my classroom. Tom helped me prop up the benches to make tables and we rounded up stools from different classrooms for the chairs. Actually, the chairs and tables are about the right height. Fortunately, COFO sprang for the book stands—that's a must so they can prop the typing booklets against the stands and look directly at the booklet instead of the typewriter as they type.

Gina, you are a wizard. I'm highly impressed with your ingenuity. Hey, I'll take any of your algebra students who don't want typing class and combine them with my geometry students. I can make it work.

Thanks, Everett. You are no slouch yourself. Hey, we better get into the auditorium. I think I hear Marla strumming her guitar to get everyone's attention. You'll have to wait 'till the singing is over to find out my second secret.

The mystery is overwhelming me.

Ha!

Everett recognized the tune Marla was playing. She strummed her guitar and sang out: *Good news: Chariot's are coming. . .*

The students belted out the lyrics, smiles on their faces.

Gina walked over and stood next to Marla. *Good morning, Freedom Students!*

Good morning, Gina!

Today we're singing only this one freedom song, because we have a special surprise for you. Have any of you ever heard of haiku poetry?

Josephia raised her hand.

Go ahead, Josephia. Haiku poems are some of my favorites. It's a patterned poem—comes from Japan. There are only three lines and each line has a certain number of syllables—the first line has five syllables, the second line has seven syllables and the third and final line has five syllables. Usually haiku poems are written about something in nature like a cloud, a rock, or the wind. But sometimes people write them about other general topics. I've written a few myself.

Thanks, Josephia. You are right on target with your definition. We all know that Samantha is patiently waiting in the Linnville Jail for her trial to start. Well, while she's been waiting, she's been writing some haiku poems. The other day when I was over visiting her, she handed me several poems that she'd written and asked if I'd share them with you. Even though she's not with us physically, she's dedicated to our mission of freedom. So, if you'll listen up, I'll read these:

> *From the mountain top*
> *Let freedom ring throughout*
> *For all God's creatures*

Endless hate abounds
As white supremacy reigns
Racial justice now

I've got me a robe
With colors of the rainbow
I'll wear it proudly

My little light shines
Shines all over Linnville, yes
My little light shines

No more Jim Crow laws
We're seeking integration
The non-violent way

Gather round my friends
Regardless of skin color
Equality now

An uphill journey
I'm going to freedom land
I am on my way

Gina looked up to signal she was done reading. Josephia jumped up instantly and applauded. Soon the entire group of freedom students was standing, shouting, and clapping. *Three cheers for Samantha,* Daniel shouted.

Hip, hip hooray! Hip, hip hooray! Hip, hip hooray!!

Everett raised his fist in the air. *Way to go, Samantha!*

Gina waved her arm back and forth to signal she wanted the group's attention again. They quickly sat back down and gazed at her attentively. *I knew you would be moved by Samantha's haikus and I was right. Now, I have another little surprise for you. Do you recall on the first day you came to Freedom School that you filled out a survey of the classes you'd like to see taught here? Well, a lot of you said you wanted to take a typing class. I contacted my father back in New York and he got his Lions Club to donate enough money for twenty brand new typewriters.*

Beatrice called out, *Do you mean typewriters for us?*

Yes, exactly. We've divided those of you who said they wanted to take typing into three groups which I'll teach in the morning in place of my algebra classes. If you

266

are in my algebra classes and want to continue with algebra instead of typing, just head to Everett's classroom at that time. If others of you decide you would also like to give the class a try, you can sign the paper by the front counter and we'll get you scheduled into a class. So, as you leave the auditorium this morning, check the lists for the three classes—if your name is on the list, then get ready to become a world-class typist.

Gina hurried out of the auditorium and down the hall into her classroom. She wanted to get there before the students so she could see the expressions on their faces when they saw their classroom outfitted with state-of-the art typewriters.

Joshua was the first to enter. *Man alive. Look at this. Manna from heaven.* He grinned and quickly sat down across from a typewriter on the first row. *Miss Gina, you be sure to tell your father thanks for getting these for us.*

Absolutely, Joshua. Better yet, once we get going, why don't you type him a thank you letter.

I will do just that.

The classroom was full of oohs and aahs as students filtered into the room and got seated. They chattered quietly looking excitedly amongst each other. After a few minutes, Gina quieted the group and began her instruction.

Okay, everyone. Let's get started. Let me explain that the goal of this class is for you to be able to type thirty-five words a minute. For some of you, this goal will be easy; for others, it will be more challenging. No worries. I will help you to improve. Your success depends on concentrating and really trying to keep your eyes on the typing booklet—not looking at the paper in the typewriter. So, let's begin by studying correct finger positioning. I'm asking you to place your left pinky finger on the a-key. Now spread your left fingers out left-to-right with one finger on each key. Next, place your right pinky finger on the semi-colon key and spread your right fingers out right-to-left with one finger on each key. This is how you will start typing every time. Please take both hands off the keyboard and then place your fingers back on in correct position. Good. Now repeat this three more times. Gina waited while the student eagerly placed their fingers in correct position and then removed them from the keyboard several times. Gina demonstrated how to insert a piece of typing paper and how to manipulate the carriage.

Good. Look over at the typing booklet on the stand. The collective eyes of the students focused on a thin booklet *How to Type Fast on a Manual Typewriter—a Freedom School Text* by Gina Lovick.

Teacher, did you make this for us? It has your name on the cover.

Yes, Daniel, I did. It has all alphabet letters in it as well as some practice activities so you can learn them. Turn to page one in the booklet. We're going to start by typing the letter c. Put your fingers in correct finger position. Your left middle finger will reach down and press the c key. The VERY important thing is now to look over at the booklet and type the c key six times. Do NOT look at your typewriter or the paper as you are doing this; look at the typing booklet. Now, turn the carriage so you are back on the left margin and type a row of c's again. Do you notice that the c's in the booklet have a space between them? Well, you are going to type two more rows of c's and this time place a space between each c. To do this, use your right thumb to reach down and tap the space bar at the bottom of the keyboard. Just a bit of information here, your thumb always taps the space bar and if you are typing a letter on the left side of the keyboard, you use your right thumb on the space bar. Likewise, if you are typing a letter on the right side of the keyboard, you tap the space bar with your left thumb. This will become automatic after a while.

Let's move on to the letter a. Any thoughts about which finger will strike that key?

Beatrice raised her hand. *I'm guessing the left pinky because it's already there.*

And you are correct, Beatrice. So, type a row of a's keeping your eyes on the typing booklet. Remember to put a space between them.

Gina loved the atmosphere in the classroom. The students had their eyes glued on the typing booklets and were remembering her guidance not to look at their papers, but at the booklets. After a few minutes of practicing the a's, she moved on to the t's.

Your left forefinger is going to reach up and type the t's. Give it a try. You might miss at first, but after a while, it will become automatic. Once you've practiced a couple of rows, you are ready to integrate the three letters we've learned today into words. So, practice typing cat, tac, and act. Type several rows of each word and just put spaces between the words this time, not each letter. Check your work after you finish and see how accurate you are. Once you've gotten pretty good at this, then repeat two rows of c's, a's, and t's and the words. Do this faster and faster without. . . .

Looking at your paper! Said Carolina.

Exactly. Gina grinned. *I'll be walking around the room and checking to make sure each of you has correct finger position. You are off to a great start in today's typing class!*

***

Beatrice and Josephia were sitting under a tree outside eating their sack lunches.

I just love typing class, don't you?

It's the best. No wonder all the white kids get the good jobs—they have typing classes in their high schools and we don't.

Not any more. When word gets back to the northern states that we are benefitting from typing instruction, I think they will send us more typewriters. I am beginning to think that people in the North have good intentions and want us to be more equal. After getting to know Samantha, Gina, Tom, and Marla, I'm convinced of it.

You're right, Josephia. Look how Samaantha took a risk by coming here—as a black person, she could have easily stayed in Chicago living her life. And Gina worked with her father to get us these typewriters. Tom called his dad to be Samantha's attorney—Marla's too, and Marla leads us in freedom songs everyday—coming down here to help us get our freedoms—freedoms she already has.

I really admire them. They are taking risks by coming here to our racist city. It would be a lot easier and a lot safer if they'd stayed back in their northern cities. Poor Marla; she got all beaten up just to help us. And Samantha's stuck in jail.

Beatrice stood up and crumpled the paper that had held her lunch. *Come on, Josephia. We don't want to be late for Miss Marla's and Miss Loretta's classes. I heard they were going to team up to teach us something new about civics this afternoon.*

Lunch break over, the small clusters of Freedom School students moved from the lawn into the building. Most afternoons were devoted to active involvement in civil rights activities. Beatrice liked the theoretical civil rights classes better than the hands on ones. *Yesterday's class discussion "An examination and comparison of Southern and Northern culture and society" really showed me how blacks in the North have a way better life than we do." I did enjoy the afternoon we handed out our Linnville*

272

Freedom School newspaper and the afternoon we talked to folks about registering, though. She continued to roll her preferences through her mind as she walked into her classroom. Miss Loretta and Marla were smiling as they walked in.

It didn't take long for the group of eleven students to seat themselves and quiet down. Marla gave Miss Loretta a friendly wave—probably a signal to start the talking.

Welcome back from your lunch break. This afternoon we are going to dig into a civic government structure: city council. You probably know that Linnville is governed by a mayor and five city council members. It will come to no surprise to you that all the figures involved are white. I've lived here in Linnville some sixty years, and it's always been that way. But imagine what might happen in our city if our mayor and council members were black. What would be different for us? What issues might be discussed and solved?

This afternoon, we are going to hold a mock election for mayor and council members. Those of you who do not wish to be mayor or on the council will still have an important role; you will be Linnville citizens speaking on behalf of the issues we take up. So without further adieu, Marla will get the election off and running.

Marla picked up her clipboard. Who of you would like to run for the position of mayor?

The classroom was quiet for a minute. Then, Joshua stood up. I would like to run for the position of mayor of Linnville. Marla jotted his name down.

Thank you Joshua. Are there any other interested candidates?

No one stood up or raised their hand. Okay, we have one candidate for mayor. Those in favor or Joshua Arnot becoming mayor of Linnville, Mississippi, say 'aye.'

Hector interrupted. Respectfully, Miss Marla. I thought all voting was done on paper ballots in secret.

You are right, Hector. But since our time at Freedom School is short and we have a lot to cover, and since we just have one candidate, we are going to have a voice vote. For councilmembers, we'll do a paper ballot. So, I'll repeat my statement: all of you in favor of Joshua Arnot serving as our mayor, say 'aye.'

'Aye,' shouted the class in unison. I now declare that Joshua Arnot is the official mayor of Linnville. I'm going to pass this clipboard around the classroom. If you would like to run for councilmember, just write your name *on the paper. In real life, you would have to go house-to-house and get a certain number of signatures from people who support you. Again, to save time, we're going to do it a different way.*

Waves of whispering moved through the classroom and students passed the clipboard around the room, some adding their names to the list of candidates. Victoria was the last to get the clipboard. She signed her name and took the clipboard to Marla.

Marla quickly counted the number of names listed. *Good,* she announced, *we have seven candidates for council members. I'll write the seven names on the board. Miss Loretta will bring you a piece of paper so you can vote for two. Then we'll tally the votes.*

Loretta passed out paper to the students while Marla wrote the names on the board. In just a couple of minutes, the students were handing their papers back to Loretta. *Go ahead and visit amongst yourselves while Marla and I count the ballots,* she said. *Just so you know, in a real city council election, there might be three or four people running for each council seat, so there would be an election in each ward of the city. We are doing an abbreviated election so we can see just how a council and mayor work together.*

I'm proud of all seven of you for running. If I don't mention your name, please don't be discouraged. You will have a very important job of representing a citizen who has an issue to bring before the council. Perhaps this role will be the most important one.

Here are the four Linnville council members: Beatrice, Hector, Daniel, and Ed. That means that these five of you will be citizens or officials speaking behalf of issues: Josephia, Shirley, Adam, Gwendolyn, and David.

Give yourselves a round of applause for your involvement, said Loretta.

Huzza, huzza! shouted Adam. The rest clapped.

Loretta waved her hand to get attention. *Your job is to get in small groups of council members and citizens and brainstorm some issues you would like to change in Linnville. Joshua, you can walk from group to group and listen in so you'll have an idea of what you will have to deal with as mayor. Remember, you will be conducting the meeting in a fair way. In reality, we would be using something called Robert's Rules of Order, a designated way of introducing actions that would then be voted on. Since you haven't read the book, you will just have to ask the council to vote on the issues and do it in a fair way.*

Actually, Miss Loretta, I did once read a book about Robert's Rules of Order. I found it at my grandpa's house and thought it looked pretty interesting. I'm not sure I have every rule memorized, but I have a pretty good idea of the procedures.

Well, I'm glad you are serving as our mayor. Let's get in our groups.. Someone in your group, make a list of your issues and. . .

Marla looked at Loretta with bug-eyes. Within seconds, the groups were formed and students were eagerly sharing ideas. Loretta decided to walk around the groups and listen in. What she heard amazed her: *Let's integrate the Linnville schools; I'm going to bring up restaurants being open to blacks and whites; we need a swimming pool—a really big one—that all kids can swim in; there shouldn't be taxes for senior citizens; people can sit anywhere in a movie theater; everybody can vote. . .*

Chapter 15

Henry Jambrowski climbed off his blue Cannondale bicycle and put down the kickstand to park the bike near his garage. *I'm going to have to speak to Carla about clearing out that stack of flower pots along the east side of the garage so I can park my bike inside. If I don't, one of these days, I'll get home from the courthouse and find it missing.*

Henry liked his position as federal judge of Dane County's fifth district. There were many reasons. *For one, I don't have to dress up—my long black robe covers whatever I decide to wear. And another is each day brings a new case with new plaintiffs and new circumstances.*

Today's case would be an interesting one. A California attorney was representing a Madison resident taking on the Linnville, Mississippi Sheriff's Department. *This one is sure to be an interesting case.*

Henry showered, dressed in a pair of slacks and a sports jacket and tie. Carla was already gone with her friends to the Monona Golf Course for a nine-hole game, so he saved time by not having a friendly goodbye chat with her. Maybe enough time to grab a cup of coffee and a bagel at The Koffee Cup. He picked up his black leather briefcase leaning against the front door and headed out to his Fiat. *Sure glad I sprang for this 1962 model. Really smooth to drive. I'll have to talk Carla into getting one for herself.*

Henry got onto the city beltline and sped along until the downtown exit. The courthouse was smack downtown and fortunately near a good parking garage. His annual parking pass was one of his valued investments.

The sun reflected off the blue Lake Mendota waves. *Madison is sure a dream city. Not only is the scenery nice with the five lakes here, but the citizens are refreshingly well-educated and open-minded about issues. I'm glad Carla agreed to let me have my wish to live here even though I know she'd prefer her San Francisco life. Maybe I should just surprise her with a new Fiat sometime—a token of my appreciation for letting me have fun here in the Midwest.*

The sidewalks were bustling with state employees heading to their offices. They seemed to be deadlining it. Most government jobs started at nine o'clock sharp. It was 8:50 and some were still walking briskly. *Don't know how they'll make it in time.*

Henry ducked into the Koffee Cup. A portly man with long gray hair was the only customer ahead of him.

The staff was always efficient here and it took only seconds for the gray-haired man to be served. *I'll have a cup of light roasted—medium, and a cherry Danish.*

Sure. That will be a dollar-ten.

Henry pulled out his money clip and took out a five-dollar bill. *Here, keep the change.* He handed off the bill in exchange for his to-go cup of coffee and pastry. The clerk thanked him for the tip.

Let's see, I'm expected in the courtroom at ten, so I have plenty of time to enjoy this in my chambers. I better look over my mail. Sure hope my copy of Law Today arrived.

The elevator operator greeted Henry. *Good morning, Judge Jambrowski. How are you today?*

Just dandy, Helen. And how about you?

I'm doing great. My sister is visiting me from Des Moines. After work, I'm taking her to Ella's Deli.

Oh, she'll love that place—all the antique mechanical toys suspended from the ceiling everywhere. You'll have a fun time.

Yes, and all the great deli food. She'll have a hard time deciding what to order. Their menu is fantastic.

I agree. You can never go wrong with the Bratwurst topped with spiced sauerkraut.

You are a true Wisconsinite to love sauerkraut on your bratwurst, Judge.

Well, I'm not originally from here, but it only took me a short time to discover that flavor fest.

My sister loves flowers, so I also plan to take her to Olbrich Gardens. She'll love seeing the rose gardens.

I'm not into flowers much, but I do go there once a year with my wife—it's one of her favorite haunts, too.

The elevator stopped at the fourth floor. Helen slid the inner door to the left with her gloved hand. *Here you are, Judge. Floor number four. Have a good day.*

And you too, Helen. Enjoy your visit with your sister.

Henry walked down the hallway to his office. He turned the antique brass door handle and walked into the carpeted office. His red-headed secretary looked up to greet him.

Good morning, Judge. You look chipper today. Are you ready for your big case? She shifted a stack of paperwork from the center of her desk to the upper right corner.

Hello, Stella. Yes, I'm prepared. Should be an interesting case. I've read over the Sheriff's defense papers and I'm ready to listen to what her attorney has to say. As you well know, the civil rights movement is sweeping across the southern part of our country, although here in Wisconsin, were' oblivious to the implications of it. Probably because we have such a minority of blacks living here.

You are right, Judge. There are a few black people who attend my church and two of the women volunteered to teach Sunday School. I hope to get to know them better. From my perspective, all black people have a harder road to travel due to the prejudice whites carry. The other day I was reading an article that said the per capita income of black workers in the Midwest was lower than that of whites. So, even here in the Midwest, we have a way to go to achieve equality.

Stella, you are a gem. Always wanting people to have a better life. I'm glad you are my secretary. Hey, would you eat half of a cherry Danishl? It's fresh from the Koffee Cup.

Stella smiled. *I know how much you love those cherry Danish, so I will pass. I just had a donut, myself.* She handed Henry a stack of mail.

Okay, if you say so. Stella, will you buzz my office when it's time to head into the courtroom? It looks like I

*got my monthly issue of Law Today and you know how
engrossed I can get reading that.*

*Yes, I will buzz you at 9:45. That will give you time
to put on your robe and give me the papers you want me to
carry into your bench. Good luck today with your case.
I'm confidant you will act justly.*

*I hope so, Stella. That always weighs on my mind—
the responsibly of finding a case based on true justice. It's
an ongoing challenge, but an exciting one.*

You will be just, I'm sure.

Henry shut his inner office door. That way he could
put his feet up on his desk and dig into his law magazine
while savoring his pastry and sipping his coffee. The inside
feature was an article called "The Law—Two Different
Interpretations Depending on Where You Live". He read
the headnote: "The Civil War fought some one hundred
years ago was supposed to create freedom and equal
opportunity for all; however, some experts question
whether there are two standards for justice—one for people
living north of the Mason- Dixon line and another for those
living south of it."

Henry was a speed-reader. Always had been. He
quickly read page one of the article before realizing he'd
guzzled all his coffee and eaten the entire Danish. The gist

of the article was eye-opening. It gave several examples of legal cases and showed that for the same legal charge, defendants got very different punishments depending on where they lived. One black man in Louisiana received a twenty-year sentence for stealing a hardware store item, whereas in Maine, the same crime's punishment was a misdemeanor with community service. The article didn't mention the races of those charged with crimes, *but I bet anything the guy in Louisiana was black.*

I'm sure race is a factor in my case today. The plaintiff, a white girl, is taking on a Mississippi sheriff. His intention is to stifle her involvement in the Mississippi Civil Rights mission—a mission designed to give blacks more rights. So, I guess Stella is right about us having a way to go to achieve equality.

Henry was surprised to hear Stella's office buzz. *Thanks, Stella. I hear you.*
He gave her his legal pad, manilla folder filled with the Linnville Sheriff's office documents, and pen to carry into his courtroom bench.

Henry stood from his desk and reached for the hangar holding his black judge robe. He took off his jacket and slipped the robe over his shoulders. The courtroom was too hot to wear the jacket under his robe. *Besides, nobody can see what I'm wearing.*

Stella came back into his chamber. *Stella, I appreciated your buzz. I was engrossed in my law magazine.*

No worries, Sir. Good luck to you this morning. If I wasn't so swamped, I'd come in and listen, but duty calls.

That's okay. I'll fill you in on the details later. You take care.

Henry sauntered down the hallway into the back of the courtroom. He'd wait there until the bailiff announced him. He'd cut it closer than he'd realized. In just a couple minutes, the bailiff opened the door for him and he walked into the courtroom to the words: '*All rise for the Honorable Henry Jambrowski, Federal Judge of Dane County's Fifth District.*'

Henry walked over to his desk on the dais. He set his briefcase beside him and removed the documents. He slid out a legal pad and mechanical pencil. Once he had his paperwork organized, he was ready to proceed. He looked out into the courtroom. Only a handful of visitors. Seated at the plaintiff's table was a sharp-dressed attorney. He needed to verify the attorney's identity.

Good morning, are you Thomas Jenner, attorney representing Marla Johnson?

Jenner stood up and straightened his tie. He looked directly at the judge's eyes. *Yes, Sir. I usually practice in California, but was asked to represent Miss White as she was mistreated in Mississippi and needed an attorney.*

And you just happened to be in Mississippi?

Actually, she was teaching there along with my son who is also from California and he called me to represent her. I am certified also in Mississippi.

Yes, I know. Our office received your documentation. And just where in California do you reside?

My family and I live just outside San Jose.

The reason I asked, Mr. Jenner, is that my wife's family are all from California, so as you can imagine, I've heard endless stories about the superiority of that state.

I'm sure you have, Judge.

Well, I compliment you for stepping out to represent Miss Johnson. You may be seated and we'll proceed.

First, Mr. Jenner, I'm going to ask you to present your charges against the Linnville Sheriff's Department. Following that, I'll share the defense statements prepared and mailed here by the Sheriff's attorney. Then, I will

286

share my findings based on the legal elements of your two sides. Any questions?

No, Judge. Not at this time.

So, you may proceed.

Jenner was used to using a lot of glitz and glamour as he presented his high profile California cases. After hearing Judge Jambrowski's folksy introduction, he decided a more casual, objective approach would be the best for his presentation. Jenner stood and shared some statements about Marla growing up on the east side of Madison, and then moved to the purpose of the Freedom School movement and how Marla had gotten involved. He stayed objective in his thoughts and was careful not to insert opinion into his narrative. He quickly got to a description of the beating she'd suffered at the hands of the sheriff. He stuck to the main points, including testimonies from the Freedom School students who'd witnessed it.

And if I may, I'd like to submit into evidence, these photos of the physical bruising Marla Johnson suffered at the hands of the sheriff. He carried a clear packet containing the photos Beatrice had taken of Marla's swollen back leg wounds and handed them to the judge.

Judge Jambrowski pretended to view the photos nonchalantly, but as he stared at each one showing the deep hose wounds on Marla's legs, he could barely hold back tears. To think a human being, especially one in authority, would strike a young woman repeatedly was unfathomable.

Jenner thought he detected a tremble in the judge's voice as he formally accepted the photos as evidence.

Please be seated, Mr. Jenner. I had previously planned to present a lengthy summary of the argument the attorney for the Sheriff's Department submitted me before my ruling. But after hearing your presentation and seeing these horrific pictures, I conclude there is no need to do that. There is no need for humanity to respond in such a cruel, harsh way. I also believe there is no need for a human being to misuse authority in the way the sheriff did. Marla Johnson went to Linnville, Mississippi to teach black high school students about freedom—freedom they simply don't have yet. Today, I'm going to send a message not only to the Linnville Sheriff's Department that their actions were unconscionable and inhumane, but also highly illegal. I want my message to resonate across the state of Mississippi that acts of white supremacy will no longer be tolerated.

Sometimes, the best way to punish people is through their pocketbooks. So today, I am finding the Linnville Sheriff's Office guilty of physical brutality to Marla

Johnson. They will be liable to pay one million dollars to Miss Johnson.

Jenner wasn't sure if he heard the judge right or not. *A million dollars?* Jenner thought he mumbled a thank-you to the judge, but he wasn't sure.

A middle- aged couple rushed up to Jenner. *Thank you, Mr. Jenner, for what you did today. We are Marla's parents and we so appreciate you representing her in this case.*

Jenner gave them each a hug.

The Johnsons walked up to Jambrowski's desk. *Your Honor, thank you for your decision in our daughter's case.*

Henry Jambrowski stood. *You are welcome. It's a small thing I can do to make our world a better place. I'm sorry it ever happened. Thank you for raising a wonderful daughter who truly cares about justice.*

Chapter 16

Mississippi morning. Lydia Struck flipped on the light switch in the Linnville Courthouse. She walked directly to the counter behind her desk and plugged in the electric coffee maker. She spooned three tablespoons of ground Folgers into the basket and added eight cups of water.. As she stood waiting for the coffee to percolate, she thought about her recent visit with the handsome California attorney. *Thomas Jenner, what a dignified name. I really do think he had some romantic desires for me.*

Lydia felt bad when her boss had reprimanded her for not reading over the summary of the case before she preapproved it going to a federal judge in Wisconsin. *What does it matter, really. Aren't all judges about the same? So what if the sheriff wouldn't be able to present his case in person but rather in writing? Just like someone in authority to have to show their power. Oh, well, I can take a little criticism now and then. They know this courthouse wouldn't run as smoothly without me, so there's no danger of me losing my job. Besides that, my family are the leading donors to the Linnville County Republican party and that's a guaranteed insulation for me always having my job*

The aroma of fresh coffee permeated the area around Lydia's desk. She poured a cup into her favorite pottery mug and carried it over to her desk. Time to fluff her hair while she waited for the coffee to cool down. *I wonder if Thomas will stop back here before the trial. Maybe I can think of a reason to give him a call.* She pulled open her center desk drawer and removed a small piece of paper with his phone number on it. She put the paper by her phone. Perhaps she'd think of a reason to call him today.

Lydia sipped her cooled coffee and gazed out the large double-paned glass window. Traffic was beginning to pick up along the avenue. People heading off to offices to earn their paychecks. A United States Postal Service truck pulled up in front of the courthouse and the driver got out. He carried an envelope with him as he walked up the steps to the courthouse entrance. *Wonder what this is all about. Our mail usually doesn't get delivered until late morning.*

The door opened and the postal worker walked over to Lydia's desk. He handed her a thick envelope. *Ma'am, I need your signature on this form. This here is a certified letter.*

Lydia glanced at the envelope. *Hmmm. . .It is addressed to our office.*

Sir, do you know what's inside?

Respectfully, Ma'am, I do not. I am only responsible for delivering the mail, not for knowing what is inside the envelopes. It must be something important, though, to have been sent by certified mail. The return address says it's from a court in Dane County, Wisconsin. Do you have a connection with that court somehow?

Oh, now I think I know. Yes. We sent up some information from the Sheriff's Department to the federal judge there. This must be a letter saying they received our information. I'll be happy to sign your form.

Lydia picked up her black ink pen and signed the form. *Here you go. Thank you for hand delivering this envelope.*

That's my job, Ma'am. You have a good day.

Lydia debated whether to open the envelope or just wait 'till later. *Okay, I better get this opened, read, and filed now before who-knows-what-else happens this morning. You never know what crazy interruptions can happen around here.*

Lydia used her fancy gold letter opener to slit the envelope open. She removed the three or four pages of folded text. She only needed to read paragraph one before her mouth dropped open.

This certified letter is to inform you, that a judgment for One Million Dollars has been levied against the Linnville Sherff's Office in a decision by Federal Judge Henry Jambrowski. The monies are payable in full by September 1, 1964.

Lydia looked up and stared at the empty coffee cup. *What? There must be some misunderstanding. I sent up all the information about the Marla Johnson case to that Dane County Courthouse. Oh, no, I think this is saying that the judge found in favor of the girl and is demanding we pay damages. One million dollars! Wherever will we get that much money? Oh, dear. I better make some phone calls.*

Lydia dialed the Sheriff's office and Deputy Glen answered. *Hello, Deputy. Lydia Struck here. I must speak with the Sheriff.*

Ah, good morning, Lydia. Nice to hear that soft voice of yours. Can you fill me in about what's going on and I'll tell the Sheriff when he gets back?

Well, where is he?

He's having some important intellectual discussions at the diner. Should be back any time.

Better yet, call the diner and tell him there is an urgent matter. He needs to come over to the court house right away.

Yes, Lydia. I'll get on it.

Tiny beads of perspiration formed along Lydia's brow. She folded a piece of paper to make a paper fan and swished it back and forth in front of her face. Herman Smith, the Sheriff's attorney had drafted the papers for the Sheriff. Lydia knew he would probably be in his office by now. She'd ring him up.

Herman, can you buzz over to the court house. I'm afraid there's some bad news I need to share with you.

Lydia, my dear, what could be bad this early in the day?

Nothing I can tell you over the phone, Herman. Hurry over here and I'll show you.

You mean I have to put down my crossword puzzle right now? It can't wait fifteen minutes.

Honestly, Herman, trust me. It's serious. Just get over here.

Lydia hung up the receiver. She clasped her hands over her eyes. *I better bring over Rodger Cook, the auditor. This is a financial issue that we'll need him to solve.*

Lydia stood up and walked across to Rodger's office. She opened the door and leaned in. *Rodger, I need*

you to come over—something big's come up. Can you be
here in five minutes?

Rodger looked up from his ledger pad. *Yes, Lydia.*
If you say it's big, then I'll come back to my bookwork
later. In fact, I'll just follow you over there.

Rodger strolled over to the door and exited with
Lydia. He put both hands in respective pockets and gave
her a friendly grin. *So, Lydia, can you give me a hint what*
big issue has come up?

Rodger, I'd prefer to wait until the Sheriff and
Herman get here. I only feel like explaining it one time.

I bet it's about our Linnville legal fees going up.
Has Herman already turned in a bill for representing the
Sheriff in the Bryant case? I'd think he'd want to wait 'till
after the trial.

You're on the right track. It is about legal costs.
Unfortunately, it's about the Marla Johnson case.

You mean the case that was tried up in Wisconsin?
Yes, exactly.

Lydia and Rodger walked into Lydia's office.
Sheriff Owens and Herman Smith were already seated in
chairs opposite her desk.

Lydia felt as nervous as the time she gave her first
speech in high school. She walked behind her desk and

stood up as she spoke. *Gentlemen, thanks for coming over on such short notice. I received a certified letter in this morning's mail that I want you all to know about.*

Owens interrupted. *Well, don't look so worried, Lydia. There's nothing bad that can come in a tiny envelope.*

Lydia looked eye-to-eye at each man as she opened the letter and passed it around, starting with Rodger. *Unfortunately, we did not fare well in the district court in the Marla Johnson case. The federal judge there is assessing us a million dollars in a settlement that is due by September 1.*

Owens jerked to his feet. *Why that no good Yankee judge. What business does he have meddling in our Mississippi law. He's a no good scheister, that's for sure! We'll have to appeal this decision!*

Herman spoke next. *Now just a minute, Owens. This is what it is. We've got to pay it.*

Rodger's face turned a shade whiter. *I sure don't know where we're going to get that much money. It's more than the county budgets for all the counties in Mississippi put together.*

Lydia reluctantly spoke up. *I see no other option than to dig into the savings of the Struck family. My brother said if I ever needed some big money, that he'd help me. This looks like the time. I'll have him write a check to us this week and then you can send one off to Madison, Rodger.*

The three grown men were quiet as they walked out of Lydia's office. How a northern judge could have that much power was unfair. They never once criticized Owens for his brutal actions—it was just part of his job.

***

Marla was excited. Her afternoon class had organized a peaceful march. The pretend city council meetings had empowered the students and they wanted to do something to show the whites in Linnville that change was needed. Beatrice had suggested a peaceful march along Main Street, past the business district. Her reasoning was that the black people in Linnville were good customers of the businesses and the white owners might notice them marching with signs. The kids had hand lettered some effective signage and were excitedly carrying them to the walk's start in front of Titan Hardware.

Joshua, come closer so I can see what's on your sign.

Hi, Miss Marla. This is supposed to be a drawing of a foot. It says, my black foot is just the same as your white foot—let me try on shoes!

Oh, I remember you telling me how blacks aren't allowed to try on shoes in shoe stores—what's that. . . you are only allowed to bring in a paper that shows the outline of your shoe. Good idea of a sign to use in today's protest, Joshua.

Thanks, Ma'am. I'm looking forward to our march today. It's about time we express our views.

Marla glanced up. *Good. I see Everett, Gina, and Tom. Looks like most of the students came, too. Can't wait to see all their signs.*

Tom walked up to Marla. *Do you mind if I give directions to our crew right now? I know you did most of the organizing for this and I don't want to overstep my bounds.*

Oh, that's perfectly fine, Tom. You go ahead and get the show on the road.

Tom waved his hand to get the group's attention. *Hey, everybody. Listen up. We're going to get started. Those of you with signs, spread out in the group. We'll walk along the sidewalk going North, then at Hen's*

Millinery Shop, we'll cross the street and come back along the south sidewalk. Any questions?

Carolina waved her sign saying 'One town—One Swimming Pool' to show she wanted Tom's attention. *Mr. Tom, what do we do if the law comes at us?*

Remember to keep your eyes on the prize. Keep marching with pride and know that even if no other people see you marching today, a COFO rep will be showing up to take photos of us marching with our signs and we'll be turning in those photos to the media. You may never see our march reported in the Linnville paper, but millions of people in Chicago, LA, and New York will know that a brave group of high school students from Linnville, Mississippi want justice.

Carolina added, *So what you are saying, Mr. Tom, is that regardless of whether anyone sees our march today, we will have a feeling deep in our hearts that we are making a difference.*

Yeah, that's a great way to say it. So, if there are no other questions, let's get this march underway.

Marla decided to walk at the back of the group. They'd talked about the teachers spreading out amongst the kids. *I sure hope the sheriff won't interfere with our march today. I don't want any trouble for the kids.* She stepped off to the side as the kids formed partnerships and walked off two-by-two. *The signs the kids made are really excellent.* She started reading several as students carried them past her: *Get a good view at the theater—any seat for any person, Why should the black library be smaller than the white library—let's have ONE library!, Integrate schools NOW!, ALL have the right to vote!.* . . Marla heard a car approaching. When she recognized it was Nels driving the COFO Dodge Dart, she let out a sigh of relief.

Nels parallel parked and jumped out of the car. He carried a camera in his right hand.

Hi, Nels, I'm glad to see you. So, you are the designated COFO volunteer who is going to record our march today?

Yes, indeed. There's also another reason I'm here: I have some good news for you.

You do?

Yes. Your parents made a call to COFO headquarters along with your attorney Mr. Jenner.

Marla wrinkled her nose. She did that whenever she was nervous. Nels said the news was going to be good, but she wasn't sure. . .

Marla, I am the lucky one who gets to tell you that the federal judge in Madison Wisconsin, Judge Henry Jambrowski, ruled in your favor in the case Jenner made against the sheriff's office.

I'm glad, Nels. It's nice to know that my home state is behind me. Now I feel I have some closure. What did my parents say?

Nels smiled. *Mostly stuff about loving you and being proud of you.*

And Mr. Jenner—was he pleased at the outcome?

Yeah, very pleased. Marla, you can't imagine how big a deal this is for justice. Thousands of people have been physically mistreated by southerners in power. This will serve as an example to other law enforcement and officials in positions of authority that such behavior will not be tolerated.

Is that what the judge said?

In a way, yes. He said it by making a monetary judgment against the sheriff's department. A judgment for one million dollars!

What?

Yes, you heard me. Marla, the Linnville Sheriff's Department has to pay you a million dollars before September 1.

I can hardly believe this, Nels. She reached out and hugged him. *Nels, I have an idea. Can you set up a foundation through COFO—I want the money to be awarded as scholarships to black kids in Linnville County who want to pursue a college education.*

Gee, Marla, that's very generous. You better talk to your parents about this first.

I know they will support me on this idea, Nels. I will call them, though. Can I come to COFO this afternoon and use your phone? Also, I'll want to call Mr. Jenner. He was a fine lawyer for me. I know he'll represent Samantha well, too.

Nels walked over to his Dart and took a megaphone out of the back seat. He walked back and shouted in it—loud enough for all the marchers to hear: *Hey, all you Linnville Freedom School students—a Wisconsin judge has ruled against the Linnville Sheriff's Department—they were fined a million dollars in the beating of our very own teacher Marla Johnson! Let Freedom Ring!*

Joshua and Beatrice were walking at the lead of the march. They clearly heard Nels' message. They started a chain reaction which led to all the Freedom School students shouting *Marla Johnson helped freedom ring! Marla Johnson helped freedom ring!*

302

Tears rolled down Marla's face. Tears of joy.
She'd been badly beaten, but her heart was full of love for
these students. She'd help them get to college.

Chapter 17

Samantha double-checked her lined notebook. She'd been careful to sandwich her notes about Freedom School teaching in small lettering between the haiku poems. Upon first glance, the poems stood out on each page. The notes were legible, but in tiny type—a few sentences between each poem. She started with reasons for her involvement in the Freedom School movement, and added notes about the actual teaching experiences. *I'm surprised that I have so much to write about being here. . .*

The aroma of warm cornbread and beans with bacon wafted through her cell. She always looked forward to the meals Hannah prepared for her. Even though she was the only inmate in the women's wing of the jail, she appreciated the careful attention Hannah put into the preparation and cooking of her meal. She varied the meals, each one having nutritious ingredients. Sometimes she tucked a tiny piece of paper with an inspirational thought written on it under the food. Yesterday, she found one that read *Be strong like Harriett.* Samantha knew instantly what she was referring to.

Deputy Glen unlocked Samantha's cell to let Hannah in.

Deputy, can you just leave me here for a few minutes? I need to visit some with this prisoner. There are some new rules about what to do with the trays when finished eating.

I don't know what that would be, but okay. I'll give you three minutes. Better be done in three.

Hanna smiled as the deputy walked out of Samantha's cell.

Good morning, Miss Samantha. I hope you got a good night's rest. I have a little song I'd like to sing to start your day. You start eating as I sing.

Hanna hummed a few bars of "This Little Light of Mine and then added her lyrics: *This little light of mine, I'm gonna let it shine, shine all over Lynnville, I'm gonna let it shine. This little light of mine. Marla's won her case, a million dollars comin' her way. This little light of Marla's she's gonna let it shine, startin' up a foundation to send black kids to school."*

Samantha sat up straighter on her cot. She cupped her hands around her face in surprise. *That's a great song, Hannah. It makes me so happy.*

I have one more verse, Dear. *This little light of mine, your lawyer's gonna make it shine, he's coming for a visit soon. . ."*

How's your Bible reading coming, Samantha? Keeping your spirits up?

Yes, thank you again, Hannah for sharing it with me. I've read the story of Joseph who was sold into slavery and instead of harboring a grudge against those who mistreated him, he forgave them. He went on to accomplish great things. I think the lesson of reconciliation is a good one, don't you?

Yes, Dear. The Bible has many good lessons. You should read about Ruth. She had some challenges, too.

Thanks, Hannah, I will.

The deputy reappeared and unlocked the door. *Come on, Hannah. You've done more than your share of singing and talking to this girl. Give her a break. She'll need her strength for her trial.* Samantha handed her empty tray to Hannah.

Samantha could barely hear their conversation as they walked down the hallway away from her cell. Something about the trial coming up very soon.

Samantha knew that the deputy and the sheriff spent a lot of their morning time eating breakfast and napping at their desk. Sometimes the sheriff left for coffee time, but generally, they didn't check the cells until after lunch, so the sudden footsteps coming toward her cell surprised her. They were the deputy's.

Bryant, your lawyer is here in the back room. Come with me.

Samantha waited until he turned away from her before she quickly took her notebook out from under the cot. She quickly slipped it inside her shirt *Mr Jenner might want my notes for the trial.*

Jenner was standing as she entered the back storage room. *Good day, Samantha. So nice to see you today.*

Ten minutes, Jenner. That's all you get with her.

Yes, Deputy. We'll chat for ten minutes.

I'll be back in ten. That's for sure.

Samantha removed the notebook from inside her shirt. She opened it and tore out the pages of her notes. *Here, Mr. Jenner, are the notes I jotted down for you. I couldn't trust the staff here, so I wrote some haiku poems in big lettering, then you can see here between each poem where I inserted notes about my reasons for coming and my teaching here at Freedom School.*

Jenner took the notes and slid them quickly into his briefcase. *Thank you, Samantha, these will be most helpful.*

307

I bring you some good news.

Is it about you winning Marla's case?

Oh, my, how good news travels.

I just know the basics that the judge ruled against the sheriff and fined him one million dollars.

Actually, that is the main part. The good thing, is it's sure to rattle the sheriff and the county officials. They'll be scrambling to scratch up the money.

Will Marla get all the money.

Yes. I'm representing her pro bono—you too. Marla wants her money to go to black kids here in the county to attend college. But, since we don't have much time, I have a couple of things to talk about with you about your case. One thing is, as expected, Judge Roanoke denied our change of venue—remember we claimed we couldn't get justice in his court. Well, he required me to send reasons why I felt justice would be denied in his court, and I just received his official decision that he's denied our request. No surprise. Just wanted to fan the fire a bit.

Now, the other thing is that we talked about you sending the sheriff on a wild goose chase about what your case is going to be about. Have you had a chance to do that yet?

Samantha grinned. She was looking forward to sharing her thoughts about this. *Yes. The other day, the sheriff asked me to answer two questions. He said if I answered them satisfactorily, he'd reduce the charges.* She pulled out the carbon copied form Owens had given her and handed it to Jenner.

Jenner studied it. *It looks like he dropped two charges. Ha! What did you tell him to get him to agree to this?*

I told him that the witnesses you would call would be national leaders in the civil rights movement. I also told him not to tell you that I knew you had the dates and times the two leaders would be criss-crossing Mississippi.

Jenner's eyes twinkled. *Samantha, Bryant, you are a rascal. You have set this up great. I'll ask for a plea deal and that will give him the opportunity to ask me for the whereabouts of the big-shot leaders of the movement. I couldn't have thought of a better guise myself.*

Jenner stood up. *Now, use your improv skills to pretend we never had this conversation. I'll take it from here.*

The deputy appeared at the storage room door. Jenner exited, followed by Samantha. She was careful to

slip the notebook back inside her shirt. Writing the haiku
was a great release; she could pen more.

On the way out of the jail, Jenner stopped by
Owens' desk. *Sheriff, I'd like to set up a meeting with you
regarding my client, Miss Bryant. I think we can come up
with a better arrangement before the trial starts.*

Are you hinting about a plea deal, Jenner?

*Well, since you mentioned it, that might be a good
option.*

Set yourself down right now and we can talk.

Owens pulled an oak chair in front of his desk. *So,
in order for me to give you an offer, you've got to give me
some good news. Got anything, Jenner?*

*Owens, you know this thing is bigger than just the
girl you've locked up. Why not let her go and I'll give you
names and dates of when the movement's king-pins will be
in your neighborhood.*

Start talkin'.

Jenner opened his briefcase and pulled out a small
pocket calendar. He ripped a piece of paper off his legal
pad and pretended to be referencing his calendar as he
wrote dates, initials, and cities on the paper:

| July 12 | Jackson |
| July 14 | Linnville |

July 15	Nachez
July 19	Vicksburg
July 20	Oxford

Jenner handed the paper to Owens.

So, what does this crap mean?

I've just given you the dates and cities where two of the big civil rights leaders are appearing. Go after them and let the girl go.

Owens folded the paper and put it in his pocket. *Naw, this isn't enough for much of a deal—well, we'll drop the jaywalking charge, and disturbing the peace, but that's the best I can do.*

You are a jerk, Owens. You know that this is fresh news for you cops. You'll be able to send your goons after the big civil rights leaders. Jenner stood up and acted disgusted.

Owens repeated himself. *There's no deal if this is all you are offering. We'll see you in court next week.* Owens put his boots up on his desk and rested his hands behind his neck.

If that's what you say. See you in court. Jenner stomped out of the jail, slamming the door.

Ah, we've got them where we want them, Glen I've got us the dates and places where the kingpins will be and still have the trial on the books—a trial that will send them Yankees north with their tails between their legs.

Chapter 18

Samantha heard some soft footsteps coming down the hallway. She raised herself up on her elbows and looked up from her cot. *But only one set of footsteps? The deputy always accompanies Hannah when she brings my meals. What's going on?*

Samantha blinked, but saw the same scene before her. Hannah was carrying her food tray in her right hand, and in her left, the ring of jail cell keys. She inserted the key to Samantha's cell lock and pulled the barred wall open.

She sat completely up. *Let me guess. The sheriff likes you cooking so much that he's promoted you to deputy.*

Hannah grinned as she handed the tray to Samantha. The blended aromas of fresh blueberry muffins, cheese-topped scrambled eggs and apple-smoked bacon wafted to her nose. *Thank you, Hannah. This looks great.*

Me the new deputy? That's a good guess, Dear. Actually, I think I'd do a pretty good job at it, but there's a different explanation. Seems the sheriff and deputy are off

*together at an important meeting, so the deputy's brother is
covering for them while they're gone.*

And he trusted you with the ring of jail cell keys?

*Well, sort of. I gave him a double serving of
breakfast in exchange for the key ring so I could clean your
cell. He's an easy one to convince, or should I say he's too
lazy to walk down this hallway with me. So, here I am.*

Samantha had eaten half of her muffin and was
eagerly devouring her eggs and bacon. *Hannah, this is a
fabulous breakfast. Did you fix this for all the prisoners?*

*Well, you could say so. There aren't many in the
jail today. You are the only woman and there are just two
in the men's wing. Dilbert Jones—he's in for drunk in
public again. Poor man. He's been drinking a lot ever
since his wife passed away. I'm trying to get some help for
him. Jeremy Brinks is here for a spell, too. According to
the deputy, he stole a ham from Happy Market. I happen to
know he's out of work and probably took the ham to feed
his young family. I talked to him this morning and told him
that my loving husband agreed he and I can make a weekly
money donation to his family until he finds work. We'll
also send over a basket of food each day. I have a cousin
in Milwaukee who may help him get a job. I wrote him a
letter yesterday. Then there's the fine he'll have to pay for*

314

stealing the ham. My church will take up a collection to cover that.

Hannah, you amaze me. You are a one-woman social agency. I don't know how you have time to work here and also help others.

It's my priority, Miss Samantha. I believe we were all put on Earth to live a goodly life. For me, that means helping out others as best I can. Nobody comes to me and says, 'Hannah, you can help so-and-so by doing this or that.' I just have to keep my eyes open and help out the folks that I think need some assistance.

Well, you sure have helped me, Hannah. You lent me your family Bible, you sing message songs to me—even though they don't always rhyme, and you keep me cheered up. Why, just the other day, you took a big risk by letting Gina come into my cell and bring me the cards from the students.

Thank you for that nice compliment. Speaking of the Bible, have you read the book of Ruth like I suggested?

I did. You were right; there are some good messages in the Book of Ruth.

Tell me, Dear, how did this scripture minister to you?

I think it described the hardships Naomi and Ruth had. First, was the fact that due to famine, Naomi had to move from Judah to Moab. Then, while she was there, Naomi's husband and two sons died. Then something good happened: when she decided to move back to Judah, her daughter-in-law Ruth accompanied her. Ruth's challenge was that when she arrived in Judah, she was a foreigner in that land. Fortunately, Boaz married Ruth and also cared for her and for Naomi.

That's a good summary of the scripture, Samantha. Now, how does that scripture give you hope?

Well, I think the message of the Book of Ruth is that God loves all people, regardless of their race, nationality or status. Ruth was not a Jew; she was a Moabite. Even though some people in Judah discriminated against her, God loved her just the same. I think that's a lesson we are trying to support in our Freedom Schools; all people are equally important, whatever their race.

Yes, that is so. You are a black woman from the North, here helping young people get justice. God loves you not only for being you, but for your dedication to helping those who are less fortunate. You keep your spirits up, Samantha, especially when your trial starts.

I wish I knew when that was.

Oh, I almost forgot to tell you. I saw a paper on the sheriff's desk. The trial starts tomorrow.

Really? Thanks for telling me, Hannah. I don't know what I'd do without you. You are a regular news source.

I better be getting back with this key ring. She reached into a shoulder bag and pulled out a clean sheet. *Here's a clean sheet for your cot; let's take off this old one and replace it. I'll actually be back to clean your room later today when the deputy's brother is gone. The same excuse will only work once with a man.*

Hannah stuffed the dirty sheet into her shoulder bag. Hannah handed her the empty breakfast tray. *I'll be back with an early supper. One more thing. My mother named me after Hannah in the Bible. Hannah devoted her son Samuel to the Lord. I don't have any children, but I do devote myself to Him.*

And you do a fine job of it, Hannah!

Chapter 19

Jenner drove his rental car slowly into Claude and Maybelle's gravel driveway. He wasn't surprised to see his son rolling around on the ground with Claude's two boys jumping on and off of his back. *Just like him to get totally involved in whatever he's doing.*

The sound of the car alerted Claude to walk out on the porch. When he recognized Jenner Senior, he relaxed his pose. *Seems this Freedom movement has brought some new surprise nearly every day. I wonder what Jenner will have to share with us at suppertime.*

Jenner grabbed his briefcase from the passenger's seat, unloosened his tie, and swung his long legs onto the ground as he opened the car door. *Hello, everybody.*

Willy and Wayne ignored Jenner's greeting and continued to hoot and holler as they pretend-wrestled with Tom. When Tom glanced up and saw his dad, he motioned for the kids to put the wrestling on pause. Tom met up with his dad and Claude on the porch. Jenner gave his son a friendly slap on his shoulder. *Hey Tom. You beat me here. I was worried that I was late for dinner and might miss out on Maybelle's good cooking.*

Maybelle heard his compliment through the screen door. She wiped some flour off her hands onto her apron, and walked out on the porch to join in the conversation. *Thank you, Thomas, for that nice compliment. I am happy to announce that you are just in time to sample my signature fried chicken, mashed potatoes, and greens. Oh, and I hope you are in the mood for some peach cobbler tonight.*

Maybelle, you don't know how delicious that menu sounds. I'm definitely in the mood for everything on tonight's menu.

Well, come on in and sit at the table. Willy and Wayne, you two need to dust off and rinse your hands at the pump before you come in. Get a move on. She held the door open to double check on the boys' hand washing.

Jenner walked to the back porch where he set down his brief case by his make-shift bed. He slid off his tie and shirt and grabbed a tee shirt from his suitcase under the bed. Time to get casual. He rumbled through the suitcase until he found a pair of jeans. He grabbed them out and hastily exchanged them for his dress pants. Claude had fashioned a clothes rack out of a large tree branch and Jenner hung his jacket and pants on separate hooks of the rack. Maybelle had washed and pressed two of his dress shirts and neatly folded them before placing them at the foot of his bed. *She's a master at laundry—sure is worth the ten-dollar bill I pay her each day for this service.*

Willy was the first to finish washing. He frowned at his mother. *Ma, I don't see why I have to wash my hands. They were perfectly fine.*

Now, one day you will meet a pretty girl and want to marry her. She will expect your hands to be clean before you sit down at the table to eat with her.

Gosh, Ma. I don't think I'll ever marry. It's too much work.

Someday, you will marry—I'm sure of that. Maybe that nice Swanson girl.

Ick! She's not for me. Too uppity.

Maybelle closed the door and walked over to the oven. She removed a large casserole pan brim full of fried chicken. After placing it on the table, she spooned out large bowls full of mashed potatoes and greens and set them in the center of the table.

Tom seated himself between the twins. *This meal sure looks dee-licious, Maybelle. We may never leave Linnville—your food is just delicious.*

Thank you Tom. You are certainly welcome to stay on. Our family has enjoyed you being here, that's for sure.

Claude extended his hands and signaled it was time for grace by bowing his hands. The group formed a circle of hand holding throughout his short prayer. *Lord, we thank you for the blessings you have bestowed upon us. We are grateful for your wisdom and power. Help us to live good lives. Be with Mr. Jenner as he leads his court case and thank you for this good food Maybelle has lovingly prepared for our benefit. In your Son's name, Amen.*

Willy repeated the 'Amen' the loudest; Wayne came in second place.

Once the bowls had been passed clockwise around the table and everyone had taken a helping, Claude spoke.

Say, Jenner, you never told us what you used those shovels for.

With the children present, Thomas knew he'd need to share a G-rated version of the episode. *I want to thank you again for lending me the shovels, Claude. They came in quite handy. I happened to overhear a couple of good-olds say they wanted to torch the Freedom School. . .*

Wayne interrupted. *Mr. Jenner, what does 'torch' mean?*

Well, Wayne. The men brought a bucket of kerosene and they planned to light a match to the kerosene right by the school.

Wayne put his fork down on the tablecloth. *They were gonna' burn the school down?*

Yes, that was their plan. But I'm sure you'll agree with me that it's not a good idea to burn down schools.

Wayne nodded.

So, to stop them, Tom and I went out to the school and we used the shovels to dig some big holes in the ground. Really big holes. We covered the holes with branches so it would be hard to see the holes at night.

Willy spoke up. *I know what happened. The bad guys thought they were walking across the grass and they fell down into the big holes!*

Jenner saw a grin spread across Claude's face.

Of course, Tom and I wanted to teach them a little lesson, so we dressed up in costumes and lassoed them. We pulled them out of the holes and led them to their truck.

Did you dress up as Superman? Wayne asked.

Nope. We looked more like ghosts, you might say.

Claude laughed so loud that tears came to his eyes. *You mean they thought you were KKKers? Oh, what a picture!*

You guessed it. We told them they were in our territory and never to come back there.

Did you keep them tied up? Willy asked.

322

Tom joined in the tale. *You kids might not know this, buy my dad can make his voice sound like other people. That night, he was able to make his voice sound like other people were there besides the two of us. We let the guys go and they scooted right out of there in their truck.*

Golly, laughed Claude. I've never heard such a funny story as that.

Wayne jumped up and down excitedly in his chair. *Can you show us how you can change your voice, Mr. Jenner? Please?*

Jenner thought for a minute before imitating Maybelle's voice. *Willie and Wayne, it's time for bed now. You go on and jump in your bed.*

Both boys looked back and forth between Jenner and their mother. They didn't see either one move their lips. *Gosh, that's good! You sounded just like our mother! How did you do that?*

It's called ventriloquism. I'm talking without moving my lips.

Maybelle pushed herself back from the table and stood up. *Actually, it IS time for you boys to head to your bedroom. Do your devotions and then get a good night sleep. School will come early tomorrow. Thank you, Mr. Jenner, for your fine story and demonstration of my voice.*

After Maybelle got the boys settled for bed, the adults slipped out onto the porch for dessert. Maybelle served large portions to Thomas and Tom. *Say, Tom, you didn't tell us much about your day teaching at Freedom School. We'd love to hear about it,* she said.

Thanks for asking, Maybelle. It was a good day at Freedom School. We took the students to the white diner and did a mock sit-in.

You mean you went inside the diner and sat down?

Not exactly. We carried stools from Freedom School over to the diner and sat on them in front of the diner, pretending to be inside the diner. Sort of like acting like we were in a real white diner. Some kids pretended to be customers; others dramatized the employees, waiting on the customers.

And the sheriff didn't come and break up your show?

Fortunately, not. We guessed that he was busy getting ready for the trial. It was really quiet for which we were glad.

I'm glad it went well for you, Son. You sure are introducing the teens to some real-life experiences.

Thanks, Dad. I have to give Samantha credit for the idea. I sat near her on the bus on the way here and she shared the idea with me. Another time, we'll go inside the white diner and asked to be served.

Claude placed his finished dessert plate on the small porch table. *I sure am impressed that you five teachers are working so well together. It's wonderful to see black and white young folk talking to each other and working together so well. We've lived in such a segregated town, that the concept of working with a white person seems so alien to me. I hope one day that Linnville will be more integrated.*

Say, Jenner, are you ready for tomorrow's trial. I imagine a lot of white Linnville citizens will be in the courtroom hoping you don't do well; but we Linnville blacks, are hoping the opposite. We'd like nothing better than for the Bryant girl to get off free and the sheriff get nailed.

I hear you, Claude. I have a few surprises for Sheriff Owens and his buddies. One of them is the reason I was a little late getting here for supper.

And what is that, Dad? You haven't told me what's up your sleeve.

Well, I had a little meeting with the judge this afternoon. I convinced him to allow a camera into his courtroom. Told him this was a historic time and that a visual record of the trial might make him well-known not only in Linnville, but around the country.

And just what do you mean by this? asked Claude.

Well, as we are sitting here right now, a friend of mine Noel Grizzard, who is a Hollywood movie producer, is over at the courthouse setting up his camera. He's going to film the case in its entirety and edit it at the end of each day. Then, he'll send the footage to the major television networks so they can show it on the evening news on every tv in the country.

That's amazing. Claude continued, *I can hardly believe that such a process can be achieved. I sure wish I could see the trial. It's sure to be a good one with you as Samantha's attorney.*

Actually, I've arranged for you and anyone else who is interested to watch the trial live. Grizzard brought a tv with him that he's going to mount in Louie's diner. He'll set the tv high on a counter so that lots of people can come in and out during the day and watch the trial.

Maybelle and Claude exchanged glances. Maybelle shook her head side to side. *Claude, we might want to do our work through the night so we can watch the trial. What do you think?*

I think you are absolutely right, Maybelle. The trial may be the biggest event Linnville has ever experienced.

Jenner stood up to stretch his legs. *I'm hoping the trial may be the biggest event the country has ever experienced. Wait 'till you see my friend's work. He'll splice the scenes together in a very dramatic way. Few people outside Linnville know what you black folks are up against. If all goes well, millions will know the injustices.*

But how exactly did you get Judge Roanoke to agree to this, Dad, Tom asked.

Easy. A coffee chat with Roanoke revealed that he once dreamed of becoming a movie star. I convinced him that his performance at the bench might lead to a movie contract.

Dad, you are the master of psychology.

Keep your fingers crossed, everyone. I hope my witnesses do a good job with their parts!

Chapter 20

Noel Grizzard smoothed the wrinkles in his gray-striped sports jacket. He checked his Rolex. *Gosh, only nine o'clock in the morning, and I'm already dragging. It's a good thing that Hans, my sound recordist came with me and helped.* Noel and Hans had spent the previous evening doing the wiring for the tv he'd dropped off at the diner. *What had Jenner referred to it as—oh, yeah, the black diner. When will people finally get it together and not have separate diners for different races?* He shook his head. *Probably never. Well, at least the blacks in Linnville will be able to follow along with the trial as it unfolds. Their version will be live, raw—not like the finely edited one I'll submit each afternoon to be edited for the national news. And how good is it that the trial will finish mid-afternoon each day (Jenner assured me) and due to the time zone difference, I'll plenty of time to drive the daily footage to the Jackson lab where it can be edited and sent over to Associated Press in time for late news shows across the country.*

Grizzard thought about the awards he'd gotten for his films. *Last year, I got the nod for an Oscar, but old what's-his-name must have been a distant cousin of the Oscars Board of Directors, or I would have gotten it for sure.*

Thank goodness my cousin helped me get started in this business—it's so cut-throat. I'll always remember when Roger called me after my bar mitzvah and invited me to visit him in Hollywood. I had no idea at the time that it would lead to this. I think I got hooked the minute he took me on the set of a western he was filming. A couple of actors were practicing a shoot-out scene in front of a saloon set. When that saloon door opened and the two burst out suddenly onto the dusty street, I was so startled that I wet my pants. . .

Then Rodger hired me to help him out each summer during my high school years. Being a go-fer, I picked up a lot of skills, especially my favorite: filming. Good 'ol Cousin Rodge—what a mentor!

A squeaky pipe returned Grizzard to the present. *I'm lucky that the janitor let Hans and me in to the courthouse last night after I wired up the diner. Fortunately, we got the camera and equipment carried in and set up lickety split. Can't believe Jenner convinced the judge to let me film the trial.*

Today, I'll focus on getting some good footage of the jury selection. Hopefully, I can zoom in on the jurors as the attorneys question them. I need to get some close-ups of jurors pondering the questions they're asked to see if they qualify. Grizzard inserted a reel of sixteen-millimeter film. He heard some conversation through the walls. *Probably the jurors getting ready to come in the court room. This should be a wide-angle shot.*

Excuse me, Sir. Do you have permission to be using your camera in Judge Dean's courtroom? A tall officer stood very close to him. *Probably the bailiff.*

Grizzard reached into his jacket pocket and withdrew a folded document. He unfolded it and handed it to the man. *Here, take a look. Roanoke signed this permission to film the courtroom proceedings. He's good with it.*

The bailiff slowly read through the paragraph, word by word. He looked up at Grizzard.

Here, you can have this back. I never would have believed that Judge Roanoke would have given his okay to let you film the proceedings here in his courtroom. But, I've judged people wrong before. Whatever.

The bailiff walked over by the door leading to Roanoke's chambers. He stood with his back against the wall and folded his hands, one over the other. *Probably waiting for the judge to enter his courtroom.*

Suddenly, a door on the east side of the courtroom opened and a group of men walked through it and seated themselves in the rows of chairs lined up near the judge's bench. *Must be twenty or so.* A middle-aged woman with fluffed blond hair entered after the men, sitting at a small table just to the right of the judge's desk. She carried a clipboard in her right hand. *You don't see short skirts and high heels like that much any more.* Grizzard zoomed in to get a shot of the woman. *Must be the clerk of court. My word, she's chewing gum.* Looking through the camera lens, Grizzard caught her gum-chomping lip movements. She seemed to have a habit of fluffing her hair with her fingers.

The attorneys' tables were to the left and right of the judge's elevated desk-bench, directly behind the podium. Jenner and the other attorney followed the woman into the room and sat at their respective tables, Jenner at the table on the right. *Jenner looks good in his suit. I'm sure they have no idea what he's got cookin' for this trial. The prosecuting attorney looks weak, though.* Grizzard was used to guessing a person's intellect and personality from his appearance. *What's a lawyer doing wearing a wool vest*

*under his suit in the middle of summer? And that shaggy
beard needs a good trim. Oh, heck, maybe his Green Acres
look impresses the locals—who am I to judge.* Grizzard
took a quick shot of both attorneys before putting the
camera on pause.

Grizzard's musings were interrupted by the bailiff's
loud voice. *All rise for the honorable Judge Dean
Roanoke.* The door to Roanoke's chambers opened and he
quickly walked onto the podium and stood behind his tall
oak desk. He glanced across the room from side to side
taking note of the people present. *No surprise; it's another
all-white jury. Maybe Jenner will object.* Roanoke lifted
the hem of his black robe and seated himself in the oak
swivel chair. He reached down into his briefcase and took
out a notepad and pen. *My photographic memory will
record every detail—no need to take notes. But then again,
with the camera running, I may pretend to so I will give the
appearance of being a scholarly judge. I'll have to sit up
straight—just like my mother used to urge me; after all, I
want to project a good image of southern judges even if the
prosecution may be biased.*

Roanoke looked up to see Herman Smith toward
his desk. His brow was furrowed and his eyes squinty in
anger. *What the heck, Judge! What's that guy doing with a*

332

camera in the courtroom? He better not be here to film this trial—we've never had a camera in here before. I'm objecting big time to this!

Roanoke waited for Smith's anger to simmer a bit. *I understand your concern, Herman. You are one hundred percent correct that we've never had a camera in my chambers before, but there are some extenuating circumstances in this case so I've given permission to have the proceedings filmed. I'm thinking that this will be a good idea to have an accurate version of the trial for history's sake. Why, ten years from now, people will still be talking about this case. We need to have footage of what actually happens at the trial so we can keep history accurate. Also, while the defendant is being tried, we have to face it that southern justice is also on trial. Whichever way this case shakes out, we want to have a true version of it.* He waited for Herman to respond.

I do see your point, but I don't like it. Hector turned away and plodded back to his table. *Doesn't Roanoke know that I'm camera shy—never did like a camera poking in my face. Oh, well, if Roanoke has already decided to let the case be filmed, I'll save my objections for something else.*

Lydia Struck picked up her clipboard and pencil. She stood and focused her eyes on the men gathered in the audience section. *Gentlemen, I am Lydia Struck, Clerk of Court for Linnville County. It is my responsibility to monitor those who are selected to serve as jurors. I'm going to call twelve of your names. When you hear your name called, please walk over to the jury box on the west side of the courtroom.* Lydia dramatically gestured with her right arm to show the designated area. She finger-swished a swatch of hair by her right ear. *So, listen-up. Here are the names: Lyle Granger, George McGrath, John Struck, Burt Nemick, Edgar Riemenschneider, Robert Danger, Evan Jochims, Roger Cook, Lyle Corbett, Benjamin C. Dorink, Stephen Gorham, and Lorne Sheffield. I have just called twelve names for jurors for the case of the Linnville Sheriff's Department vs. Samantha Bryant. Case #3421.*

The men slowly stood and moved to the jury box as Lydia continued speaking. *To the rest of you seated before me, I'm informing you that you need to remain seated right where you are until the full jury has been selected. If one of the twelve people just named is not accepted for the jury by one of the attorneys, then I will need to replace that juror with one of you.*

Hans recorded several boos from the disappointed men. Grizzard swiveled the camera on its tripod to face Judge Roanoke. *I know from all my filming of movies about trials, that the judge will be up next. Time for his statement to the jurors about the type of case.*

Grizzard was right. Roanoke put on a pair of dark-rimmed reading glasses and began to read the case description. He tried looking up from time-to-time to establish eye contact with the jurors. *Today, you are here to begin the first step in legal case 3421, also known as the Linnville Sheriff's Department vs. Samantha Bryant. This case is a case put forward by the county government alleging that the defendant, Samantha Bryant from Chicago, Illinois was on the wrong side of the law. She is being charged with inciting unrest. Because of the seriousness of this charge, you will be commissioned with making a determination of her guilt. You will be asked to find her guilty of inciting unrest with intent which has a twenty-year jail term, guilty of inciting unrest as a participant in a group which has a five-year jail term, or innocent. Listen carefully to the evidence that both sides present. You will need to distinguish the level of intent Miss Bryant demonstrated when committing this crime. Now, before the attorneys begin questioning you to see if you can serve fairly on the jury for this case, I need to ask if any of you have a reason you cannot serve.*

The juror seated at the south end of the second row in the jury box raised his hand. *Your Honor, I am Stephen Gorham. I am a very busy farmer. In the next few days, I'm going to have some calves born on my farm and I need to be there to help. May I be excused.*

Roanoke tried not to grin. There always was someone who tried to get out of jury duty with some lame excuse or other. *I'm sure those mother cows would like nothing better than to have you assist them with their births, Mr. Gorham. However, it is your civic duty to serve on a jury when called, and I'm going to have to deny your request. You'll need to ask a neighbor to help you out while you are here.*

Gorham lowered his head and pouted.

Judge Roanoke continued. *The attorneys will now take turns asking you questions to determine if they think you will be representative of the nature of this case. This questioning is referred to as voir dire. In case you are not a Latin scholar, these words mean 'to speak the truth.' I am reminding each one of you that you will need to tell the truth when asked a question. Mr. Jenner, you may begin.*

Jenner briskly walked up to Roanoke's table. *Respectfully, Sir,* he spoke softly. *I see that all potential jurors in this room are of the white race. My client is black. How can she receive a fair trial with an all-white jury?*

Look, Mr. Jenner. I capitulated on letting you film the trial, but I'm not budging on the race of jurors. For your information, throughout the twenty-seven years I have served on this bench, we have always had a jury comprised of white males. It is the way it has been. Save your objections for something else. Mr. Jenner, please proceed with your questioning of the jurors.

Jenner walked back to the table. *Well, when the film footage rolls across the good ol' U.S.A., they'll see what blacks are really up against. It's a good thing I've got a few things up my sleeve.*

Jenner looked the first candidate in the eye. *Mr. Struck, do you think you can give a fair judgment in this case?*

Struck thought he was supposed to stand up to answer. *You may remain seated during my questioning, Mr. Struck.*

Yes, I do. I am a fifth-generation landowner in Linnville. I serve as Treasurer of the Linnville Republican

Party. I certainly can look at something in an objective way.

Thank you, Mr. Struck.

Jenner knew that all the potential jurors were racist to some degree. *I'm not going down that line of questioning. Mr. Cook, do you work for Linnville County?*

Cook raised his head and looked directly at Jenner. *Why, yes. I am a veteran county auditor here.*

And how many years have you been working for the county?

Proudly, thirty-one.

Jenner walked up to Roanoke. *Your Honor, I move to strike Roger Cook as a juror. He works for the same county that is trying the case.*

The judge pondered Jenner's remarks for a moment. *Motion denied. While in the same county, the courthouse is clearly a different government body from the jail. Mr. Smith, your turn to question a potential juror. . .*

Noel Grizzard happily slapped the wall behind him. In the two hours of jury questioning, he'd gotten some great close-up shots of the attorneys and jurors. Movies about underdogs triumphing were always a hit. Throughout the jury selection process, Jenner got the short end of the stick. The judge seemed to favor Smith, not

338

letting Jenner strike any jurors. I can't wait to get this footage to Jackson. I'm pretty sure, we''ll get a few million to watch the trial based on just today's jury selection fiasco alone.

Chapter 21

Marla looked over the students in the auditorium. They were abuzz in conversation. *Are they excited that our march went well? Had they heard about how Tom and his dad curtailed the burning of our school? Are they simply glad that Gina is teaching them to type?*

She strummed a few C chords on her guitar, her signature signal that it was time to get the beginning-of-the-day freedom song session underway. *Hey, you stellar Freedom School students, let's channel your energy into the singing of a favorite song of ours: "This Little Light."*

Hector belted out some measures with his harmonica. Beatrice shouted out her wishes for the first verse: *Shine all over Freedom School. . .*

Instantly, the guitar, harmonica, and voices blended into harmony.

'This little light of mine,
I'm gonna let it shine,
This little light of mine,
I'm gonna let it shine
This little light of mine,
I'm gonna let it shine, shine shine.

Shine all over Freedom School,

I'm gonna let it shine

Shine all over Freedom School,

I'm gonna let it shine,

Shine all over Freedom School,

I'm gonna let it shine

Let it shine, shine, shine.

Joshua shouted out the next idea for a verse. *Shine all over Samantha's trial.*

Marla couldn't believe the volume and emotion of the students' voices on this verse.

Shine all over Samantha's trial

I'm gonna let it shine

Shine all over Samantha's trial

I'm gonna let it shine

Shine all over Samantha's trial

I'm gonna let it shine

Let it shine, shine, shine.

Joshua stood up and faced Everett. Mr. Everett, will we be able to attend Samantha's trial. The group's collective cheers echoed throughout the auditorium.

Marla glanced over at Everett. *Aha! That's why they are so excited today—Sam's trial. . .*

Everett raised his hand to signal he wanted to give the kids an answer to Joshua's question. *As usual, Joshua, you are asking a good question; a question that all of you are probably wondering about. The answer is that we hope we can send a contingent of Freedom School students to watch the trial. It would be good for several reasons. Number one: it would show Samantha that we are supporting her. Number two: since not many black people attend trials in the Linnville Courtroom, it would be another way we can integrate Linnville. Today is the selection of the jury; the actual trial starts tomorrow.*

Everett was interrupted by every student standing and shouting, *I'll go, I'll go. . .*

He raised his hand again to get the group's attention. *Wow! We couldn't ask for more support than that you are showing today. Unfortunately, the Linnville Courtroom is not a roomy place, and we'll need to limit the number of students we take. If you are interested in being one of our school reps, then sign your name on this paper.* He placed a piece of notebook paper and a pencil on the table by the door. *While, we'd like for all who are interested to be in the audience, we'll have to limit the*

342

*number to five students. I'll have the other Freedom
teachers help me decide on a fair criteria to select the five.
We know that all of you are supportive and will understand
that even if you are not selected, you will support Samantha
with your thoughts and prayers. Does that sound fair?*

A chorus of yeses filled the room.

*Now, because many of you have not attended a trial
before, today, we are going to spend time in our classes
talking about the procedure of a trial. Even if you are not
selected to attend Samantha's, you may one day be asked to
serve on a jury of a trial, so it's important for you to know
the procedure.*

Hector stood up. *Respectfully, Mr. Everett, don't
you think that it's more likely we will be defendants in trials
than jurors?*

*I hear you, Hector. Sadly, because of the color of
our skin, it IS more likely that we will be falsely charged
with crimes, or harshly judged for simple misdeeds in
society. I wish that weren't so. But, even if you are
misjudged by society, you should also know what to expect
in the courtroom. This is also a function of our Freedom
School: to inform you as a citizen of how the legal system
works—whether it is legitimate or corrupt.*

Hector blurted out. *We all know, Mr. Everett, that here in this state, the legal system is corrupt. If it weren't, Miss Samantha would never have been arrested.*

Everett knew it was important to address the teens' questions. *Hector, you are speaking the truth. Remember, we are engaged in a power struggle. Throughout society, people have struggled with acquiring power. Often, those who are not at the top of the intellectual or economic ladder, find that they can achieve power by keeping others at the ladder's lower rungs. The whites in Linnville are part of this power struggle. They know that throughout the northern states, that blacks are more involved in decision making. Here in Mississippi, ever since the institution of slavery, whites have tried to keep blacks on the lower rungs of the ladder. You see this in the segregation of schools, movie theaters, and voting opportunities. We are at a turning point.*

There is a third reason it is important for us to have a delegation at Samantha's trial: A friend of Tom's dad is a Hollywood movie producer; he is filming the trial and sending the footage to news outlets across the country. It's highly possible that millions of people around the country will watch this trial and respond to it at some level. If whites in northern states see that Freedom School students care enough about justice to attend a trial on behalf of one of their teachers, they will be moved.

Everett didn't remember dismissing the students to their first class of the day. He witnessed the immediate forming of a line to sign the paper he'd placed on the table by the door.

***

Tom scrambled to his classroom after the freedom song session. He enjoyed sitting at his desk and watching the faces of the Freedom School kids as they walked into his classroom. *At first, I was challenged to see the distinctive features on each of their faces. It seemed like they all looked the same. Now, each one has identifying appearances: Joshua is tall, very muscular, and has a square jaw. Beatrice is thin, with a rounded face and a nice wide smile. I bet the reverse might be true—white people might seem to look the same at first. . .*

Joshua was the first to come through the door. *Hey, Mr. Tom, I was the first to sign the paper to be in the audience for Samantha's trial, so does that mean I'm selected as one of the five?*

Nice try, Arnot. Just because you probably muscled your way to the front of the line, doesn't automatically put you on the list. On the other hand, you've written some pretty convincing pieces for our Freedom School newspaper. I certainly have been impressed with the logic and examples you use in your writing.

Thanks, Mr. Tom. I'll keep my fingers crossed that I'll be chosen. Don't forget that I plan to study law and this would be a good experience for me.

I get your drift, Arnot.

Tom stood up from his desk, his hands inserted into his pants pockets. He hadn't needed to prepare for today's civics class; teaching the lesson about trial procedure was second nature. *When Mom had to take a night shift at the hospital, I remember as a kid, Dad taking me to his office and getting me involved in whatever case he was working on at the time. Sometimes, I was supposed to take the role of a juror, sometimes I got to pretend I was the judge as Dad practiced his closing argument in front of me. . .Yeah, this lesson will be a fun one to teach.*

So, as Everett explained just now, it's important for you to know just how a trial works. Let's start with a little background, then I'm going to make up a case where you will take the roles of attorneys, jurors, and judge.

346

Beatrice raised her hand. *Mr. Tom, will the case you're going to have us decide be like Samantha's case?*

Close. No two cases are exactly the same, but I've concocted one that will be similar. Stay tuned.

Tom grabbed a piece of chalk and wrote some key terms on the board as he explained the jury selection process, opening statements, direct and cross examination, objections, and closing arguments.

Mr. Tom, just how do you know so much about this? You aren't even using notes to explain this, said Josephia.

Tom chuckled. *When I was a little kid, my dad would have me pretend to be one of the people in a trial that he was working on.*

Did you ever get to be the bailiff and pretend to toss someone out of the courtroom? Daniel asked.

Ha! I would have loved that, but no, I had some tougher roles.

What could be tougher than throwing someone out of the room?

You have a point, Daniel. It would take some muscle. But actually, there's a lot that goes on before the trial begins that prevents negative things from happening in the courtroom.

Do you really think the judge will let us be in the courtroom? I've heard that only whites are on the jury and in the audience.

We can't be one hundred percent certain that the judge will let us seat ourselves in the audience. However, because the trial is being filmed, the judge will want to at least give the appearance that he's fair. We're going to give it a try, that's for sure.

Now, it's time for us to do a simulated court case. Our case is Linnville County vs Joshua Arnot who has been arrested for trying to order lunch from a white diner.

Joshua grinned. *Gee—I was hoping to play the part of an attorney, Mr. Tom.*

And you'd be a fine attorney. But you will also be an excellent witness, so get started thinking about why you wanted to get lunch at the diner. After all, there's a perfectly fine diner in town for 'people of your kind.'

I see your point, Mr. Tom. I will be a great defense witness.

Tom continued to assign roles for the trial simulation. Every student eagerly accepted his or her role and the case of Linnville County vs. Joshua Arnot unfolded. *How could a teacher have more fun than this. I wish my old man were here to see that all his babysitting techniques really paid off. . .*

***

Gina took a second look at the list of students who'd signed up to be at Samantha's trial. *Everett, if I'm counting right, it looks like EVERY student signed up to be at Sam's trial. How are we going to decide who gets to go—draw names from a box?*

Everett grinned. He placed his hand gently over Gina's. *Gina, Gina. Let's think of what's really important. It's not who we select, but that we select five people to be our representative students. In fact, we have no guarantee that the judge will let us seat the students in the courtroom.*

Do you think some of us should accompany the students in the audience?

Definitely. I think you and I.

But don't you think Tom should be there—after all, his dad is Samantha's attorney?

No. Precisely for that reason. We want to seem that we are a diverse group of teachers and students that are part of a movement. Some blacks will be surprised that a white teacher like you would care enough to get involved in the Freedom Schools and likewise, some whites would be surprised that a black man who enjoys the good life in the North, would be willing to get involved. We are perfect choices.

I see your point. She squeezed his hand. *But back to my question, Everett, how are we going to choose which five students are selected.*

I say we don't stress too much about our choices. What's important to me is that we choose kids who are totally committed to the movement. Certainly, those whose writings and actions are forward-thinking and dedicated should be the ones we choose. Think about the passionate writings in our school paper, the perspicacious questions students ask. The leaders in our peaceful demonstrations. With that in mind, here are my five nominations: Joshua, Josephia, Daniel, Beatrice, and Victoria.

Gina nodded as she folded the paper with all the students' names. *Everett, you are so astute. I agree completely with you.* She stood and placed her hands on his shoulders. *Did I tell you how much I admire you?*

Everett encompassed her with a hug. You know that you are a very special woman, Gina. . .

Chapter 22

Samantha heard the twin sets of footsteps coming down the hallway. Hannah was talking with the deputy in her soft, persuasive voice.

Hannah, you seem to have a reason to talk to the inmates at every meal delivery. And today you want to stay and scrub the walls? Do we really care if the walls of the Linnville jail are scrubbed?

But, Deputy, we want to go after that national jail contest this year, and the inspectors will definitely look at how clean our facility is. If I don't do a little wall-scrubbing each day, it will get ahead of me and I won't have time at the last minute. . .

Enough, enough. Hannah, you've convinced me. But I'm only giving you fifteen minutes. Get the girl's breakfast meal served and scrub the walls. I'll be back in fifteen minutes.

Samantha sat up on her cot. Hannah stood outside her cell carrying a breakfast tray in one hand and a bucket of soapy water in the other. A sponge was floating on top. Her shoulder bag looked thick.

Click, and the door opened for her to enter the cell. *Click*, and the deputy locked the door behind her. *Good morning, Dear. Today is a special day. There's no need for me to sing to you, I'll just come right out and tell you that the deputy will be here soon to drive you over to the courthouse. Today is the official first day of your trial.*

Good morning, Hannah. So, do I get to wear regular clothing, or do I have to wear this jail suit?

Hannah handed her the food tray and set the bucket down beside the wall. She reached into her shoulder bag and pulled out a neatly folded stack of clothing. *Here, my Dear, is your outfit for today. Your lawyer, that nice Mr. Jenner, argued with Sheriff Owens and won. Sheriff wanted you to appear in your jail garb, but Mr. Jenner convinced him that the trial would be on national tv and it would make the jail look good if you were wearing regular clothing—sort of like the rest of trials in the northern states. I overheard the discussion—you could say it was more of an argument—and Jenner stood firm for you to dress up. So, Marla selected a set of clothes for today and I washed and pressed them nicely for you. As soon as you finish eating my fluffy flapjacks and fruit, wash up and put on this outfit. I'll fix your hair so it will look especially nice.* Hannah reached into her shoulder bag and took out a

352

jar of hair gel. *In fact, if you don't mind, I'll just stand behind you and start styling your hair as you eat.*

Hannah's soft hands took strands of Samantha's thick, black hair and combed through them. She spread a thin layer of styling gel on each strand before braiding them. She finished her braiding as Samantha took the last bite of fruit.

Hannah reached into her shoulder bag and pulled out a small mirror. *Now, take a look at this beautiful young woman's hair style.*

There was no mirror in her cell, so this was her first look at her reflection. *Oh, Hannah, you are a woman of many talents! Not only are you a great cook, but you are a top-notch hair stylist.* Samantha twirled her head from side to side, gently flinging the braids. *This looks great.*

Now, quickly, get changed. I'm going to wash one wall while you are changing. Don't be modest. I've seen many people change clothes. I'll be focused on the dust on this west cell wall, anyway.

Samantha unfolded the dress Marla had picked for her to wear. *Wait a minute—this isn't a dress I brought with me.* A navy- blue shirtwaist dress with white trim. *Very stylish.* As she pulled the dress over her head, she felt a scratchy price tag. *It's definitely not one I brought with*

*me. Somehow, Marla must have gotten hold of a brand-
new dress in my size.* She pulled the lightly attached string.
*I'll have to find out for sure if Marla is the nice 'elf' who
got me this new dress.*

Below the dress, was a pair of black slip-on shoes.
They looked brand new, too. She slipped them on.

Hannah turned around after washing the wall. She
set her bucket down and dropped the dirty sponge inside.
Her face glowed. *Why, don't you just look dignified,
Samantha. That dress suits you just fine! You will set a
fine example in the courtroom.*

Time's up, Hannah. Miss Bryant, you need to come
with me; we're driving over to the courtroom to begin the
trial. Do I need to cuff you, or do you promise to behave?

*No, Sir. You will not need to. I promise not to
cause you any trouble.*

Samantha felt the soft hand of Hannah resting on
her shoulder as she walked out of her cell and down the
hallway.

*Here I go. I can't wait to see how my trial will
unfold.*

Hanna released her hand and whispered, *my church
is praying for you. May God give you strength at this time,
Samantha.*

Chapter 23

George McGrath pulled on his jeans and cinched his leather belt. *Morning seems to show up earlier each day. I better get myself down to the sales barn and get set up.*

McGrath wasn't looking forward to serving as a juror. When the judge had asked if anyone had a good reason for not serving, he'd been tempted to speak up. After all, the sales barn was a time-consuming business, one that required a 24/7 kind of effort. *But I know that Owens is counting on me putting in my time on this case and I don't want to let him down.*

McGrath had moved to Linnville in the late fifties. He'd gotten wind that the sale barn was up for sale and had scraped together enough dough to make a down payment on it. *One of my best decisions ever. Why, I've already doubled my investment.*

At first, area cattlemen were hesitant to take their cattle to McGrath. Some drove over twenty hours to cities where they felt the long-established sale barn would give them a better price. McGrath had done his homework, though. He researched all the surrounding barns and offered the locals a more competitive price. That was one thing he'd done right. The other, was getting to know the local guys—both the farmers and the businessmen. He didn't always agree with their politics, but he could listen to their ideas and nod now and then to seem to agree.

But now I'm worried. Owens asked me in front of the others to step up and be the jury foreman. I'm not looking forward to putting my neck out in a case about race. After all, my ancestors who had slaves were the first in the county to treat them fairly and the first to set them up in their own businesses. I think in their hearts, they knew the system was unfair and wanted to do something to make-up for the indignities slaves had suffered. Of course, Dad felt the same way. He always seemed to lend a hand to black folks who needed it. I'll always remember him helping Amos Caldwell get a lumber yard started. Dad was the financier of the business and a frequent customer. Because of his involvement, Dad's other white friends also bought their wood from Amos. And Dad made sure that each one of Amos's kids had support for businesses they wanted to start.

George tiptoed downstairs to the kitchen. He carried his boots so as not to wake up Nan and the kids. *I'll just grab a slab of bread and peanut butter for now. That and a cup of coffee will keep me going until I can get a hot beef sandwich at the sales barn's restaurant.*

A set of soft footsteps approached the kitchen. George looked up from the kitchen counter to see his youngest son, Ben, standing in pajamas. *Good morning, Son. My, you are up early today. What woke you up?*

Hi, Daddy. I just couldn't sleep right. Can I go with you to work today?

Well, I'd love to say 'yes', but I'm only going over to the place for an hour or so.

Why, Dad? You usually are there all day until supper.

I've been asked to help out with a trial that starts today. I'll get things started at work, then head straight over to the courthouse.

What's a trial, Dad?

It's when someone is accused of breaking the law and twelve people called jurors have to decide if they are guilty or not.

Gee, that sounds exciting. Can I come watch.

Naw. You have to be much older to be in the audience. Besides, you need to help your mother in the garden today.

Aw, that's women's work. I want to be with you.

Now you know, you like to eat, so the least you can do is help your mother pull some weeds around the vegetables.

Gosh. So, what did the man do to break the law?

Actually, the person is a woman.

What did she do?

George thought about how he could explain the case in an objective, child-version way. *It's because she came down to Linnville and did some things that made the white people here upset.*

Like what?

Well, she took some of the newspapers into the white bank and white diner. And she bothered the white librarian.

Is she black?

Yes, Son.

In my Sunday School class, my teacher said that in God's eyes, people of all races were considered the same. She said it was some new thinking that people in the northern states were talking about. What do you think, Dad? Are black people as good as white people?

Well, your Grandfather McGrath sure thought so. He often helped blacks get started in business. They always

were appreciative of his help and paid him back for giving
them money to start their businesses.

There's a kid I've been talking to who's black—his
name's Robert. He watches us play baseball. One day I
asked him to join in and he hit a home run. Now, we argue
about who gets to have him on their team. He likes playing
with us.

I'm proud of you, Son, for looking at the good in all
people. Unfortunately, the older people—adults—in town
aren't as open-minded about including black folks. It's the
way Linnville has always been—separate things for whites
and blacks. I don't think you and I can do much about it.

You could vote for the girl to go free, Dad.

Thanks for your advice, Benjamin. I'll try to
represent the McGrath family values in my decision. Say,
I've got to run. Give me a hug.

George slipped out the back door and climbed into
his pickup. His discussion with Ben was still fresh in his
mind. *Funny how kids can get right down to what's*
important. Hope I can keep my business going and still
represent the McGrath way. . .

***

Tom scooted out of the auditorium before the students. He wanted to get to his classroom to put on a serape and sombrero. *Kind of corny to wear these stereotyped pieces of clothing, but at least it will set the scene for my Spanish lesson. Thank goodness Mom got the package to me pronto.*

Beatrice was the first to enter her classroom. *So, are you supposed to be a pioneer explorer?*

You're close, Beatrice. Actually, I'm wearing the clothing of one of our country's neighbors, Mexico.

Ooh, are we studying about Mexico today?

Sort of. Many of you said that you wanted to learn a foreign language in Freedom School since you aren't offered that elective in your high school. So, bienvenidos. Welcome!

Josephia moved from a bench in the back of the classroom to the front row. *This is exciting, Mr. Tom. Spanish is one of the romance languages and is one of the most melodic languages I've heard. . .*

Joshua interrupted. *And tell me, Josephia, just when have you ever heard someone speak Spanish in Linnville?*

You may find this surprising, but Miss Loretta knows a little Spanish. The other day she showed me a poem written in Spanish—she even read it to me.

The texture of the roughly-woven cloth serape against his skin, brought back memories of his teen years and the trip to Mexico he'd taken with his buddies. *It seemed like just last week that I convinced my old man to fund the excursion there. The dollar was strong, so we convinced local families to host us for a few bucks a night. And boy the food—there's nothing like home-cooked enchiladas. There was the art in Mexico City, and the rustic bus rides through the mountains where indigenous people were poor but happy. Yep. Lots of lessons learned then. . .*

Tom waited until everyone was seated. *Hey. Let's get our Spanish class off and running!*

Daniel raised his hand. *Mr. Tom, where did you get that outfit? The Linnville General Store?*

Tom joined in the laughter. *Actually, these fine articles of clothing are from Tiajuana, Mexico. Not everyone in Mexico dresses exactly like this, but I picked these things up on my way home from a visit there. Many of the men do wear hats to ward off the sun's strong rays and both the men and women wear bright-colored clothing—colors like you see in this serape. Another interesting thing is that many of the people there are quite poor—poor but happy.*

Kind of like us, Mr. Tom, added Daniel.

I won't argue with that statement, Daniel. And while this clothing is stereotypical and not representative of all the people in the country, it gives us a glimpse of a different culture. So, today, I'm going to teach you a little bit of Spanish. Who knows if you'll ever have an occasion to use this language, but the sign of an educated person is that they are eager learners. So, you eager Freedom School learners, let's practice a little conversational Spanish.

> *Repeat after me:*
> *Hola! (Hello)*
> *Como estas? (How are you?)*
> *Bien, y tu? (Good, and you?)*
> *Bien (Good)*
> *Adios (Good-bye)*
> *Adios (Good-bye)*

The unfamiliar words rolled off their collective tongues. *Good job, guys. Now partner up, and practice the conversation. We'll be dramatizing these conversations in front of the class.*

Josephia quickly finished practicing with Beatrice and the two walked up to Tom. *Mr. Tom,* Josephia said, *I want to thank you for teaching us a foreign language. I*

362

was one of the kids who put the request for it on the opening day survey and I sure like the way you teachers are teaching us things we want to learn.

Beatrice nodded in agreement. *Me, too, Mr. Tom. You're giving us learning experiences that we've never had before.*

Well, thanks. Can I ask you two to be the first to do your conversation in front of the class?

Sure, we'll go first. Do you want us to go now?

Tom looked around. *I think so. Hey, everybody, voices. Let's have each partnership come to the front of the classroom and pretend you are walking along the street and randomly come upon a friend you haven't seen for some time. Use some expression as you greet your friend.*

Tom listened intently as Beatrice and Josephia dramatically recited the conversation. Josephia hugged Beatrice and went a little overboard with expression.

Nice job, girls. Let's give them a round of applause. Ah, Daniel and Hector, will you be next?

Both teens stood up. Daniel grinned as he walked behind Hector to the front of the room. We are ready to do the skit, Mr. Tom, but you can be sure of one thing, there won't be any hugging in ours!

Chapter 24

Samantha had held her head high as she entered the courtroom with Mr. Jenner. He had said something to calm her, but she couldn't recall the exact words now. As she walked into the room, she tried to get a good look at everyone without seeming too obvious. Her eyes first focused on the jury box. Twelve lily white jurors, most of whom had a scowling expression were already seated. The prosecuting attorney sat at a table to her left. He reminded her of the drawing of Rip Van Winkle in her senior English lit book. *There they are! My colleagues Everett and Gina.* Tiny tears of joy came to her eyes as she recognized the five Freedom School students: Joshua, Josephia, Daniel, Beatrice, and Victoria. *I can't believe they were allowed to be in the audience!*

The bailiff took a step forward from the wall. *All rise for the Honorable Judge Roanoke.*

In unison, the entire courtroom stood up as the judge walked through his chamber door, and took a seat. Samantha focused on the judge's eyes as he announced, *You may be seated.*

When Samantha sat back down, she noticed a half-sheet of paper in front of her. *Jenner must have slipped this*

in front of me while the people were focused on the judge.
The message was brief, but calming.

>*Good morning, Samantha. This is Day One of your*
trial. We will begin with opening statements. Listen
closely to Herman Smith's statement—it will give both of us
a clue about the direction they are proceeding in your case.
Maybe you can pick up some details that we can talk about
later. After the statements, there will be a recess during
which Smith and I will present evidence to the judge and
the three of us will have to agree on what is accepted.
After the recess, Smith will begin to present his side of the
case in direct examination. I will get to cross examine any
of the witnesses he calls. I want you to be ready for some
theatrics as I'm going to ask their witnesses some tough
and revealing questions. Can't wait! If you need anything
during the trial, just whisper to me. Sincerely, Thomas
Jenner

Samantha gave Jenner a nod and half-smile. *Nice of*
him to give me this background. She leaned back in her
chair.

Judge Roanoke began a discourse full of procedures
for the audience, attorneys, and jurors. *Today, we are*
gathered in this court room to hear Case #3421: Linnville
Sheriff's Department vs. Samantha Bryant. Members of the

Jury, I remind you to be objective in your considerations about this case. Listen attentively to the witnesses and the explanations of the evidence. The case will begin with the opening statements of the prosecution and the defense. The opening statements must be confined to facts that will be proved by the evidence. The prosecution will be first to present their opening statement because they are the party with the burden of proof. Remember, that in this case, the government must prove beyond a reasonable doubt that the defendant is guilty.

To the prosecution and defense attorneys, I remind you to follow accepted legal procedures in your questioning of witnesses. I will listen to objections to certain lines of questioning, but you must give me a reason for your objections.

And, lastly, to the audience, I direct you to remain silent during the court proceedings. If you need to leave the courtroom, please do it during moments of recess so you will not disturb the proceedings. Are there any large concerns before we begin our opening statements?

Herman Smith rose and walked to the microphone in front of the judge. Your honor, with respect, I wish to challenge the appearance of Freedom School students and teachers in the audience at this court case. Today's case is a legal case against a teacher at that school, and the presence of her students and two teachers may cause undue distractions.

Judge Roanoke looked at Smith over the rim of his glasses. *While it may appear out of the ordinary, Mrs. Struck researched the ages of these five students. All are seventeen years of age or older, so they meet the age requirement for audience members in my court. It is the responsibility of the students to maintain proper decorum so as not to interrupt court proceedings. Should one or more of them become unruly, the bailiff will remove them.*

Smith frowned. He knew he lost on this point. As he turned and walked back to his table, he realized he might be facing a challenge or two. *Oh, well, when the jury looks out and sees all those black faces in the audience, they will be solidified in their resolve to find the girl guilty.*

Roanoke waited a minute while looking from side to side in the room. *Seeing no one else approaching the microphone, I hereby declare the court proceedings to continue in this case. Herman Smith, you may proceed with your opening statement.*

Smith gathered a note pad from in front of him and walked back to the microphone.

Your Honor, May it please the court. He waited a
moment for the customary judge's response.

You may proceed.

*The sheriff's department is forwarding a legal case
against the defendant, Samantha Bryant, Case #3421.
Your Honor, law and order is a necessary prerequisite for
any community to be successful. When the law and order
of a community is threatened, the community becomes less
safe. In this trial, the prosecution will prove beyond a
reasonable doubt, that Samantha Bryant, from Chicago,
Illinois, infiltrated into the city of Linnville and proceeded
to use illegal means to create unrest. She has caused
undue unrest by theft, harassment of the Linnville library
staff, and by distributing commie newspapers in our white
businesses. While these actions by themselves may not
seem overly egregious, we ask you, the jury, to see them
collectively as a blatant attempt to disrupt the way of life in
Linnville, Mississippi. We will provide evidence and first-
hand testimony that will support her alterior motives and
illegal actions. We challenge you, the jury to find
Samantha Bryant guilty of inciting unrest in Linnville
Mississippi.*

Smith turned to the jury and smiled. A long smile.
He picked up his notepad and trundled back to his table.

Well, that went well. I saw quite a few grinning back at me. This should be a push-over of a case. We'll send a message to those Freedom agitators that they are not wanted here in our town. A guilty conviction should do the trick. . .

Jenner stood up and slowly walked to the microphone empty-handed. He looked directly at the judge, then sideways at the jury. *Your Honor, may it please the court.*

Roanoke responded. *You may proceed, Mr. Jenner.*

We are in a remarkable time in history. In our country, the founders declared that 'all men are created equal.' This seemed to be a good principle, but unfortunately, it did not pertain to a large percentage of our southern population, the blacks, who had been illegally brought to America to forward the white agricultural industry. Even though Abraham Lincoln delivered the Emancipation Proclamation in 1865, there remains in place a white systemic structure of racism which prevents blacks in Linnville and throughout the South, from enjoying the basic freedoms our country offers whites. Why, here in Linnville, there are separate schools, libraries, swimming pools, and businesses for blacks and whites. Why is this? In my travels throughout the Deep South, I have concluded that white folk simply do not like blacks because of the color of their skin. While appearing to be religious, the whites are actually negating the belief of their Savior that 'we should love our neighbor as ourself.' This morning, we witnessed the attorney for the prosecution even try to remove teens from the audience because of the color of their skin. We all know his claim that it was due to being a distraction is false. White people don't like to admit it, but we are racist. People like me and you have the advantage of white superiority. And others of you who are white, may not be extremely wealthy, but the money you do have has been acquired off the backs of blacks.

As I previously said, we are in a remarkable time in history. It is a time where whites can own up to our racism. We can admit that slavery was evil. We can admit that conscious actions that keep blacks in poverty are wrong. And we can admit that efforts like the Freedom Movement and Freedom Schools are the beginning of that accountability. Why does Linnville have a smaller library for blacks? Why can't Linnville blacks eat in the same diners as whites? Why are the schools segregated with fewer resources for blacks. And why is voting by blacks suppressed? All across the country, whites are beginning to own up to this racism. It's time now for you in Linnville to step up to the plate and make some changes for the black

citizens—changes that will lead to equality of all races. My
client, Samantha Bryant, is a symbol of your hesitancy to
admit the truth: you are trying to hang on to your racist
ways.

Samantha Bryant came here to offer black teens
some educational opportunities that you whites are denying
them. She and the other Freedom Teachers like Gina
Lovick and Everett Jackson, that you see in the audience
have come to help you find the path to racial equality. She
is not guilty of the charges accused of her, but rather is a
fine young woman who wants black teens to be able to
learn to type, to be able to study law, to be able to buy a
sandwich in the same diner you do. I ask you, if you were
black, wouldn't you want these same opportunities. So, to
those of you in the jury, I challenge you to find Samantha
Bryant not guilty. She should be celebrated, not sentenced.

Grizzard's heart jumped. *Jenner's opening*
statement was just what he'd hoped for. A slap in the face
of racism. Maybe it will make the jurors angry to hear the
truth, but the truth isn't always pretty. If they can begin to
see themselves as who they are, then that's a huge
accomplishment. . .

Grizzard realized he'd been lost in thought. He
heard Roanoke's voice announce, *We'll take a one hour*

371

recess. Both attorneys, please remain in the room so we can resolve the entering of evidence.

The bailiff walked over to Samantha and escorted her out of the courtroom. She wasn't sure where he was taking her, but it didn't matter. *I'm over-the-top proud of my attorney. He's making this trial about racial justice. . .*

Chapter 25

Judge Roanoke picked up his heavy wooden gavel and slammed the table. *The morning recess is over and we are proceeding with the case of the prosecution. Herman Smith, you may now begin calling witnesses for the state for the purposes of direct examination. Mr. Jenner, you will have an opportunity to cross examine the prosecution's witnesses. Remember that no new evidence may be introduced, other than the items you, Mr. Jenner, and I approved during the recess. Mr. Smith, you may call your first witness.*

Herman walked to the microphoned podium. *I call Hunter Radley as the prosecution's first witness.* Lydia Struck noted his name on her ledger. She prepared herself to take notes about the proceedings. Noel Grizzard slipped a film reel into his camera. From his position in the northeast corner of the room, he could zoom into all the actors—judge, attorney, jury, and audience. He was looking forward to today's taping. He'd edit it afterwards for the news, and then reflect on how he could use the footage for a cinema that was formulating in his mind.

Hunter Radley walked over to Lydia's table. She placed a Bible on top of her right hand and reached it out towards Radley. *Mr. Radley, place your hand on this Bible, raise your other hand, and repeat after me: I Hunter Radley swear to tell the truth, the whole truth, and nothing but the truth, so help me God.*

Radley mumbled the words.

The judge spoke up. *Mr. Radley, I could not hear a word you said. Please repeat the swearing in. Mrs. Struck, please note in your summary of today's proceedings, that the witness had to repeat the swearing in.*

Radley didn't want to have to repeat the silly ceremony another time , so he belted out the words. He strode up to the witness box and sat down. Smith approached the microphone with a yellow legal pad and began questioning Radley.

Mr. Radley, will you state your name and address for the court?

Yes. My name is Hunter Radley. I live at 3605 Pembroke Lane.

And where is your place of employment?

I work for the city.

And what is your job for the city?

I'm a lineman.

And what are your duties as a lineman?

I check the area's telephone lines from time to time. If a line is down, I phone in to get a back-up worker to help me do the repairs. People depend on me to keep communication going to their houses.

Thank you, Mr. Radley.

Mr. Radley, do you know the defendant? Smith turned and glared at Samantha.

Yes, Sir.

And would you tell us how you came to know her?

Yes, certainly. I was driving along County Road X, the afternoon of July 2, when I spotted her putting wood from Fred Dodger's barn into a cart and pushing it down the road.

She was stealing the wood, wasn't she?

Jenner punched the air with his fist. *Objection, Your Honor, leading the witness.*

Judge Roanoke didn't hesitate. *Objection sustained. Remember, Smith, to use those open-ended questions you learned about in law school.*

Yes, You Honor

So, Mr. Radley, did you see how the wood got into the cart?

Yeah, I did. I saw her using a hammer to pry boards off the shed and put them in that cart.

Did you see all this happen while you were driving?

Not exactly. I stopped by the shed when I saw her and some others ripping off the wood. I wanted to see what was going on.

And you saw Miss Bryant tearing the boards off herself and loading them into the cart herself?

Yes, that's what I've been trying to say.

And where was she headed with the cart of wood?

Objection, Your Honor, speculation.

Objection overruled. But again, Mr. Smith, I remind you to question your witness more directly.

Yes, Your Honor. Mr. Radley, did you follow the witness to see where she was taking the wood?

I did. I stayed back fifty yards or so and drove slowly so I could see for myself what she was doing with the wood.

And where was she taking it?

She pushed the cart all the way to where their Freedom School is. She dumped it on the ground, then walked back toward the shed with the empty cart.

And you followed her back?

Yeah. It was a slow day for me, so I wanted to see how many loads she was stealing?

And how many times did you observe Miss Bryant pushing the cart from the shed to the school site?

I saw her take two full loads, but then I got a call on my cb radio and had to head over to Anover to help a guy sink a pole, so I couldn't stay and see how much she was stealing.

And Mr. Radley, can you tell the court whose shed she was removing the wood from?

Yes, everybody knows that the shed is the property of Fred Dodger.

No further questions, Mr. Radley.

Noel Grizzard zoomed his camera in to get a shot of Hector Smith grinning at the jury and walking back to his table. Grizzard knew Jenner would get a shot of cross-examining Radley. *I can't wait until he gets his chance to break down this weak witness.*

Jenner walked over to Lydia's table where the admitted evidence was resting. He picked up a clear envelope containing a document and walked over to Hector Smith. Smith nodded his approval for Jenner to use the exhibit. *I can't believe Smith didn't object to me using this document during our evidence selection with him and Roanoke—he must not have seen Dodger's signature.*

Jenner quickly approached Roanoke, showing him the exhibit. Another nod.

Your Honor, permission to approach the witness. Roanoke nodded.

Jenner raised his voice to make sure Grizzard's mike caught his voice. He held the exhibit labeled Defense Exhibit 1 close to the witness. *Mr. Radley, would you describe this document?*

Looks like some kind of note signed by Fred Dodger.

Thank you Mr. Radley. Would you please read the note aloud?

I don't see why I have to do this. Why don't you just read it?

Roanoke straightened his neck. *Mr. Radley, I remind you that Mr. Jenner is in charge of this cross examination and that you need to follow his directions.*

Radley frowned, then began reading. *To COFO: I give you permission to tear the shed on Lot 57 down and use the boards for rebuilding your Freedom School. I am donating this wood. Sincerely, Fred Dodger*

Radley looked up angrily. *There's no way you can prove that this is authentic. You could have made up this note yourself.*

Mr. Radley, do you see the pressed seal in the lower right corner of the note?

Yeah, so what?

What initials do you see by that seal?

Radley studied the letter. *Looks like an M and a B*

Correct. The embossed seal is a legal symbol pressed into the paper by a notary public. The initials MB are the initials of May Burns who works at the Bank of Linnville, Linnville's only bank.

Radley stood up in the witness box. He started to step down.

Ah, Mr. Radley, you are not dismissed yet. I have a few more questions for you. You said that you witnessed Miss Bryant removing and transporting wood. One week later, after the school had been opened for one week, where did you go in the evening?

Objection, Your Honor, Lack of Foundation.

Jenner, you need to give some background that ties this question into the prior testimony.

Yes, Your Honor. I will show that Mr. Radley participated in an activity the evening following the one-

week opening of the Freedom School that links his negative
views of the Freedom School to the legal transporting of
wood by Miss Bryant.

Jenner had barely finished his sentence before
Roanoke announced his 'sustained'. *You may proceed, Mr.*
Jenner.

I met up with my friend Burt Nemick for an evening
drive.

What time was this drive?

Pretty late—about ten or so.

And did you go by the Freedom School on your
drive?

Yeah. So what?

Did you get out of your truck at the school.

Yeah, just to check one of the tires on my truck.

Did you have a can of kerosene in the bed of your
truck?

Yeah. I always carry one.

Did you go to the Freedom School with the intent of
burning it down?

You can't pin that on me. You have no proof.

Jenner took a risk. He walked back to his brief case
and took out the white costume he had worn the night of
the KKK impersonation. He put on the costume and used

his ventriloquist skills to repeat the warning he'd given Radley and Nemick while pretending to be the KKK klavern's regional leader.

Grizzard wasn't sure the order of the mayhem. He filmed a few frames of Burt Nemick standing up in the jury box shouting expletives at Jenner. He got a shot of Lydia Struck tugging at her hair and dropping her pencil. Then he swiveled the camera to include a frame of Radley's facial expression and comments. *So YOU were the lowdown sun of a gun who tried to scare us away from the school that night! Why, we should have stayed and burned that nigger rat trap down! You are as bad as the infiltrators who are trying to take over Linnville. . .*

Grizzard swung his camera around to get a final shot of Roanoke slamming his gavel on his desk to get control. Hans captured Roanoke's words. Court is adjourned for today. *When you return tomorrow, I caution you all to display better decorum! That includes YOU, Mr. Jenner!*

Grizzard thought he filmed Roanoke slamming his gavel five times.

Chapter 26

Claude held the door to Louie's Diner open for Maybelle. He tried to do gentlemanly actions for his wife whenever he could—*after all, Maybelle's been my precious wife for fifteen years. It's the least I can do.*

Thank you, Claude, for your kindness.

Yes, Dear.

Claude's eyes nearly popped out of his head when he stepped inside the black diner. Louis was packed full of customers whose eyes were glued on a big tv that appeared mounted on a board on the west wall. *Jeepers, Maybelle. I think just about everyone is here watching the trial.*

Maybelle reached out for Claude's hand. She didn't want to get separated from him in the crowd. *Let's stick together, Claude.*

I hear you, May.

Why, I see some folks here who I haven't seen for years. Somehow the word got out that this trial would be shown on tv. Sure is nice of Mr. Grizzard to wire us up to the courtroom.

A portly woman turned around and shushed Claude. *You've got to whisper, Mister. We want to hear every word that crooked Hunter Radley has to say.*

Sorry, Claude whispered.

It had taken Claude and Maybelle a little longer than they'd expected to get their work done at night and get ready for the trial. Claude thought, *even if we get to see a part of what's going on in the courtroom, it will be worth it.* He pulled Maybelle toward a table nearer the tv. He spotted two empty chairs at Perry and Mila's table. *Mind if Maybelle and I join you at your table?*

Sit yourselves down. Happy to share with you.

Claude smiled. *Thanks, you're a decent fellow.*

Claude pulled out a chair for Maybelle, then gently pushed it in towards the table. He sat between her and Perry.

Great view of the tv from here. Thanks again.

Claude and Maybelle leaned back in their chairs. A young waitress noticed them and walked over carrying a pot of coffee. She held the pot up to signal she was wondering if they'd like a cup. Claude and Maybelle both nodded and as she moved closer, Maybelle turned both of their upside down coffee cups right side up to further signal their wishes for a hot drink. Claude fished in his pocket for two dimes and a nickel tip. By the time the waitress maneuvered her way to the table, he was ready to place the coins squarely in the center of her left hand.

She thanked him for the nickel tip as she filled both cups to the brim. Mable took one sip, and whispered, *One good thing about Louie's is that he always brews a good cup of coffee—not watery like your mothers, Claude.*

Claude pretended to be surprised by Mabelle's accusation, though he knew she was right. *Ma always waters everything down, not just coffee, but gravy, grits. . . everything.*

After a couple of sips of coffee, the duo focused their eyes on the mounted tv. The screen showed Hunter Radley seated in the witness box. Jenner was walking up toward him to show him something. It was hard to hear each word Radley was saying, but Claude could tell that Jenner was showing him a paper and questioning him about what it said. He was making Radley read a note from Fred Dodger saying he'd donated the wood in the shed to the kids fixing up the old community center into a school. *That's good, Maybelle,* he whispered. *They won't be able to pin stealing on the girl.*

Maybelle waited until Jenner was done finishing up a thought before whispering a message back to Claude. *Now, you know that the law doesn't need any real reason to pin a crime on a black person. If they can't find something legitimate to say a person's done wrong, why, they can simply make it up.*

Perry leaned over to Claude to whisper. *The California attorney's doing a fine job, don't you think?*

Yes, he is. I'm proud to say that Maybelle and I are hosting him in our home. He's been an excellent house guest and by the looks of it, a mighty fine attorney, too.

Maybelle put her hand on Claude's wrist. *Why is he walking over to his table and reaching down into his briefcase?*

Beats me.

The tv screen showed a close-up of Jenner putting on a KKK robe and walking back to Radley. Jenner was imitating someone else's voice. Then, he made his voice sound like other people.

Ooo-eee, Maybelle. He's using his ventriloquism skills right there in the courtroom—remember when he showed us them at supper last week?

Maybelle put her hand over her mouth. *Why, he's using theatrics to get a rise from Mr. Radley.*

***

The crowd at Louie's Diner quieted to see Burt Nemick jump up from the jury section to shout at Jenner and to get an earful of what Hunter Radley was shouting at the white robed attorney. Maybelle thought she heard every word: *You were the lowdown sun of a gun who tried to scare us away from the school that night. Why we should have stayed and burned that nigger rat trap down.*

Claude wasn't sure how it started, but almost every customer in Louie's Diner raised their fisted hand and cheered and shouted. Jenner had successfully gotten Radley and Nemick to admit to trying to burn down the Freedom School. Attempted arson would get a jail sentence in most cities, but not Linnville with the white racist hierarchy in place. The customers lowered their voices and their arms. They were still elated even though they knew that Owens would never charge Radley and Nemick with the crime, but at least they had the satisfaction of seeing Jenner get the two men to openly display their racism in front of the people of Linnville and maybe the rest of the country. A step in the right direction.

Sheriff Owens bee-lined his way from the courthouse to the Linnville Downtown Diner. After

Radley's testimony, he'd given the two left-finger tap on his forehead signal to the regulars to meet him at the diner. He wanted to recap the trial's first day. He didn't want to waste any time by calling Mabel to see if the crew could meet in the private dining room, but he doubted she'd care.

Theresa greeted him as he rushed in. *Hello, Sheriff. Having a good day?*

Yeah, you could say that. Are any of the others here?

Actually, you are late. They're already in the back room. Do you want me to bring menus?

Naw. Just a round of coffee and some pie—what's today's flavor?

Mel baked up a bunch of cherry pies today.

Sounds good. Can you heat 'em up and put a scoop of vanilla ice cream on top?

Sure, no problem.

Owens headed down the hallway past mounted pictures of all the previous owners. Mabel, the current owner, had told him she refused to have her picture displayed. She said it would make her feel old to have her face next to the other dead owners.

Owens pulled open the private dining room door. Hector Smith was saying something and the others were laughing and slapping their legs.

Hey, everybody. What's all the noise about?

Herman stopped laughing wiped the tears from his face. *I thought I'd seen it all in my courtroom experience, but I never would have imagined a defense attorney would put on a KKK robe in front of a judge and jury!*

Owens felt relieved. He hadn't been able to decide if Jenner's drama scene helped or hurt the case.

Herman gestured to Nemick and Radley. *Now, whether or not you realize it, your actions really helped our case today. Tomorrow, I'm going to question you in redirect, Radley. You'll convince folks that you and Nemick felt the school—made from all those beat-up boards was such an eyesore in the community, that you were going to burn it down. You meant no harm to anyone, just wanted to get rid of the eyesore structure. So, let's have a toast to a successful first day of the trial.* He raised his coffee cup and the others followed. Owens heard a chorus of *cheers*. The cheers got even louder when Theresa brought in a tray full of cherry pie ala mode.

***

Josh, Beatrice, Josephia, Victoria, and Daniel watched as Jenner led Samantha out of the courtroom. Victoria gave her a short wave.

So, loyal students of Samantha Bryant, follow us, Gina said. She gestured to them to follow her and Everett out of the courtroom. As the group walked together down the three sets of stairs, they reflected on the day's proceedings.

Everett got them talking. *So, what do you think about the courtroom proceedings today?*

Joshua broke the ice. *It certainly was an interesting day. I thought Smith's opening statement was pretty weak. Jenner did a good job on his. Then, I was pretty impressed how Jenner put on a KKK robe to dramatize the good-olds attempt to burning down Freedom School. . .*

Josephia interrupted. *I agree that what Jenner was doing was to counter the sheriff's claim that Samantha stole wood and at the same time show how bigoted the white people of Linnville are.*

He took a pretty big risk, though, Daniel said, *at the end, the judge yelled at him for putting on the robe and pretending to be a KKK leader.*

Joshua wanted to make a point. *Say what you will about Jenner's risk, he got the jury—and the millions of people who watch the trial at home—to see that racism is an integral part of Linnville's fabric. He's making the case about the whole Freedom movement. People will have to decide whether they are for white supremacy or racial justice. It's just that simple.*

Everett turned to face the students. *I commend you for your astute observations. And I agree with you.*

Chapter 27

The bailiff nonchalantly stepped away from the door by the judge's chambers. *All rise for the Honorable Judge Roanoke.*

The door opened and Roanoke strode confidently to his desk. *You may be seated.* He sat down in his brown leather chair and bent down to remove a yellow legal pad from his briefcase. Grizzard pressed the zoom button on his camera. He captured a close-up shot of Roanoke putting on his glasses and writing the date on the top of the blank pad.

Roanoke leaned into his microphone and began with an agenda. *Because the plaintiff's first witness, Mr. Radley's credibility may have been damaged during yesterday's cross examination, he may be questioned by his attorney. Mr. Smith, I caution you to only ask questions related to the cross examination—you know those nice open-ended ones I like.*

Mr. Radley, come forward for your swearing in and this time, please speak up so all of us in the courtroom can hear you.

Radley walked forward, but complained. *Aw, Judge. I don't see why I have to do this swearing all over again—isn't once enough?*

Roanoke remained silent. Lydia held out the Bible Radley slapped his hand on it and reluctantly repeated the oath.

Smith approached the miked podium. He placed a piece of notebook paper on the incline. Grizzard's camera captured some messy handwritten notes on the paper, but the writing was too illegible to decipher. *So, Mr. Radley, in yesterday's cross examination you said that you went to the school late at night. Did you think there would be any students or teachers there at that time?*

Naw. Me and Nemick didn't see any lights on. We know the school clears out by four or so in the afternoon.

You also mentioned that you had plans to burn the school down. Is that true?

Yeah. Several men in Linnville had said that the school was an eyesore—the outside looked real shabby in appearance. We have high standards here in town about what a building should look like. So I decided to show my community support and get rid of it.

No further questions.

Roanoke waited a minute before dismissing Radley. *Witness dismissed.*

Now, we'll proceed with the prosecution's next witness. Mr. Smith, please call your next witness to testify.

Hector Smith remained at the microphone. *Your Honor, I call Sheriff Riley Owens to the stand.*

Grizzard caught an image of Owens with a big grin on his face. When Owens placed his hand on the Bible Lydia held out to him, he slowly looked around the courtroom, his eyes staring at Samantha as he took the oath.

Mr. Owens, would you tell the court your name and address?

Of course. My name is Riley P. Owens and I live at 125 Maple Lane here in Linnville.

And what is your occupation?

I am the sheriff of Linn County. My office is here in the Linnville Jail and I've been well-regarded as one of the state's best sheriffs, winning the state award seven times.

Jenner spoke up. *Objection, Your Honor. Speculation. The witness is using hyperbole to describe his qualifications.*

Objection sustained.

So, Sheriff Owens, can you tell us about a phone call you received recently from the Linnville Public Library?

Yes. I was in my office the afternoon of July 9th when the phone rang. It was the head librarian calling me to tell me that Samantha Bryant had harassed her.

And what exactly did she do?

She and one of the other teachers brought some black students into the library for the purpose of checking out books. As you all know, Linnville has a perfectly good library for those people; they do not need to use ours.

And how did they harass her?

Well, in addition, to agitating her for just being there, they demanded to check out some books. She was a nervous wreck and called me because she was afraid they might come back again. We can't have this agitation here in Linnville. It all started when Miss Bryant and her buddies came here with the intent of integrating our town. .

.

Smith felt that the sheriff had made his point. *Thank you, Sheriff. That's all.*

Roanoke waited a minute before calling Jenner to cross examine the sheriff. *I don't know why Smith's witnesses are giving such short testimonies. Smith must*

think he has a slam-dunk case and doesn't want to waste
his time dragging out the trial. Whatever. . .

Mr. Jenner, you may cross examine the witness. No
funny business this time.

Jenner walked up to the exhibit table and picked up
Defense exhibit #2. He got the customary nods from Judge
Roanoke and Smith before handing the document to the
sheriff.

Sheriff Owens, can you describe the two pictures
you see on this paper?

Well, this one looks like the Linnville Public Library
and this one on the right is the Linnville Black Public
Library.

That's correct. Why do you have two libraries here
in Linnville?

Owens frowned. *That's a stupid question. It's*
always been like this. Both the whites and blacks like to be
with their own people rather than mixed together—or
integrated as you call it-- so we've got a library for both of
them.

Are the libraries the same size?

Not exactly. The white library is larger.

Yes, that's true. The white library is twice the
square footage of the black library.

And according to the population of Linn County, what percent is black and what percent is white?

I'd say it's about 50% for both.

Actually, according to the recent census, the percentage of whites in Linn County is thirty-three per cent and blacks is sixty-seven. So, does it make sense that the whites should have a much bigger library when they have a smaller percentage of population?

I don't think this has anything to do with my arrest of the girl.

Actually, it is directly related. You arrested Samantha Bryant, not because she broke any laws, but rather because she is here in Linnville to bring changes to justice. She didn't physically threaten the librarian; she merely took some students to a nicer public library so they could get a choice of books that is not available in their modest black library. You might be surprised to learn that Dale Carnegie, the benefactor of both libraries did not wish to have segregated libraries, but the white board which supervised the building of libraries after his death was pressured to help maintain the status quo in the South. Well, the time has come for you and the power structure to realize the limitations you have placed on black citizens in your county. I have no further questions.

Herman Smith sat silent, unable to shout out an objection to Jenner's ramblings. *I didn't realize the percentage of blacks was that high in our county. . .*

Roanoke continued. *Sheriff Owens, you are dismissed. Mr. Smith, do you have another witness?*

Yes, Your Honor. The plaintiff calls Billy Rae Jones to the stand.

Billy Rae had dressed up in his dark blue jeans and long-sleeved shirt. He'd written some notes down on a napkin from the diner, but *I think I better just speak from the top of my head. Might look too hokey to look up and down at my notes.* He kept the napkin in his pocket. As he approached Lydia, he started to feel droplets of moisture form on his forehead.

Lydia thrust out the Bible and he put his hand on it. *Don't know why they insist on using a Bible—don't make sense for us folks who don't attend church regularly.*

Billy Rae repeated Lydia's oath and followed her gesture to the witness stand. He had to undue a small latch to open the small wooden door in front of the witness stand. *Doggone it, seems to be sticking. I'm usually pretty good at figuring out things like this.*

Lydia walked over and pressed the metal latch, allowing the door to swing open. She relatched it once Jones was seated.

Grizzard zoomed in and got a close-up of Lydia assisting Jones. *I predict that Jones will be a weak witness—oh goody!*

Hector Smith brushed his fingers over his beard. *This boy is making me nervous. Hope 'Ol Billy comes through.*

So, Mr. Jones, will you state your name for the court?

My name is Billy Rae Jones.

And are you employed in Linn County?

Yes.

Where do you work?

I'm assistant manager at the Linnville Downtown Diner.

And would you describe your duties there?

I keep everything stocked up. I open up in the morning, and clean up at the end of the day.

So, can we conclude that you are at the diner every day?

Yes. I even work there Christmas Day.

Were you there the afternoon of July 15?

Like I say, I'm there every day.

Is that a 'yes' or a 'no'?

It's a 'yes'.

And what did you see on that afternoon?

Billy extended his arm and pointed at Samantha. *I saw her come in the diner with a big stack of Commie newspapers.*

And how could you tell what was in the newspapers?

After she left the diner, I went over and got one to read.

And what topics did you read about that proves the paper was a Communist one?

I knew from the first article I read about blacks wanting to get equal rights in Linnville, that it was Commie inspired.

How many papers did she leave?

I counted thirty-four.

And why did you think these newspapers should not be distributed at the diner?

Can you please explain what you mean by 'distributed'?

Yes. Why should Miss Bryant not have brought the papers in the diner?

Grizzard anticipated Jenner objecting, so he swung the camera over in his direction.

Objection, Your Honor. Opinion. Billy Rae Jones is not the spokesperson for the entire town of Linnville.

Objection sustained.

Herman Smith picked up his page of notes and started back to his table. He almost forget to say the 'no more questions' expression.

Judge Roanoke glanced down at his Rolex. He really wanted to be home in time to call his cousin about moving to Linnville. *I'd like him to check out the two-story house next to Irma and me before someone snatches it off the market. Maybe I should call the trial over for the day. . . well, maybe Jenner will be quick about his cross. I'll give him a chance.*

Mr. Jenner, you may cross examine the witness.

Jenner walked to the evidence table and picked up Defense Exhibit #3. He got the nods and showed it to Jones.

Mr. Jones, would you identify this for the court?

It's one of the Commie papers she put on the diner counter.

Would you read the headlines of the articles on page one?

All of 'em?

Well, choose any three.

Okay. This one says: 'Justice Should Be Fair for All'. This one says Freedom School Teaches Typing. And let's see. . . my third one is Josephia's Original Poetry.

So, let's start with the first article about justice being fair. Do you think if your friend stole a pig that he should get the same penalty as if you stole a pig.

I guess.

Do you think it is bad for students to learn how to type?

Not really.

Is reading poems Communistic?

Well, you're trying to trap me. The whole idea of a paper written in that school and distributed in our white diner is just plain wrong.

Thank you, Mr. Jones for your thoughts.

I do have a few more questions. Last year in the fall, you paid a visit to Ebidiah Green. You were with two other men, weren't you?

I can't recall exactly who was with me.

Was Ebidiah able to drive his car after your visit?

I haven't seen him around.

That's because the three of you tied him to a cross and set him on fire, wasn't it.

Herman knew he better stop Jenner from his line of questioning. *Objection, Your Honor. Lack of Foundation.*

Mr. Jenner. Explain how Mr. Jones' actions last fall tie in to this case, or I will have no choice but to sustain the objection.

Yes. Gladly. In my opening statement, I explained that Samantha Bryant's arrest was symbolic of the efforts to stifle racial justice here in Linnville. Each witness today has supported this theory. Mr. Radley wanted to get rid of the Freedom School—not because of it being an eyesore, but a reminder that racial change is coming. Sheriff Owens testified that Miss Bryant harassed the librarian because she simply gave her students an opportunity to check out a book—at a white library. And Mr. Jones is labeling a freely distributed student newspaper as Communistic. What's even worse, is the lynching you did to Ebidiah Green was cruel and heartless—the most racist behavior a man could do to another man.

Judge Roanoke leaned very close to his microphone and looked directly at Thomas Jenner. *Objection overruled. You may proceed, Mr. Jenner.*

So, Mr. Jones, did you or did you not tie Ebidiah Green to a cross and set him on fire?

Billy Rae grasped his forehead with his right hand. *I know I'm supposed to tell the truth—I'll just tell my part in it.*

Mr. Jones, I'm waiting for your reply.

All right, all right. I was there. I used my rope to tie him up, but I wasn't the one who poured kerosene on him or lit the match. Besides, none of got arrested.

No further questions, Your Honor. This witness is dismissed.

Judge Roanoke looked back at his watch. *Court is recessed until tomorrow.*

***

Ethan Bryant turned on the family TV to channel WGN. His mother liked that channel's evening news presentation the best. *Ma, Dad, hurry up. It's starting.*

Betty and Herb Bryant dashed into the living room and sat beside Ethan on the plaid cloth couch. *Do you think they'll have anything about Samantha's trial on today?*

The news anchor was an attractive woman with an Afro-style hairdo. *Welcome to tonight's news. We have an update on the Samantha Bryant case. Stay tuned for a brief commercial and then we'll dive into the story.*

Betty sat with her eyes glued to the screen lost in thought. *Would Sam's attorney have done a good job today? Would he be sharing her story to the world? How is she holding up?*

Betty couldn't remember what product the commercial was promoting. When the news story came back on, she saw a close-up shot of her daughter sitting proudly by her attorney at the legal table. *Herb, today, she's wearing the two-piece maroon suit we sent her. Doesn't she look beautiful?*

Yes, Dear. And look at the confidence in her face.

Ethan focused on the camera zooming in at Jenner questioning a witness. *Listen, Mom and Dad! Her attorney is saying that racial justice is coming! That's good news—Sam really does want racial justice to come.*

Chapter 28

Hannah's shoulder bag was pretty heavy. She picked up the breakfast tray for Samantha and waited patiently for the deputy to get out of his chair and go with her to unlock the cell. *Deputy Glen, you could save a load off your feet and just let me take that key ring down to the cell and unlock it myself.*

I'm thinking about it, but something might go wrong and I'd get on the wrong side of Sheriff Owens. He pressed both hands down on the chair rail to ease his standing up. *Besides, if Owens steps down, I want to be next in line.*

What are you saying? That Owens is going to quit being our Sheriff?

Now, don't go saying that to anyone. It's just my own thinking. Things don't seem to be going our way. He lost the Johnson case and from what I've heard around town, this case is up in the air.

Hannah couldn't believe what she was hearing. *Whites always keep a lid on justice for blacks. What could be any different in this case?*

But don't you trust the jury to side your way?

Yeah, you're probably right. We got all our people on it. Probably no matter what the sharp shooter attorney for the girl comes up with, the jury will vote our way.

Hannah knew not to press any further. If the deputy felt she was giving her opinion, he might not trust her as much.

As my father always said, 'Only the Good Lord knows.'

Well, let's get this breakfast tray delivery over. Nobody's in the men's side, so we just have the Bryant girl to deliver to.

Samantha was walking her laps as the cell door clicked open. She waited until the deputy left before walking to Hannah and giving her a big hug.

And just what do I owe for such a nice welcome?

Nothing. You deserve a nice welcome. Every day I'm here, I see how you use your behind-the-scenes influence to make my stay pleasant.

Just doing my job, Samantha. She held out the breakfast tray.

Yum. Your fluffy blueberry pancakes today. I love these.

Hannah sat beside her on the cot. *Samantha, have you given any thought to what you'll do when you get out of here?*

Do you think I will be released?

I've got a hunch that your case is a big one. It just might be the straw that breaks the camel's back. The law here in Linnville has been racist because they've been able to get away with it. But because you are from the North, where folks are more open-minded, there's a lot of sentiment that the Sheriff is wrong in arresting you. If enough people put pressure on the Sheriff's office, he might want to convince the jury to say you are innocent.

Hannah, that's an amazing thought. Thank you for your support.

Oh, no need to thank me. She reached into the shoulder bag and took out a bright green dress. She removed a tiny note from the left sleeve. *Your parents have been sending these pretty clothes to you—they mail them to Marla who gets them to me. While I was pressing the dress last night, this little note slipped out. Here.*

Samantha read the letter aloud. *Dearest Sam, we have been so worried about you and how you are doing. But the last few nights, the evening news has been sharing accounts of your trial. People here cannot believe how the*

opportunities for blacks are so limited in the South,
especially in your area. They also are upset at how whites
are perpetuating supremacy. In last evening's news show,
the mayor of Chicago pledged to personally call the mayor
of Linnville and complain that you were falsely arrested.
He even said he was going to launch a phone campaign to
mayors and governors around the country to urge them to
do the same. So, hang in there, dear. We are 100% behind
you. Love, Mom, Dad and Ethan.

Hannah lifted Samantha's chin. Now, we can't
waste any time. *I'm going to style your hair a special way*
today so you will look stunning for your day at court. I've
learned that the Sheriff's done with his side and now it's
time for your side to be on deck. I can't wait to hear what
happens.

Hannah chattered incessantly as she spread gel on
Samantha's hair and styled it. *You know that they're*
showing the trial at Louie's Diner. Perry told me that Mr.
Smith didn't do so well. . . Mila said that Mr. Jenner put on
a KKK robe and scared the wits out of Burton Nemick and
Hunter Radley. . . They admitted to trying to burn down
Freedom School. . . And that no-good Billy Rae Jones said
that he was in a gang of three who lynched Ebidiah Green.
. . I wonder who the other two were. . .

Samantha slipped on the long-sleeved green dress. Her long braids framed her beautiful face. *Between Mom's note explaining that the whole country has its eyes on my trial and Hannah's commentary, I feel that something good is about to happen.* Her cell door clicked open and she proudly walked down the hallway with Hannah and the deputy.

***

Sheriff Owens lingered outside the courtroom. He wanted to share the good news with one of his friends. He caught sight of McGrath coming up the stairs. *Hey, McGrath! How ya doin'?*

Well, I have to admit, I'd rather be at the sale barn. There's a lot I'm missing out on. Hope today's the last day.

It might be the last day of testimony and then you'll be sure to get the jury decision worked out quick as a wink.

You'll enjoy today's testimony. Jenner's going to call in some civil rights big shots—Martin Luther King Jr. and Dick Gregory. I got wind of it. I'm even more excited that I squeezed out the dates these traitors will be touring our county. We can arrest them—piece of cake.

Wait a minute. You think Jenner will ask them to be witnesses? What does it have to do with the Bryant girl?

Don't you see, McGrath, Jenner isn't really representing the girl; he just wants to make us look bad because we have separate facilities for whites and blacks here in Linnville. His strategy to bring in a couple of big shots is going to backfire. I bet you five bucks, it will.

Well, I'm not so sure. That California attorney is pretty cagey. He seems to be going somewhere with his line of questioning. Always asking the witnesses about other things they've done.

Trust me, McGrath. You'll be foreman of one happy jury very soon.

I better get in there. See you later, Sheriff.

Sheriff Owens opened the courtroom door and followed McGrath inside. The attorneys and audience were already seated. *Doggone those Freedom School kids—they never should have been allowed in. I can hardly wait for today's witnesses.*

Noel Grizzard set up his camera. He rubbed the dark circles under his eyes. Not much sleep last night. It hadn't taken long to drive the footage to Jackson after yesterday's trial, but last night, he'd gotten the big idea for his feature length film. It would be set in a mythical town

410

in Mississippi in the summer of 1964 and feature the experiences of young Freedom School teachers. It seemed that everyone knew the facts about the Freedom Movement—the boycotts, marches, the police brutality. . . but not many knew the behind-the-scenes—the dreams of the black families, the desires of their children to get a good education, the support and love of blacks for whites who tried to get them justice. In the film, he couldn't ignore the feelings of the blacks who'd been treated inhumanely. He'd wired his production company late and told them he'd be staying in Linnville to interview and film locals. He hoped they would come through and get behind his film dream. The Freedom Teachers might give him some tips of who to interview and film.

Grizzard saw the bailiff step forward and he swung his camera to get a close-up. *Roanoke looks a little haggard today. This case might be taking its toll. Hmmm. . . maybe I can offer him a few quid to play the judge in my film. . .*

Today, we begin the defense part of the trial. Attorney for the defense, Mr. Thomas Jenner will call witnesses and Mr. Herman Smith will have an opportunity to cross-examine. Remember, jury members, to listen carefully so you can make a fair judgment in the case. So, Mr. Jenner, will you call your first witness.

Jenner walked to the miked podium. *Your honor, I call Joshua Arnot.*

Owens opened his eyes wide in surprise. *What? He's calling one of the Arnot kids to be a witness? He must be saving his big guns—King and Gregory—for later.*

Joshua stood and stepped out of the audience section. He stood proudly in his sports jacket, tie, and dress pants. He gazed at Samantha before approaching Lydia Struck. Lydia hesitated before holding out the Bible to Joshua. She wasn't used to a black person touching it.

Joshua unlatched the low door in front of the witness stand and climbed inside. Jenner took his time approaching the podium. He started with the customary comment of respect to the judge. *Your Honor, May it Please the Court. . .*

You may proceed.

Please state your name for the court.

Joshua Arnot.

And how old are you Joshua?

I'm eighteen years old, Sir.

Thank you, Joshua.

And where do you live?

I live at 103 Timmons Road

Is that in what the people here refer to as the 'black part' of town?

Yes, Sir.

And are you a student at the Linnville Freedom School, Joshua?

Yes.

Why did you decide to attend this school?

I attended the school for Linnville black students and wanted to see what this Freedom School was all about.

Do you have a summer job, Joshua?

Yes, I do. I work for my uncle on his farm.

How can you work on his farm and still attend the school?

Oh, I arranged with him to let me work in the evenings so I can attend school during the day.

You seem motivated. What is your goal?

I plan to study law and become a lawyer.

So, have you found it worthwhile to attend Freedom School?

Yes, very worthwhile.

What are you able to study in Freedom School that you couldn't in your public school, Joshua?

So many things. For one, we were asked what courses we wished to study. Many of us have never been offered foreign language classes or typing classes, so they are great because they can help us be well-rounded students and do better in college. And even more exciting, is that Freedom School teaches us to learn the principles of rights and freedoms that all people should have. It's unique that the school allows us to learn about these rights and freedoms by participating in community events.

Can you give some examples of activities you've found meaningful?

Yes. Mr. Everett guided us in creating a newspaper—we've never had a newspaper that represented our point of view. Miss Samantha showed us that the white library in town had law books—there aren't any law books in the black library. And one day we went to Louis Diner and registered people to vote. Voting by blacks is suppressed here in Linnville.

Joshua, compared to the teachers in the Linnville schools, how do you think Miss Bryant compares?

That's a tough question. We have dedicated teachers in our black—may I say segregated—schools. But they have limits. For one thing, they have very limited budgets and have to use discarded textbooks from the white

414

schools. *Our teachers try their best, but they know they would be reprimanded if they had us do marches, boycotts, or other real-life activities. So, I would say they do their best as part of a society where systematic racism exists.*

About Miss Bryant. She is one of the best teachers I've had. She puts effort into her teaching plans and has great lessons for us. I admire her also for her bravery. She took a risk to come down here from Chicago and try to make a difference for us. I am embarrassed that she got arrested for simply trying to give high school kids a chance to experience what other high school kids in the north do. I will always respect and admire her.

No further questions, Your Honor.

Roanoke looked at Smith. *Do you wish to cross-examine this witness, Mr. Smith?*

Smith thought for a minute. *Jenner really didn't get anywhere with this witness. Just some smaltzy feel-good thoughts from one of her students. Naw. . . I'm saving my cross for the big shots who are coming up.*

He nodded 'no.' *Your Honor, the prosecution does not wish to cross examine this witness.*

Roanoke rested his head on his left wrist. *What's going on? Smith is giving the defense witnesses a pass?*

He must be pretty confident that whatever Jenner presents,
that the jury will have their blinders on.

    Mr. Jenner, do you have another witness to call?

    Your Honor, I call Samantha Bryant to the stand.

    The row of Freedom School kids sat up straighter. They collectively wished that Samantha would speak from her heart and influence the jury in a positive way.

    It was the second consecutive time that Lydia had to hold the Bible under a black hand. Her saying of the oath showed her disdain.

    Samantha's green dress was a good contrast with the light oak wood surrounding her on the witness stand. She calmly folded her hands in her lap.

    Jenner took his time walking to the podium. His peripheral vision caught a surprised look on Sheriff Owens' face.

    Please state your name for the court.

    Samantha Bryant.

    And what is your address? 4578 Bridgewood *Drive, Chicago, Ilinois.*

    And what is your age?

    I am twenty-two years old.

    Do you attend college?

    Yes, I attend Northwestern University in Chicago.

And what is your major field of study?

I'm majoring in secondary education.

Please tell the court why you decided to be a Freedom School teacher.

I've been following the Freedom Movement and learned that there was a need for volunteers to come to Mississippi to be teachers in Freedom Schools. I was surprised to learn that black students in the South did not have the same educational opportunities as those in the North, and even more surprised to learn that black students in the South did not have the same educational opportunities or even community opportunities as white students living in the same community. Black kids here are segregated from movie theaters, schools, swimming pools, libraries, restaurants, and even drinking fountains. And their parents are blocked from society by not being able to vote.

Do you think you broke the law and should have been arrested?

What I broke, was the code of systematic white supremacy that exists in this town. In the North, there's nothing illegal about dismantling a shed and carrying the wood in a wheelbarrow to rebuild a building. There's nothing illegal about going into a public library—our

417

libraries are for people of all skin shades. And in the North, there's nothing illegal about publishing a newspaper and distributing it. I grew up believing that I was a citizen in the United States of America. The rights and privileges that I have in Chicago, Illinois, should be the same ones that Joshua Arnot, Josephia Nebbs, Victoria Williams, Beatrice Anderson, and Daniel Brandon should have here in Linnville. I did not know these find young people before I moved to Linnville, but after getting to know them, I developed a deep admiration for the ways they master the racist challenges they face on a daily basis. Systematic racism is deeply embedded in southern culture. To be honest, I've faced some racism in Chicago, but nothing like the deep-seated systematic racism I've witnessed here.

To those of you who are white, I say that it's embarrassing to admit that you are racist. You know, though, deep in your hearts that you are benefitting from a structure that sees those with white or light-colored skin to be superior to those with darker colored skin. This structure began as a justification for slavery and has continued to today. Even though slavery ended in 1865, the Jim Crow laws that subjugate blacks are alive and well.

So what can we do about it? I challenge you to extend your world view. Build authentic relationships that interrupt self-superiority. When you internalize these assumptions, not only will personal relationships change, but so will our institutions. Only whites can stop white supremacy. It is YOUR responsibility.

Everett wasn't certain who started the applause, but it spread down the row of Freedom School students. Jenner joined in and he thought he noticed Burt McGrath clap a couple of times.

Roanoke didn't allow applause in his courtroom. He slammed the gavel on the desk. *I remind you that while the message of this witness has been a powerful one, this is a courtroom, not a movie theater. Please refrain from any applause.*

Mr. Smith, do you wish to cross examine?

Not this witness.

So, Mr. Jenner, do you have any other witnesses to call?

Yes, Your Honor. I have one more witness.

Owens looked over at the door. *Maybe only one of the big shots came today—I hope it's King.*

Your Honor, May I approach the bench?

Yes, you may.

Jenner spoke quietly, so only the judge could hear his request, but Grizzard caught the hushed whisper on film. And he heard the judge agree.

As if on cue, Jenner walked over to the side door to hold it open for his witness. At first no one was visible. Then every eye in the courtroom focused on the scene. Perry Green was pulling a wheeled bed into the court. Stretched out on the bed the courtroom inhabitants could see the very scarred face and arms of his father, Ebidiah Green. Green's arms were atop the bed sheet covering his torso, and his fire-webbed fingers were clearly visible. His wife Bea followed a few steps behind the mobile bed. Perry rolled the bed close to the witness stand and then walked back to the audience section.

Hector Smith was aghast. This was no place in the courtroom for the mangled Green. *Folks don't need to see the results of a failed lynching. . .* Smith stormed up to Roanoke's stand. *Roanoke, what's going on here? Ebidiah can't even talk—there's no way he can be a witness. I won't allow it.*

Mr. Smith. That's not for you to decide. I'm going to overrule your objection to this witness. Mr. Green can mumble, and his wife will repeat what he says.

But your honor, she could just make up comments.
It's unheard of!

Mr. Smith, please take your seat. I want to hear
what this witness says. In your witness's testimony—Mr.
Jones was accused of participating in Mr. Green's lynching
and Mr. Jenner in his opening statement said that this case
was broader in nature. I'm going to allow it for those two
reasons. You will have an opportunity to cross examine.

Smith stomped back to his seat. Sheriff Owens got
up from the audience and walked over to the door. He
wanted to distance himself from the drama. Lydia wasn't
sure what she should do with the Bible. Bea slipped it
under one of Ebidiah's scarred hands and repeated her
husband's mumbled oath.

May it please the court?

You may proceed, Mr. Jenner.

Please state your name.

Ebidiah mumbled and Belle spoke in a loud, clear
voice.

I am Ebidiah Green.

Ebidiah. We are talking today about this defendant
Samantha Bryant. She is a Freedom School teacher that is
being accused of inciting unrest in Linnville. The reasons
for her arrest are: taking wood from Fred's shed when he

421

gave her permission, taking some black kids into the white library, and putting a stack of student newspapers on the counter of the Linnville Downtown Diner.

My first two witnesses, Joshua Arnot and Samantha Bryant have testified that Samantha's actions are legal and that she has been challenged because of racism here in Linnville.

My question to you is, have you been a victim of Linnville racism?

Grizzard couldn't believe what happened next. He focused his camera lens on Bea. Bea shared that three white-hooded men stopped by their house and along with two others dressed in white hoods, tied him to a wooden cross and lit him on fire. Bea said she put out the fire after they left, but Ebidiah was badly burned.

And did you recognize the voices of any of the men that did this?

Bea looked lovingly at her husband as he mumbled his answer.

Yes, Mr. Jenner. Two of the men were Burton Nemick and Billy Rae Jones. And now, Mr. Jenner, what I have to say is from my own experience, not my husband's. Before Hannah worked at the jail, it was my job to clean and cook. When Ebidiah got injured I had to quit work.

422

But when I worked there, I often heard Sheriff Owens say the expression, 'Gol dang bolwevils' when he was nervous. Well, that night, I heard his voice shout, 'Hurry up, let's get out of here—you 'gol dang bolwevils!'"

The courtroom erupted in conversation. Sheriff Owens slipped out the door as Judge Roanoke slammed his gavel to regain order. *I declare the trial of Samantha Bryant over. There has been plenty of evidence presented. Burton Nemick, I am dismissing you from the jury. Jury members, you are to go immediately to the jury room to deliberate the verdict in this case: guilty of intentionally inciting unrest, guilty of inciting unrest in a group, or innocent.*

Grizzard thought he heard Roanoke slam his gavel seven times. He wasn't sure. When he reviewed the film, he'd know the exact number of times.

Jenner gave Samantha a hug. His hunch was to remain in the courtroom until the verdict was rendered. He knew that was within the law. The students sat back down. They would wait, too. Samantha turned around and gave them a friendly wave. The teens waved back.

***

McGrath joined the other ten jurors at the table in the jury deliberation room. *If no one objects, I volunteer to be our foreman.*

One of the jurors broke the ice. *You go right ahead.* He saw the others nod.

McGrath spoke in a clear, confident voice as he summarized the trial and the witnesses' comments. *Okay, it's time for a vote.*

They went around the table. He couldn't believe it. Somehow the testimonies had struck a nerve in each witness. There was rawness and discomfort and justice as ten people raised their hands when McGrath said 'innocent.'

Roanoke asked McGrath to say the verdict as the jury reassembled themselves in the courtroom. McGrath stood up and looked at Roanoke. *Your Honor, we the jury, find the Defendant Samantha Bryant innocent!*

Tears of joy flowed down Samantha's face. She felt Thomas Jenner's warm hug and then the hugs of Everett, Gina, and her Freedom School friends.

Chapter 29

Judge Roanoke remained at his desk. He glanced downward to disguise his smile. He lightly tapped his gavel once on his desk and spoke softly.

Miss Bryant, I am pleased that justice triumphed today in my courtroom. Normally, I instruct someone who is found innocent of a crime, to return to the jail for out-processing. This involves returning jail-issued clothing and then receiving back the personal items you had with you when you were arrested. However, the nature of your case leads me to re-examine this procedure. Today, I am going to decree that you may leave the courtroom immediately to wherever you wish to go and return to the jail at your leisure to pick up your goods. Is this solution acceptable to you?

Samantha heard the judge clearly explain her option. *Yes, Sir. I would like to return to get my items at a later time. I've missed the delicious peach cobbler my host mother, Loretta Mays fixes, and I can't wait one minute longer to taste her good home-cooked food.*

I don't blame you, Samantha. I am also a fan of peach desserts. I hope you enjoy a double-serving of it tonight. And I have something I would like to say to those of you left in the courtroom—Lydia, please add this to the court record. My message to all of you here is regardless of how you look at justice, the main precept of it is that people are treated in a fair way. For too long, we white folks here in the South have ignored the realization that people with darker toned-skin have not had the same opportunities. I myself have tried to pay the blacks who work for me a fair wage, not realizing that they do not have the opportunity to have one well-paid full-time career and must depend on several part-time jobs to make a go of it. And even these multiple part-time jobs do not give their families enough of an income to have a good quality life. Black adults find themselves eeking out a low living that denies them some of the pleasures that are expected by whites all over the country—indoor plumbing, telephone service, comfort devices like TVs, and opportunity for travel, retirement plans-- to name a few. Today, Samantha, I personally pledge to actively work with business organizations in the state to make changes in this area. I pledge to work with the system in place to enlighten whites to fully dissolve Jim Crow and give overt assistance to blacks in their quest for a good life.

You came here, Samantha, a black person to make a difference for Mississippi blacks and were shamefully arrested. While the locals resented whites coming here to make change, they resented you even more, for being a black person trying to make changes. On behalf of our legal system, I deeply apologize for your arrest and incarceration and Miss Johnson's shameful beating. I believe that because you were black, you were singled out from the other Freedom Teachers. I challenge to step away from this shameful treatment and continue to pursue you dreams of racial justice. If I can be of any assistance to you in your future, don't hesitate to contact me.

Samantha nodded. *At least he's remorseful and trying to set things right.*

Sir, I thank you for your comments. And I thank you for your offer to help me. There IS one thing I can think of right now that you can do to help—here today in the courtroom is Joshua Arnot, a top student at our Freedom School. His goal is to become a lawyer—a difficult path for someone who is black. If you could pull some strings to help him get in college and law school, I would appreciate that.

Roanoke stood up and walked down to where Samantha and the students were standing. *Which of you is Joshua?*

She opened her palm and extended her arm to identify him.

Roanoke walked directly to Joshua and looked him in the eye. *Young man, I just happen to have a friend on the board at Drake University in Des Moines, Iowa. I plan to give him a call tonight and grease your path to becoming an undergraduate student there. They have a fine law school as well. And Joshua, my wife and I (well, I'm going to speak for her), will personally pay for your tuition and living expenses to attend Drake for your undergraduate and law school years. As I recall, there are some nice apartments near the campus—we'll cover the cost of that, too. What do you think?*

Samantha wasn't sure if Roanoke extended his hand to shake Joshua's first, or if it was the other way around. It was a hearty handshake. A small chug forward along the slow- moving train of racial justice.

***

You don't say! Loretta slapped her knee when Samantha repeated Jenner's dressing up in court to get a rise out of Burt Nemick and Hunter Radley. *I can't believe he did that in a court of law and I can't believe that it made those two culprits admit their guilt. I guess humanity can be gullible at times.*

Samantha, Marla, and Loretta were sitting in her living room. She'd fed them her signature beans and ham and now they were enjoying a big dish of peach cobbler.

I can't believe that you told the judge about my peach cobbler, Samantha. Perry was watching the trial at Louie's Diner and he drove right over here to tell me. It was such wonderful news to learn that the jury declared you were innocent—of course, we kept hoping for that all along—but then he gave me a heads up that you missed my cobbler, so I got busy and mixed up a pan of it. I'm so glad you like it.

And it sure was nice of Mr. Grizzard to set up the tv in Louie's Diner so people could get a first-hand view of the trial. Perry told me that lots of people were excited to see the comings and goings. Evidently, Mr. Grizzard got lots of great shots—especially some close-ups of the good-olds. I was glad to be teaching for you, Samantha, but it would have been a hoot to see that one scene!

Marla finished the last forkful on her plate. *Samantha, you really have been brave during this trial. I'm not sure I could have persevered as well as you.*

You had it harder than me, really. I'm glad you got justice, too.

Thanks, friend. Say, the kids are going to be absolutely over the top when you come back tomorrow.

Loretta stood up to collect the empty dessert dishes. *I agree, Marla, the students are going to be thrilled when she returns tomorrow. Do you suppose I can come to the opening activities in the auditorium just to see their reactions? I know you don't need me to substitute any more, but I would like to see how happy they will be. . .*

Samantha stood and walked over to Loretta. She gave her a hug, careful not to knock the plates out of her hands. *Oh, Loretta, of course I want you to be there tomorrow—every day if you wish. You have been a huge supporter and I can't thank you enough for subbing for me.*

Well, you know, teaching has been my life. I put my heart into it and never regretted one minute of the time I spent creating lessons. Being able to teach with you young teachers at Freedom School has reopened my eyes to the importance of teaching lessons—especially lessons that will prepare our youth for the future—a good future. I can't thank you enough for staying with me and including me in this wonderful project. I'm sure Freedom Schools will be included in future history books. And look at me—hosting two of its finest teachers.

Group hug time! Samantha and Marla walked over and gave Loretta a hearty hug.

Now, Miss Loretta, Samantha said, *we want to thank YOU for not only hosting us with your fine food and hospitality, but for your assistance when we needed you back in the classroom. You are a model of goodness here in Linnville, and I'm sure I can speak for Marla that you are one of the best people we've met.*

Mississippi hospitality. Spending time in a southern home with well-worn floors, cupboards, and curtains. Torn screens, chipped dishes, outdoor plumbing. No matter. Love, hope, and good home cooked food abound, making the world seem rich and purposeful. Seeing through the outer layer of humanity into its core.

***

Gina was the first to arrive. She'd been on a joyful high ever since she heard George McGrath announce Samantha's not guilty verdict. Then when Judge Roanoke had extended the olive branch to Joshua and offered him sponsored education for college and law school, she felt even lighter. *Sometimes when you feel that racial justice is spinning in a circle, it surprises you and it moves a few steps forward. I better focus right now and get ready for my first period class.*

Gina opened her spiral notebook and looked over her lesson plans. She'd decided to add a lesson about America's many cultures—cultures that enhanced the richness of the country. She thought about her own Italian roots—all the stories she remembered from her ancestors. *Maybe I'll start with immigrant groups like the Italians. I guess my vagabond trip to Venice might be something to share . . .*

The door to the school opened and Gina wasn't surprised to see the other Freedom Teachers arrive early as well. Like her, they were abuzz with excitement.

Tom grinned as he walked past her chair. *Hey, Gina! What great news about Samantha, don't you think?*

It's spectacular news, Tom! Say, is there any way we can get your dad to stop by this morning—I know the kids would like to thank him for what he's done—the trial and all.

As a matter of fact, he does plan to come by. He wants to say a few words to everyone. He can't stay long because another case is awaiting him back in sunny California, but he should be here during our opening in the aud.

Everett walked in with Samantha, Marla, and Loretta. They were abuzz in conversation.

Everett's bass voice could be heard above the others. *So, Samantha, what will you do next to top the excitement you've brought our Freedom School?*

Frankly, Everett, I've had more excitement the last few weeks than I could have ever imagined. I need to show my gratitude to Mr. Jenner for getting me freed—without his clever legal presentations, I would probably still be stuck in the Linnville Jail. Then, there's you guys for all of your support and for carrying on with the teaching while I was, shall we say, 'indisposed.' You could have easily closed the school because of all the turmoil, but you kept coming here to teach; that makes me really glad. And when I go back to the jail after school today to pick up my belongings, I plan to give a 'thank-you' to Hannah for how she kept me fortified physically and spiritually. Gee. . . my list of who I want to thank just keeps getting longer and longer.

Loretta was standing by the window. The distant sound of chanting caught her attention and as some dust clouds formed from the gravel road, she seemed to make out the figures of people walking toward the school. *And just what are they carrying—some signs?*

She opened the front door and pointed. *Look out there, everyone! Why, there are our students all walking together carrying signs! I do believe they are singing 'We Shall Overcome,' as well!*

Everett gave some friendly pushes to his colleagues. *Well, I'll be! If that isn't our kids leading a march! Just look at the signs they're carrying: Linnville Justice—Slow-Moving, but Moving Forward, The Freedom Train is Leaving the Station, Samantha Bryant—Freed!, A Salute to our Great Freedom Teachers!. . .*

The teachers gathered in a semi-circle on each side of the door. Loretta held the door open as each student walked inside and through the foyer into the auditorium. They clapped and called each student by name. As the two-by-two line of students walked past Samantha, they grinned. She gave each student a friendly wave while simultaneously smiling and shedding tears of heartfelt appreciation. Samantha led the group of educators into the auditorium and continued to gaze gratefully across the room.

Marla picked up her guitar and pulled a plastic pic out of her pocket. A strum of the C-chord was all the hint the students needed to start belting out the lyrics to "This Little Light of Mine."

The singing continued in the auditorium with the teachers joining in. Marla accompanied the voluminous group with her guitar straddling her knee and Hector played a descant on his harmonica. No one wanted to stop the magic, but Josephia stepped forward and raised her hand for attention—just like she'd seen the teachers do.

Hey, everyone, listen up. Today is a special day. Our teacher Miss Samantha is back. For all of you teachers, we want you to know that we just did a march through town on our way here. We walked through the white section and the black section. While more of our black sisters and brothers waved to us, there still were some in the white section who opened their doors and stepped out on their porches. And we saw some smiles on some of their faces.

We don't want to take too much more time from our classes today, so before we get dismissed to our morning ones, I want to share a poem with all of you that I wrote.

435

It's not haiku or a rhyming poem—it's free verse, so don't expect any of the lines to rhyme. I wrote this poem to capture all of our student feelings about our Linnville Freedom School. Miss Samantha, would you come up and stand by me as I read it?

Samantha walked to the front of the auditorium and put her arm around Josephia's shoulders.

Josephia reached into her pocket and took out a folded piece of paper. *My poem is titled, 'Microscopic", and no, it isn't about science.*

Microscopic

In our giant universe
Wander creatures large and small,
Creatures seeking justification
For their existence.
Human forms abound
Inhabiting, seeking, growing
And In their quest for equality
They seek justice for all.
But barriers interfere—greed, power, discrimination
Barriers that slow the quest
Barriers that limit greatness

So, my friends, what can be done
To push the barriers into oblivion?
It's simple:
Reach out to someone unfamiliar
And make them familiar.
Freedom Schools give us the power
Now, take it!

Why, this is a wonderful poem, Josephia? May I have a copy of it?

I thought you might like it, so I made you a copy. Actually, I made all of you teachers a copy—kind of like a souvenir on behalf of all of us kids. She reached into another pocket and took out four more folded sheets of paper. *Daniel, will you help me pass these out?*

Let's give three cheers to our Freedom Teachers, shouted Joshua. He raised his fist in the air and shouted to guide the others.

Hip, hip, hooray!
Hip, hip, hooray!
Hip, hip, hooray!

The timing couldn't have been better. Thomas Jenner strode into the auditorium and walked to the front.

I'm not exactly sure what is going on, but it sure looks celebratory.

Hey, teachers and students, I just want to say a few words before I take off for California. Students, I can't thank you enough for helping me with Samantha's and Marla's cases. I know you all wanted to be in the audience at Samantha's trial and even though that wasn't possible a representative group of you did come while the rest of you were there in spirit. And teachers, including my rowdy son, Tom, thanks for setting up this fine school—a school that is teaching you students how to get the rights and freedoms you should have. I've had a great time here in Linnville, and one thing I noticed, is that you are on the fringe—the fringe of change. Even the whites who have resisted change for so long are opening up to change. You have a big mission to continue to expect change and to courageously step forward to make sure it comes. My friend Noel Grizzard who filmed Samantha's trial will be putting together some footage into a feature length film. We hope the movie will convince even more people to find equality and racial justice. So, keep up the cause, my friends.

Joshua jumped up from his bench. *Okay, everyone, you know the ropes! Three cheers for Mr. Jenner, our favorite KKKer!*

Hip, hip, hooray!

Hip, hip, hooray!

Hip, hip, hooray!

Thomas Jenner glanced down at his watch. *Time to split the scene. That new case is waiting for me back home.* He walked over to his son. *Hey, kids, keep an eye on my son, will you? He can get pretty rowdy!*

Joshua grinned. *Naw, Mr. Jenner, he's just a chip off the old block!*

You know, Joshua, you are one-hundred percent correct. One more thing—I hope many of you will take advantage of the college scholarships. From what I've seen here, you are dedicated students who want to achieve a lot in life. College isn't the only path to follow in life, but it is a good one. And I challenge you to keep up your work for racial justice—it's been a pleasure to have been here to do my small part. . .

Joshua interrupted. *With all due respect, Sir, you have played a very significant role here in Linnville. Your networking got Noel Grizzard here; your talent and creativity led to a successful settlement for Miss Marla and a very good verdict for Miss Samantha. You have shown us that there are many ways to make changes, and just like Martin Luther King, Jr., these nonviolent ways are very effective. On behalf of all of us here at the Linnville Freedom School, we thank you for all you've done.*

Jenner didn't quite know how to respond to the compliments.

Tom decided to bail out his dad. *Hey, don't give my old man too many compliments; they'll just go to his head. He's a pretty good egg, but he does have some flaws.*

Like what, for example, Daniel asked.

I'll let you in on a little-known secret about Thomas Jenner, my favorite father. When he gets really angry, a tiny patch of skin on the back of his neck turns bright red.

So, what's so bad about that? Daniel asked.

If his court opponents knew this secret, then they would have the satisfaction of knowing they had gotten under his skin and they could have a legal advantage in their court arguments.

Josephia stood up. *You know, I did see that red patch of skin on the back of your neck, Mr. Jenner, when you were questioning the prosecution witnesses at Samantha's trial.*

Aha! You now know my Achilles heel. I'll be honest with you kids. When Herman Smith called his sorry lot of witnesses to the stand, it made me hopping mad that those poor excuses of human beings could be a part of deciding justice for Samantha. But sometimes, when a bloke gets angry, he or she rises up to a level that transcends anger—a higher realm where clarity and reality collide. That realm was where I hovered when Joshua, Samantha, and Ebidiah were telling their stories. I think deep in my heart that their stories—and all of yours—will transcend injustice.

Beatrice raised her voice. *Mr. Jenner. We sat behind you during the whole trial and we never saw that red patch of skin during the defense part of the trial. You got over your anger and really did hover in a good place.*

Hey, you said it, Beatrice. Sorry, but I've got to run. Peace!

It was a standing ovation.

***

Nels pulled up in front of the Linnville Jail. Samantha wanted him to stay in the car. *I want to go inside myself, Nels and collect my belongings. It shouldn't take*

441

long. If I'm not back out in thirty minutes, then come inside. But I'm not worried.

Samantha pressed the buzzer on the jail door. A familiar voice responded.

I'll be right there.

Hannah opened the door wide and gave Samantha a big bear hug. *Bless your pea-pickin' heart, Miss Samantha! I didn't know if I'd see you again. I bet you are here to get your belongings. You come right in. Sheriff and his deputy are away—I hear they might be out job hunting. Do come in.*

It's so good to see you again, Hannah! I want to thank you so much for all your caring while I was here. You fixed me such good food and you kept my spirits up by challenging me to read Bible stories.

Hannah reached for her hand and led her to a shelf beside the Sheriff's desk. She reached up and took off a small cloth bag. *Here you go, Dear. Your watch and clothes are all in this bag. There's a little surprise in there from me, too. Don't look now—wait until you leave.*

Thanks, Hannah. I can't wait to see what the surprise is. You really didn't need to get me anything. Those fluffy blueberry muffins you baked for me were enough of a treat.

Now, you're flattering me unnecessarily. I want you to have a wonderful life, Miss Samantha. They treated you bad here in Linnville, but I want you to know that you made a difference for so many people, especially the children. Yes, the children.

I've learned so much by being in Linnville, Hannah. And don't worry, I'll leave here with lots of good memories—memories of meeting wonderful people like you who work hard and make changes in the world around you.

Thank you, Miss Samantha. My world is not too big, but I do enjoy making it a better one.

Well, I better get going, Hannah. Thanks again. Best wishes to you and your family.

The hug was long and tight and loving.

Nels opened the passenger door for Samantha.
Well, that must have gone pretty well. You weren't in there long.

You're right. It was just Hannah. The sheriff and deputy were out somewhere.

Samantha pulled open the drawstring on the cloth bag Hannah had given her. Her hand rummaged through the bag feeling the cool metal band of her Timex watch. Her fingers rummaged more until she felt soft fabric—*must be the outfit I was wearing when the sheriff arrested me.*

Then her fingers caressed a soft leather book. She pulled it out of the bag and recognized it as the Bible belonging to Hannah. A note written on a small piece of paper sticking out of the Bible got her attention:

My dearest Samantha,

You are a special person—and I love you like you were my child. I want you to have this Bible to keep as a reminder that God loves you, too. And I want you to read the book of Exodus when you have time. It tells the story of the Israelites who were released from slavery in Egypt and took a round-about way across the wilderness to their old homeland. While traveling, they did a lot of complaining to Moses. But when you read this book, you will discover that God never forsook them, He was always with them. He is always with you, too. No matter how long it takes to get racial justice, God will be with us.

So is there something special about that Bible, Samantha?

Yes, Nels. Hannah, the jail cook wanted me to have this. While I was jailed, she gave me assignments to read about the people who faced challenges. It helped me cope with my imprisonment.

I see. You know, people like Hannah are the most important people in the world.

Epilogue 1

*Samantha Bryant finished her summer teaching stint at the Freedom School. She returned to Northwestern University in Chicago to complete her education degree. She got her first teaching assignment at Atwood High School in Madison, Wisconsin where she had earlier spent a semester with Marla. She gives speeches across the country about her experiences being a Freedom School teacher.

*Marla Johnson completed her degree in political science and history at the University of Wisconsin. She also earned her master's degree and got hired as a teaching assistant there. She and Samantha meet monthly for a friends' dinner at Ella's Deli. From her case settlement, she has already sent over one hundred black Mississippi students to colleges. She made a bus trip with her mother to visit Loretta and like, Marla, Mrs. Johnson enjoyed Loretta's hospitality.

*Everett completed his BA and JP at Harvard. He returned to Linnville, Mississippi to start his own law firm. He actively solicits black clients

*Gina Lovick returned to New York where she started a foundation for underprivileged children.

*Thomas Jenner II, aka Tom, got a referral from Noel Grizzard and entered the Hollywood film academy. He waits tables at an oceanside restaurant while waiting for movie role calls.

*Josephia Youds published a book of poetry: *Poems from My Heart.*

*Joshua Arnot attended Drake University in Des Moines where he earned his BA and JP. He specializes in business law.

*Beatrice graduated cum laude from Harvard University. She married a man she met her sophomore year in college. She and her husband are both chemists.

*Daniel joined a blues band, The Royals, and recorded three top-selling albums. He continues to play the harmonica.

*Victoria stayed in Linnville and opened her own bakery. She supplies baked goods for the Linnville Downtown Diner.

*Hannah still works at the Linnville Jail. Her cooking ministry helps those who continue to find themselves incarcerated there.

*George McGrath sold his sales barn and moved to Omaha, Nebraska where he and a partner opened a successful cattle barn. His son Ben was proud of his vote in the Bryant case.

*After the trial, Sheriff Owens resigned and moved his family to Mobile, Alabama where he became a security guard at a warehouse.

*A wealthy anonymous donor offered to pay for Ebidiah Green's plastic surgery and physical therapy. He is now able to talk, eat, use his hands, walk, and drive a car.

*Noel Grizzard stayed in Linnville after the trial to produce a full-length movie about Freedom Schools. He hired Loretta Mays as his assistant director and Dean Roanoke for the role of judge. The name of his film: Good Hearts.

Epilogue 2

Samantha's haiku poems (and reasons for wanting to be a
Freedom School Teacher which she gave to her attorney,
Thomas Jenner):

Children—innocence

Enjoy interracial friends

Then taught prejudice

I've been following the Freedom Movement and learned
there was a need for volunteers to come to Mississippi to be
teachers in the Freedom Schools.

Less funding in black schools

Better job market for whites

Slow for us—Jim Crow

I was surprised to learn that black students in the South do
not have the same educational opportunities as those in the
North, and even more surprised to learn that black students
in the South did not have the same educational
opportunities or even community opportunities as white
students living in the same community.

Freedom Schools

Define Civil Rights Movement

Desegregate schools

Black kids here are segregated from movie theaters, schools, swimming pools, libraries, restaurants, and even drinking fountains. And their parents are blocked from society by not being able to vote.

Student activists

In the Freedom School Movement

Helping blacks to vote

The rights and privileges that I have in Chicago, Illinois, should be the same ones that Joshua Arnot, Victoria Williams, Beatrice Anderson, Josephia Nebbs, and Daniel Brandon should have.

Freedom School students

Experiencing justice

Wanting to get more

I have developed a deep admiration for the ways these Freedom School students master the racist challenges they face on a daily basis.

Endless hate abounds

As White supremacy reigns

Racial justice now

I didn't break the law; I broke the code of systematic
racism that exists in this town. It's time to stop white
supremacy now. According to Martin Luther King Jr.,"All
people of good will must work together in a very vigorous
determined manner to solve this problem of racial
discrimination."

An Afterward

Freedom Schools played an important role in the Civil Rights Movement: In the summer of 1964, over forty Freedom Schools all over Mississippi gave some 2,500 students of all ages opportunities to learn about freedom. Students were active in classes, boycotts, marches, and getting adults registered to vote. A few days prior to the opening of the schools, on July 2nd, 1964, Congress had passed a far-reaching Civil Rights Act that solidified voting rights across America and prohibited discrimination on the basis of race, color, religion, sex and national origin. Freedom Schools opened on July 7, and served as a time to test the tenets of the Civil Rights Act. Great achievements by civil rights leaders like Martin Luther King Jr. and Dick Gregory coupled with awareness of the harsh treatment of peaceful protestors by the police and the murders of civil rights activists, had led to the passage of this far reaching act. Leaders such as John L Lewis and Barack Obama have kept up racial injustice awareness with speeches, marches, and leadership, However, the challenge of white supremacy has lingered.

Both overt and covert examples of racism continued to persist in our society. And then, just like the summer of

1964, the events of the summer of 2020 spawned a new awareness of the continuing racism in America. The events didn't just start in 2020, they've been ongoing; but in 2020, there was an increased awareness that white supremacy and systematic racism are problems whites need to help solve. It is for you, dear reader, to do your part in having a good heart. In the words of Dr. Martin Luther King, Jr., "All people of good will must work together in a vigorous determined manner to solve this problem of racial discrimination which includes the problem of economic deprivation."

And how am I, a white woman, qualified to write a book about Freedom Schools? Like many, I do not accept the systemic racism I see around me. An injured knee prevented me from participating in the Summer 2020 Black Lives Matter marches, so I offer this book as a token of my respect for every black life—you matter to me!

About The Author

I've always loved words and the power they hold. As a young child, I penned short stories about imaginary places; these emerged into thoughtful essays as I grew older, and more recently into teen fantasy and adult literary novels. My high school English teacher once told me that to write a novel, you first need to read avidly, and I will admit, I followed her advice. Besides enjoying reading, I like writing haiku poetry, riding the bike trails in Des Moines on my blue Cannondale bike, and playing an occasional round or two of golf. I live in Des Moines with my husband Jerry, and enjoy the city's cultural and recreational opportunities.

Inspired by the Summer 2020 Black Lives Matter Movement, I recently wrote Good Hearts, a women's upmarket fiction novel set during the summer of 1964. The book features a trial that changes the systematic racism in a small mythical town in Mississippi where five Freedom Teachers introduce new subjects and freedom activities to black students attending the Linnville Freedom School. Like the classic novel, To Kill a Mockingbird, Good Hearts reminds us that changes in systematic racism chug forward slowly.

For more information, please visit: www.cranberrypen.com

Books by this Author

Nobbins Series (Teen Fantasy Series)

Under Exposed - Nobbins in Turmoil – Book 1
Following a ski accident, two Midland teens, April and Jessica, find themselves under Earth in an alien civilization. The alien Nobbins reprogram the teens with new identities, just as they have done to millions of other humans they've "borrowed" to live in Under. Riley Billman, a bright teen leads a Midland rescue effore for the girls. Other smart teens in Under begin to piece clues together to learn they are living in a sham world. Will the humans free themselves from Under? Will the Nobbins try to stop them?

Mars - Nobbins in Conflict – Book 2
Following the collapse of Under, the alien Nobbins flee to Mars and set up a new civilization under the planet's surface. After a celebration kayak adventure, the teens (yes, the same ones you met in Under Exposed), find themselves victims of Nobbin character Frieda's time travel shenanigans. How does Rine, a college friend, help solve their dilemma? What happens to Nobbin Frieda when she loses favor from the other Nobbins?

Planet Rhea - Nobbins in Transition – Book 3
Rine, a college sophomore, thinks he discovers a new planet orbiting between Venus and Earth. The Planets existence is confirmed by astronomers Herb Schall and Deke Winthrop who learn that the planet, Rhea, was moved into the new orbit by Nobbins. The Nobbins invite Rine, Schall, Winthrop, and Rine's Midland high school friends to travel to Planet Rhea for an action-packed visit. Nobbin Frieda has a surprise for all of them!

Made in the USA
Coppell, TX
06 July 2021